KNOCKOUT NOEL

Knockout Noel

NOBUTARO MASAI

Nobutaro Masai

Contents

ISBN: 9781735094106

Cover Art and Illustrations: Overlord (@overload_th)
Editing: Nic Lyons, Alexandra Ott, & Cheymongeon (@cheymongeon).

First Printing, paperback edition August 2023
Printed in USA

Acknowledgements

I would like to thank my father for his love and support while writing this book. I also thank Mrs. Michelle Skipper for her time and energy reading this book's countless iterations and recommendations. Nic Lyons provided a constructive editorial assessment, and Alexandra Ott furnished important developmental edits and assessments. Cheymongeon did a fantastic job with the proofreading for this story. The wonderfully creative Overlord did the amazing cover art for this book and its illustrations. My professional colleagues, Patrick Wills, Anna Sanders, and Kathryn Hessi, offered great insight and suggestions. Aaron Boyd, anime connoisseur and friend of a lifetime, provided excellent advice. Mrs. Lavoun Boyd enjoyed reading the story and has told others about it. Tasheeta Boyd, avid reader, and writer, supplied excellent counsel as I began this project. Sharon Williams' kind words helped move the project along. She is also one of several to nominate Alex as her favorite character. Fellow writers Elmon Dean Todd and Craig A. Price Jr. provided vital information regarding self-publishing, and I couldn't be more grateful for their insight. And thank you to my girlfriend, Brittany, for reading and being so supportive.

Prologue

Loud cracks bounced off the wooden walls as stone-like fists crashed into those within range. Bodies flew as a symphony of flesh on flesh filled the air. All of the soft groans of the fallen were drowned out with hearty laughter, followed by the loud clanging of glasses.

In most places within the world of Luxcium, this would be the definition of barbaric, but here at Stan's Soda Shack (as well as the rest of Battletown) this was typical, if not a little lackluster. If you couldn't enjoy a cold beverage with the scent of blood in the air, then you couldn't call yourself a true citizen of Battletown.

"Truly, a time-honored tradition," a dark-skinned man said merrily as he finished the rest of his drink with a content sigh. Several brawls were happening around him in the rustic Soda Shack, and he couldn't get enough of the violent entertainment in all of its gory glory. After a hard day of work, he loved nothing more than to spend time here amidst the chaos at Stan's. It always got his heart racing with an intense combination of excitement and bloodlust that drowned the day's troubles.

The right knuckles of his free hand gleamed red from those who'd crossed fists with him that night. While he savored both victory and refreshing beverages, those who challenged him tasted only the dirty grime on the wooden flooring their bodies now occupied.

Slowly, several of these moaning bodies arose from their crumpled state with raised fists and staggered towards the man still sitting calmly at his usual spot at the front counter. An intense gleam blazed in his eyes as he gently set down his glass.

"Ajax Attack!" he yelled as he swung his crimson fist with a loud crack. Dumbfounded lips uttered soft groans while every approaching person hit the ground before flopping twice helplessly in a manner resembling fish on dry land.

"Ha!" The man snorted as he wiped his mouth before looking at the fallen bodies lying before him. "You're not ready for this! If you know what's good for you then stay down. You wouldn't survive a third Ajax Attack."

He looked to his empty glass, feeling his other thirst return to him.

"Give me another round!" the man yelled as he crashed a fist on the wooden counter.

The barkeep, Stan, slightly raised his red left brow. While cleaning a dirty glass, he turned his attention to the rowdy man. His piercing green eye was matched only by the intimidating, dull green eyepatch he wore over his right.

"You do recall that all we serve here is soda, right?" Stan replied with a slightly annoyed tone. His colossal figure towered over the counter. He wore a simple, form-fitting black t-shirt with blue jeans that failed to hide the bulging muscles underneath.

"Yes, I know that," the man replied in a huffy tone as he looked up to meet Stan's gaze. Most of sound mind would have been intimidated by Stan's menacing figure, but not Ajax. They had quite the exciting history together as close friends and former rivals. The two had been in countless fights; during their younger days, many of the "newer" rock roads had been constructed from bloody boulders they had smashed apart with only their bare fists and the oozing bodies of the defeated.

Ajax felt a familiar craving course through him, thanks to the memories of the past. "But any chance that you've got anything stronger than grape soda on you today?"

"Afraid not, Ajax."

"Fine," Ajax grumbled. "Give me the usual then."

"Coming right up!" Stan yelled as he filled a glass mug with the bubbly purple liquid from the dispenser behind the counter. With precise movements, he slid the glass until it stopped before the barbaric man who ordered it.

"Thanks!" Ajax said gruffly before grabbing the mug and downing the contents in a single gulp.

"Whoa, take it easy, Ajax. Aren't you refereeing at Kearce Stadium tomorrow? You really should take it easy with the soda. It'll affect your performance, and you need to be at your best, especially since the other three gyms are dead set on victory. I hear the referees from those gyms consume nothing but red meat and mammoth milk to keep up their strength, especially around big competitions like the national qualifier."

"You worry too much, Stan." Ajax bellowed with a hearty laugh. "I've been coming here for the last twenty years, and I'm still as robust as when I first began refereeing."

"Ajax, you still need to be careful," Stan said with concern. "I've heard the White Caps have been active lately. You know the degree of brutality. If that ghastly group of glowing suits attacks you and wins, they have a right to claim anything that is yours."

"Those dainty cowards," Ajax said while flexing his impressive arms. "Would be lucky to last ten seconds with me. Let them come, and I'll show them the true strength of a citizen of Battletown. I'll teach those squirts how things were done back in my day when proud sidven fought others openly and at full strength without any of this guerrilla warfare nonsense and needless theatrics."

Stan sighed as he stared into the distance. "Times have changed, Ajax. The inhabitants of this town have always craved bloodshed and violence. The mighty always have the final say in how things work here. The only difference is how the mighty choose to operate."

"Just give me five yosmins alone with those false phantoms, and I'll beat the forgotten principles of the past into every inch of their being."

"If only it were that simple. It's not called the never-ending battle without good reason."

"Ha! The battle never ends only because we choose to keep fighting. We long for bruised knuckles, bloodied lips, and broken ribs from brutal battles against both friend and foe."

"Careful with your words, Ajax. You might exacerbate the violent frenzy in here," Stan said as he turned his head, narrowly avoiding an oncoming chair before flashing a smug smile at Ajax. "Care to have more Noels in your life?"

Ajax's eyes widened as the glass within his hand fell and clattered noisily on the wooden counter.

"Ugh," Ajax groaned as he brought a hand to his forehead. He could feel the events of this evening as well as everything from the past couple of months, violently swirling around his cranium in a headache like no other. It felt like a tiger was mercilessly ripping apart his brain. "Don't remind me about her. She has been the cause of my reoccurring migraines for the past three months."

"You mean your rising star in the female boxing league?" Stan asked while stroking his chin. "Since her debut match against Miny Megan, she obliterated every boxer who entered the ring with her, even securing one of the eight coveted slots to fight for a chance to represent the Stadium during the NFBQ in record-breaking time. I've heard others say that her gloves are stained crimson from the blood of her opponents."

Ajax rolled his eyes as he gave a great sigh.

"She has both talent and drive for boxing, training nearly every moment she's not in the ring. That alone makes her an incredible boxer. However, her ruthless personality makes her an absolute terror to anyone who faces her," Ajax said, both frustrated and impressed by the young rookie. "Thanks to her brutalities, many of the girls who've fought against her required immediate medical attention after their matches. Naturally, this has made her a fan favorite."

"The townsfolk here are drawn to violence and bloodshed. She carries the spirit of Battletown. Her tenacity burns brighter than any fire," Stan said with a sigh while wiping another dirty glass quietly. After a moment of silence, he turned to face his sulking friend. "Hey, Ajax, what was the nickname they finally gave your rising star?"

Ajax returned his empty glass to Stan before responding with a single word. "Knockout."

"Her goal is ambitious, from what I hear," Stan said before handing Ajax another glass of grape soda. "Do you believe in her? Do you believe she has what it takes to defeat not just her fellow Kearce contenders but also defeat those from Bagor, Ragwine, and Crosslock?"

"Those animals from Crosslock are a beast of their own, but I believe"--Ajax poured the purple liquid down his throat--"that this year's qualifier will be talked about for many generations to come."

"Hmm," Stan said thoughtfully as he turned to gaze outside a nearby window. It was pitch black, but he swore he could make out a single figure lurking in the darkest patch of shadows staring at him. Stan glared at the darkness before returning his attention to Ajax. "It looks like a menacing shadow is upon us, and we are about to learn what happens when the endless night encounters the torch fueled by the flames of never-ending rage and tenacity."

"Now, what nonsense are you babbling about?" Ajax asked with a perplexed look.

"Nothing really," Stan said as he stepped away from the window to face Ajax with a small smile that soon became plastered. "Now, will you be paying for your drinks tonight, or shall I add this to your ever-growing tab?"

Ajax groaned dismally as he reached into his pocket to dig out a few brilocks. He couldn't afford to let his tab get any bigger.

Chapter 1

The Battle Begins

"Ladies and gentlemen!" a voice boomed through the speakers.

"This is Jesse B, and I'll be your announcer for the evening! Tonight begins round one of the national qualifiers for the female boxing championship here at Kearce Stadium, and boy, are things about to get heated!"

The chocolate-colored young man with a flat top leaned towards the microphone. He wore a loud maroon suit with a purple tie matched only by his tongue, which spoke with great passion as spit shot out of his mouth like machine gunfire.

"Before we get started, I just wanted to remind everyone all boxing matches held here are clean, with the use of performance-enhancing chemicals strictly prohibited as regulated by the ZHSAA. Every fighter on the roster is tested regularly to ensure that everyone relies solely upon their strength and determination."

"Tonight, you'll see our top eight female boxers from our high school division here at the stadium, competing for the opportunity to represent our district on the regional, if not national, stage! An honor Kearce Stadium hasn't had in several years. But enough about that, headlining us is a fierce battle between two of the finest female boxers from Battletown. In the blue corner, we have the ferocious young lady, whose strength is matched only by her appetite, the Mighty Mac-en-Clobber!"

The light-skinned girl known as Mac-en-Clobber sat cross-legged on a stool in her respective corner, wearing a black-and-yellow sports bra with matching athletic shorts and sports shoes. Her long, blonde hair was tied back into a ponytail. On each hand was a yellow boxing glove that smelled strongly of macaroni and cheese.

She wasn't paying attention to the speaker, her wingman, or anyone in the arena. Captivating her solely was a giant bowl of ramen that resided in her lap. With joyful motions, she buried her head into the bowl and scarfed down the noodles within the blink of an eye. She possessed a scraggy body and lanky arms and strongly resembled the noodles she was eating. After seeing that her food supply was now depleted, she leaped off the stool and tossed her bowl into the audience before giving her opponent a menacing smile.

The girl in the other corner returned this smile with an irritated glare. Wearing a red-and-black sports bra with matching shorts and athletic shoes, she began tapping her foot impatiently.

"Her competitor also has quite the fearsome reputation. Despite being the youngest addition to the female boxer's roster, she has displayed skills on par with even our most experienced veteran boxers. Please give it up for our upcoming boxing star in the red corner Knockout Noel! Boxers, please meet in the center of the ring with the referee and the best of luck."

Finally. I thought he would never shut up, Noel thought as she stepped toward the ring's center. The ring's flooring was covered with a thick rubber mat. At each of the four corners were a ring post, one blood red, one a breathless blue, and the remaining two whiter than a corpse.

A few drux beyond were the towering stone bleachers surrounding the ring and filled with cheering spectators. Several were munching on food from the snack bar with amused looks, while others sat on the edges of their seats with eager anticipation. The gathering crowd was diverse, full of different races, beliefs, and walks of life. To those in the audience: none of those things mattered in the grand scheme of things.

What everyone did have in common was an excited gleam in their eyes. This twinkle unified the audience with bands stronger than the most durable metal. This shimmering fervor grew in intensity as Noel and Mac-en-Clobber approached each other. Truly, nothing riled those within the audience more than a violent battle of strength, speed, and prowess between competitors in the ring.

Noel only half-listened while the referee, Ajax, went over the rules. It wasn't anything new, and it wasn't like any of the regulations had suddenly changed. After grunting to the ref that she would play fair, she quickly fist-bumped Mac-en-Clobber with her crimson gloves before both returned to their respective corners. Noel sighed inwardly. She wanted to hurry up and get this fight over with.

It was the ringing of the bells that caused the switch to flip in her head. In a flash, her thoughts focused solely on Mac-en-Clobber as her mind transitioned to combat mode. She put her gloves in a defensive stance and hopped from side to side on her toes.

Mac-en-Clobber ran towards Noel and launched a frontal assault. Punches rained down on Noel, but she intercepted all of them. The strength and speed of her gloved fists were impressive. They were a true reflection of her time and experience in the ring, but her simple-minded and straightforward way of thinking made them so easy to read. Mac-en-Clobber may have been her senior in boxing, but Noel was out of her league.

Moments into her barrage of punches, Mac-en-Clobber's movements began to slow. Perspiration dripped down her face as she struggled to remain on the offensive.

Mac-en-Clobber fired a right hook toward Noel's face, but Noel ducked and launched her glove into Mac-en-Clobber's stomach. Mac-en-Clobber gasped in pain as the air was knocked out of her lungs. She stumbled with a grimace. One of her gloved hands held her aching abdomen as she tried a defensive stance with her remaining arm.

Seeing this moment of weakness, Noel unleashed a swarm of jabs, which Mac-en-Clobber futilely attempted to guard. The blows landed and caused Mac-en-Clobber to hit the ground with a thud.

"Get up!" Noel yelled as she kicked Mac-en-Clobber's body. "Get up, so I can finish you!"

Ajax suddenly blew his whistle as he slowly approached from the outskirts of the ring.

"Foul! Unsportsmanlike conduct for Knockout Noel!" he yelled as he threw his arms straight out, resembling a giant T.

Noel glared at the referee, but he only crossed his arms, unaffected by her menacing gaze. Those massive, muscular arms covered with scars clearly indicated that you didn't want to mess with him.

"Fine, Ajax. How about this, then?" Noel said while she clasped Mac-en-Clobber's head with her gloves and launched her into the air.

As her body descended, Noel's glove zoomed into Mac-en-Clobber's face. The mighty force behind Noel's blow caused Mac-en-Clobber to fly into the blue corner.

The defeated, lanky warrior now resembled a scarecrow as she hung lifelessly against the corner, her outstretched arms entangled with the ring's ropes. Blood trickled out of Mac-en-Clobber's busted lip. A few of Mac-en-Clobber's pearl-like teeth landed on the ring floor with a light clang. Her eyes crossed before closing in defeat.

"Knockout!" Jesse screamed into his microphone as the crowd roared in excitement. Nothing evoked a more extraordinary passion within the audience's hearts than seeing a brutal KO followed by the scent of spilled blood in the air.

"Looks like our winner tonight is Knockout Noel!" Jesse continued to enunciate throughout the stadium.

"The rage-filled rookie has easily claimed yet another victory under her belt! Does anyone stand a chance against the gloves that have seen more blood than a serial killer?"

Not a chance, Noel thought to herself as she stared through the crowd as if they weren't there. *I will be number one, and no one will keep that from happening.*

She turned her back to the cheering crowds and headed to the stadium's exit. While leaving the ring, she passed Ajax. He was crouched down to check on Mac-en Clobber and gave a visible sigh of relief after he felt her steady pulse. While delicately picking up Mac-en-Clobber's teeth, he sternly shot Noel a look, indicating that she would hear more about this later.

I could care less. Mac-en-Clobber knew what she was signing up for. This isn't a competitive eating contest, it's boxing! She should have forfeited the match if she didn't want to get hurt. I came to win and would knock that chick out again without hesitation. Only the mighty make it here by mercilessly crushing their opposition. Sympathy only makes you soft, and I ain't no marshmallow.

Noel had one goal that she was determined to achieve, so she vowed never to carry compassion for anyone who opposed her.

Finally, the NQFB has started. If I win, I can compete in the national tournament and get my hands on the 4000♭ brilocks prize money. With those, I'll be set.

Noel kept her menacing expression as she entered the dark corridor that led to the female locker room. She glanced at the ticking clock on the wall as both hands indicated it was getting late.

"It won't be much longer. I'll be back soon." She muttered while heading towards her locker. With a grunt, she yanked off her boxing gloves and unwrapped the crimson hand wraps underneath. She quickly opened the metal locker and pulled out her street clothes. Much to her surprise, a small, clear plastic bag fell from the pocket of her hoodie. It landed on the tile floor with a plop. Noel picked up the baggie with a curious expression, and to her delight, she saw three sugar cookies covered in red sprinkles. A small smile formed as she opened the bag and happily munched the cookies.

After finishing the pastries, she noticed a small piece of white scratch paper at the bottom of the bag. In big, messy letters was a short message.

Good *luck with tonight's match! Beat Mac-en-Clobber and hurry home so we can celebrate! I hope you haven't forgotten what today is, Noel!*

The image of a certain little girl's eager smile filled her mind vividly as Noel's smile widened before quickly glancing around for spectators. She sighed after seeing that she was alone in the locker room. Her thoughts returned to her fight with Mac-En-Clobber.

I won tonight's match, but I have three more rounds before I make it to the final round of the qualifier to compete for the right to compete in nationals. I can't afford to lose my focus. I know what's at stake. She thought as she slipped the note into her hoodie pocket, her expression returning to its prior seriousness.

"I will be the number one boxer," She declared while quickly changing her clothes, "and nothing is going to get in my way."

Chapter 2

Late Night Fight for Food

Noel was furious. She stood in the front office of the stadium with its proprietor and couldn't believe what she was hearing.

"What do you mean you're reducing my cut!"

Ajax, who also happened to be the owner of Kearce Stadium, sat behind his desk. His hands formed into a steeple. He met Noel's glare with stern eyes.

"You were out of line tonight. Your opponent was already defeated, and you continued to attack her."

"Of course! I had to make sure that she wasn't going to get up again!"

Ajax facepalmed in exasperation.

"My gosh, girl, this is competitive boxing, not a bloody fight to the death!"

"Victory is never guaranteed unless you make sure your opponent can't get back on their feet again."

"How have we not gotten sued yet?" Ajax moaned. He turned a stern on Noel.

"Regardless." he said firmly tone, "I've warned you repeatedly that you need to tone down the brutality with your fights. If you weren't so popular with the audience, I would have removed you from the roster, but I think using a portion of your compensation to cover Mac's dental fee will help the message soak in."

"That's not fair! You know what today is! I need that money!"

"What you need is to learn restraint! Listen," he said, his tone becoming softer. "When you first came here, all you sought were strength and the means to provide for your younger sister. You've nearly lost sight of both in the bloodlust of your pursuit for the number one title. You need to stop before you enter the point of no return. Is this the kind of behavior you want to model for Alex? Do you want her to grow up thinking it's okay to continue to attack a downed opponent?"

Noel's irate expression softened. The tension in her arched shoulders and clenched fists bled away. For a brief moment, the angry gleam in her eyes dulled as it was replaced by tenderness.

"No ... But it's for her sake that I can't pull my punches. Since Mom left us three months ago, life has been more difficult. I can handle anything this town throws at me, but my kid sister isn't built like me. I'm the only family she has left that can protect her. No matter what, I'll do what our mom failed to do and keep Alex safe and provided for, and nothing or no one will stop me, Ajax."

"I know," Ajax said softly. He put his hand on her shoulder and gave it a firm squeeze. He met Noel's gaze with a look of gentle understanding.

"But," he said as his expression hardened slightly, "there is still a big difference between winning and what you did to Mac tonight. Believe me, I know your heart is in the right place, Noel. If I thought otherwise, then we would be talking more severe repercussions. Here, take this." He reached into his pocket, pulled out a handful of smooth crimson rocks, and laid them on the desk in front of Noel.

"Here are your brilocks from tonight's match with deductions for Mac's upcoming dental appointment. This will still be enough to live off of frugally as well as getting Alex something special for tonight's occasion. Just keep what I said in mind, you hear me, Noel?"

Noel's expression hardened as the two locked eyes briefly. After an intense battle of wills, Noel looked away first. After a moment of stubborn silence, glaring to the side, she nodded slowly before grabbing the brilocks and putting them in her pocket. She stormed out of the office and into the indoor training gym.

Whatever, Noel thought as she crossed the gym in a huff.

If Ajax thinks that I'm going to start taking it easy on those I face in the ring then he's out of his mind. The only way to win is to be ruthless. I will achieve victory, even if I have to beat it out of the crumpled, bloody remains of every opponent I battle. End of story.

Normally, she'd take her frustration out by exercising on the machinery until the equipment broke down, but tonight she had something important that she needed to do. She crossed through the patch of punching bags with quick strides against the vinyl flooring; any bag that blocked her path was sent flying across the room with a single punch. Each bag landed with a loud thud, but Noel paid it no heed as she made her way to the outdoor exit. She grabbed the door's handle with a tightly clenched fist and loudly swung it with a clamorous crash.

"Noel," Ajax said with a look of disapproval and a slight shake of his head, "be careful when going out with your sister at night. The White Caps have been active around these parts lately."

"I'm not afraid of ghosts, real or not! If they mess with my sister or me, then I'll punch them straight back to the Den of the Defeated!" Noel yelled as she stormed out of the stadium and slammed the door behind her.

"And stop slamming my door. If you break another one, it'll also come out of your wages!" Ajax yelled from inside the building, only for Noel to ignore him as she made her way down the street. The temperature outside was chilling, but the flames of her inner rage kept her warm. The sound of her heavy steps echoed throughout the empty street made of rocks and dirt as she made angry strides down the unlevel walkway.

It was nearly pitch-black outside, the only source of illumination coming from the flickering streetlights. Changing the old bulbs was on the to-do list of the city management, but they still hadn't come around to fixing them yet. It didn't matter to Noel, though. She could still travel down this familiar road even if all the lights went out.

All boxing matches began late in the evening, so she never got to leave till the sky was darker than a badly bruised eye. That was the primary reason she had become accustomed to these darkened roads, and that wasn't the only thing she had become familiar with.

The growl of her barren stomach caused the fires within her soul to smolder as the gentle ache reminded her of an important task that she had yet to complete.

On the way to her house, a small grocery store named Jab-en-Grab was open thirty-two hinos a day. It stood sixty drux tall with white concrete walls and red brick pillars. Hanging on the front of the building was the store's well-known logo: a fist punching a star.

Rocks within the store's dirt parking lot scattered with melodious chimes under the force of Noel's heavy steps. Clouds of dust billowed around her as she crossed the nearly vacant lot. There was a handful of Rock Rumblers, a mighty brand of automatic vehicles designed to handle the harsh, jagged terrain, within the lot. Not because there were only a few shoppers in Jab-en-Grab, but because most who resided within Battletown were against the use of heavy machinery during the grind of day-to-day living. To them: if one had to rely on external equipment, foreign substances, or labor-saving devices to overcome daily struggles, then they weren't a true citizen of Battletown, a sentiment Noel wholeheartedly agreed with.

A loud gurgle resonating from Noel's stomach interrupted her thoughts as she stood before Jab-en-Grab's double-door entrance. She ritualistically purchased what she considered "muscle chow" or food for the journey home, and today was no exception. However, today was special.

She entered the store just like she did every day and found herself immersed in a tension thick enough to be felt. Loud pops filled the air as fists flew, kicks whizzed, and shopping carts zoomed at ramming speed as the customers inside fought with a vicious intensity. Groceries were a precious commodity meant to sustain those fighting in this life from the cold, perilous grip of deprivation. Those with unyielding strength not only got to wrestle out of starvation's grasp, but got their choice of what to purchase.

The rules were simple. While in the aisles, it was first-come, first-serve to whatever was on the shelves. If someone wanted something grabbed by another, they could battle that sidvan for the right to purchase it instead, providing that they could pry the item away from them. If two sidvans grabbed the same object simultaneously, they had to fight for it unless someone backed down. External weapons from outside the store weren't allowed, but anything within the store could be used for combat. Once someone had safely made it to the checkout registers, they were no longer allowed to be pursued for their groceries.

Noel saw many proud sidvans with cracked lips and bruised faces smiling merrily. They held their Brickbuster's cereal boxes, trays of rumble bee gizzards, and colorful assortments of mouthwatering mudclairs as trophies of their victory today in Jab-en-Grab.

A small smile formed on Noel's mouth as she glanced at a cardboard cutout of Bricky, the mascot from Brickbuster's cereal, right next to an aesthetically pleasing, stacked display of the popular breakfast cereal.

Alex loves that cereal brand, mostly for the toy inside, but she likes the cereal too. It's hard to chew, though; I swear it's like they use real bricks. Alex always has to drink it with pink mammoth milk just to soften it up a bit. I need to remember to purchase the regular kind next time. She was bouncing off the walls more than usual after eating the chocolate ones with triple the amount of sugar-coated marshmallows, Noel thought before shaking her head and refocusing.

There were many with shopping carts filled with impressive bounties from various aisles within the store. Noel eyed the shoppers with an unimpressed look as she strolled through the busiest checkout lane. Just like usual, she chose to go through the one most crowded with customers, each with buggies filled with many groceries. Many shot dirty looks as Noel made her way abruptly through the line, but the glare she returned had such an intensity that they quickly looked away while sweating profusely.

Her first step: prime ribs. She approached the meat aisle, located in the middle of the farthest wall from the front entrance, and began looking over the different cuts. She loved ribs and how the meat made her muscle get bigger. It was a win-win for her. The most enormous and juiciest looking of the selection was what she always went with.

Her nose led the way as she followed the hot scent of fried grease and flavorful fat until she set foot on the meat aisle. Once she crossed the brown tile boundary line, an intense heat came over her. Perspiration poured from her body as it instantly evaporated onto the hamburger-colored tiles.

Indifferent to the fire-like temperature, she turned towards the scent of the prime ribs, which came from one of the heated racks against the back wall. Above these racks was a wooden sign painted in big red letters that read, "Eat the meat of the fallen! Make their strength yours!"

As Noel approached the racks, she saw a sight that made her heart dance joyfully. Many platters of cooked meats were on the metal racks, each with a savory, mouthwatering aroma that turned the well-fed hungry with a whiff. Before Noel knew it, her mouth began watering. She quickly wiped the drool away as she ambled briskly towards the delicious meat fried to perfection in the heat of never-ending animosity and seasoned with the salty tears of the defeated.

Many choice cuts of meat were available that tempted her palate, but before coming, she had steeled her resolve. Without hesitation, she reached for the platter with the largest cut of ribs, only to brush up against another set of fingers. This vast, well-muscled hand belonged to a dark-skinned girl who stood a good two drux taller than Noel and held a notorious reputation as the hatchling behemoth of Crosslock Stadium. In terms of popularity, she was slightly below the stadium's current number-one contender, Never-Stop Natascha, but that didn't imply she was inferior. Natascha relentlessly attacked her foes with a flurry of punches until they could no longer stand. Meg, on the other hand, attacked her opponents until the paramedics could arrive to retrieve their battered remains. This kind of brutality resulted in severe physical and psychological trauma, with some of her former opponents never entering the ring again.

This girl's grip on the rib platter tightened, her fingers wrapping over the entire plastic container as if she were palming a small toy. With narrowed eyes, the girl slowly turned to face Noel. Her thick, waist-length brown hair swayed like a wild beast on the prowl. This giant sized up Noel and spoke with a loud, booming voice.

"Knockout Noel, you've got a lot of nerve trying to take these ribs from me. You should let go of them before I take the ribs you keep in your chest."

"I'd like to see you try, Monstrous Meg," Noel growled as she firmly held onto the back of Monstrous Meg's hand. Her nails dug into Meg's coarse skin as Noel shot her a menacing glare. "I'd knock you on your blurfing butt with one punch."

Meg shrugged off the glare with a smirk as she leaned closer until they were face-to-face. "Not before I shatter your perfect winning streak, Noel. Tonight feels like a good night to put an end to Kearce Stadium's rising star. After I crush you, you'll end up like this platter of ribs: torn to pieces and devoured by me."

While keeping her left hand over Meg's right, Noel struck a fighting stance. "Bring it on, blit; my ribs are getting cold."

Meg cracked her left knuckles. "I'm so going to enjoy ending your career here. Which rack do you think they'll store your ribs in after I rip them out?"

"Next to the premium platter on the top shelf. Yours will be tossed into the rank trough they use to feed the livestock behind the building if even that. I'd hate for those poor, blood-thirsty creatures to get stomachaches."

"Blit! I'll end you!" Meg yelled as she raised a clenched fist overhead, but before she could bring it down, they were inter-rupted by another presence.

"Excuse me, ladies," one of the meat-department workers said politely. He wore a simple red shirt with a matching red headband. His brown buckskin pants with blue fringe had a rustic scent as he hoisted a giant platter of ribs the size of a table over his head with a grunt. "If you two are going to fight over the best prime-rib platter, then it would have to be none other than this beauty that came from one of our prized killer cows."

With a mighty thrust of her free hand, Meg pushed Noel, who quickly lost her balance. Noel grunted as she hit the ground hard. After tumbling a few times, her body collided with a display of Phil's Fiery Rage dipping sauce bottles. The sharp sound of silicate striking the ground, followed by the shimmering display of crystal-like condiment containers, re-verberated as the glass bottles burst into a sea of jagged shards across the tile around Noel. She sat up with an annoyed grunt and winced as the last bottle landed on her head with a loud crack. The spicy, brownish-red liquid dripped down her face and burned her eyes while an unbridled rage blazed within her soul. Fight fruit was a key component in Phil's sauce, which invoked violent tendencies in whomever it touched. Noel crawled on all fours with an enraged growl until she was in a beast-like crouch.

With frightening speed, she pounced towards Meg, or tried to, but slipped and landed flat on her face, thanks to the sauce covering the floor.

"Not a bad look on you, Noel," Meg said as she took her hand off the original platter. "But this is a sample of what will happen to you next time we meet."

Meg snickered as she walked towards the worker, snatched away the giant rib platter, and sent him sprawling across the meat department with a mighty kick. The worker groaned as he flew headfirst into the wall with a loud crash. He kicked his legs helplessly while stuck halfway through the wall but appeared unharmed, much to Meg's amusement. With one arm, she carried the platter overhead with bold strides as she slowly made her way to the checkout registers at the front of the store.

Noel rolled away from the sauce spill and jumped up to her feet in a huff. With mighty motions, she shook the fiery rage sauce off of her body in a manner similar to a dog after a heavy rain. She closed her eyes and took a deep breath. Slowly, the artificial rage dissipated as her inner rage quickly replaced it.

She shot an intimidating glare at the departing Monstrous Meg. Noel's initial thought was chasing after that towering brute and pounding her face into the parking lot, but she decided against it. Ajax had already scolded her today for unnecessary violence, and she didn't want to get another earful if he found out, and he **would** find out if she broke one of the sacred, unspoken social rules here at Jab-en-Grab. Besides, she was running late for an important celebration and had no more time to waste.

You won't be so lucky next time, Meg, Noel thought before returning her gaze to the prime ribs that had initially caught her fancy. She was more than a little hungry, but now, these ribs felt ... underserved, like some kind of shallow consolation prize. Regardless, she still grabbed them and quickly exited the meat aisle as she continued her late-night shopping.

It was the next item that was a little more problematic.

She quietly crept throughout the store until she had gone around the outskirts of the inside perimeter. She ducked into the empty killer canned vegetable aisle and slowly peeked her head out. After looking both ways twice to ensure the coast was clear, she cautiously advanced towards her most vital objective: the bakery.

Noel had a big sweet tooth, and her love for pastries was second only to ribs. It was common for her to get a case of donuts or cookies, but today her order was different. She quickly went to the warm glass counter to pick up her order. Thankfully, no other customers were present due to the buy-one-get-one-free sale for packs of nautical, never-ending noodles.

"I'd like to pick up an order for Jennifer Smith," Noel said while glancing around for onlookers. She used the alias whenever she didn't want to draw attention to herself. Her reason for being here was top secret, and she meant to keep it that way.

"Sure," the boy across the counter replied. With a wrinkled nose, he tried to overlook the globs of spicy sauce that adorned her hoodie as he turned to find the correct order. Several white, rectangular packages lined up across the racks at the back of the bakery. Each parcel had cake, cookies, or some other delicious confection. Delicious scents seemed to seep out of their packages and permeate the air with all of their calorie-saturated goodness. The aroma was so sweet within the bakery that it was a wonder no one contracted diabetes just from breathing in the atmosphere.

The boy adjusted his yellow glasses and quickly reviewed the different orders' names until he found the one.

"Here you go," he said as he grabbed one of the packages from the back and handed it to her. Someone had written "Jennifer Smith" in sloppy handwriting, but Noel barely noticed. All that mattered were the contents of the box. She opened the top and grimaced.

"This isn't the correct order."

The boy looked confused. "Pardon?"

"This isn't the correct order!" she yelled as she slammed the box against the counter. "These are cookies! I ordered a b," she started to say before cutting herself off. "Something else."

"Okay," the boy said, nervously shuffling back to the rack. Under Noel's piercing glare, he went through the orders in record-breaking time and discovered another order for Jennifer Smith. Without a moment's hesitation, he grabbed this second package and went to hand it to Noel. Before he had a chance, his eyes fell upon a poster on the wall. It read:

There are two regular customers, both of whom go by the name Jennifer Smith. If the person picking up looks like the person at the bottom of the page, it'll be under Jennifer Smith.*

The picture on the bottom of the notice was of Noel. Under it, there was an additional notice.

P.S.

Don't give her the wrong order. It will NOT end well for you.

His eyes widened his arms trembled. He approached Noel with slow, shaky steps while carrying the parcel with extended arms. Noel rolled her eyes at the boy's delay while tapping her foot.

If he doesn't hurry it up, then I'm going to...

Unfortunately, the fidgety boy tripped over a loose tile and stumbled into a rolling cart, with the parcel taking a mighty leap into the air.

"No!" Noel yelled as her order flew overhead like a comet in the sky.

She dropped her ribs. With a determined expression, she dove forward and grabbed the box, but the parcel opened, and a cake somersaulted in the air and hit the ground with a loud splat. It strongly resembled a skydiver whose chute failed to open during a jump.

Wide-eyed, Noel sank to her knees as she gazed at the crumpled remains of the cake. Ice cream oozed out of its wounds, forming a chocolate puddle. She stared with eyes full of anguish at the message on the cake that she had been trying so hard to keep hidden.

Happy Birthday, Alex!

Love, your big sis

Noel!

Slowly, Noel's attention transitioned from the deformed remains of the cake to the clumsy boy who had dropped it. Beads of perspiration drizzled down the boy's face as he became the focus of Noel's uninhibited fury. He was a dead man.

Chapter 3

WHAT THE ...?!!!

"I'm so sorry about that, ma'am!" the boy said, nearly in tears.

Noel immediately shot back on her feet and made her way to the counter in a slow, menacing manner. Gradually she leaned over the counter until she was inches away from his face and muttered, "Oh, you will be sorry."

Immediately she put her hand on the counter and leaped over it. Her right bangs swayed up, briefly revealing a brown birthmark shaped like a fist, which caused the boy's eyes to widen. With slow, heavy steps, Noel sauntered towards the shaking pastry chef. "Sorry that you're still alive once I'm done with you."

"Wait! Please! I can make it up to you!" the boy said desperately, waving his hands. It was like he was standing before some unmerciful judge who was moments away from giving the death penalty. Clearly, it was time to beg desperately for his life. He grabbed an icing pen, but Noel aimed a fist right toward his face before he could do anything. Noel saw it connect but was surprised that she felt nothing but air.

I must be off my game tonight; is it because of the rage sauce?

Immediately she pulled off her hoodie before launching a barrage of punches, all of which seemed to hit, but she felt no impact. As she looked closer, she became shocked at what she saw. The boy stood before her in a panicked state, but he appeared blurry while she was throwing punches at him. It was almost like he was made up of vapor.

Noel kept firing away, trying to figure out how the boy remained unscathed when it suddenly hit her.

The boy wasn't getting hurt because she was attacking his afterimage. Somehow, his body was shifting so fast that Noel couldn't register his movements.

"Look, I can tell you're upset, so let me make it up to you," the boy said while he continued to blur through all of Noel's punches. He showed no signs of fatigue. In a fraction of a second, he disappeared from Noel's vision. The clattering of several cabinet doors opening and shutting and the clanging of pots and pans filled the bakery.

Noel looked around wildly, trying to pinpoint the source, but couldn't. The noises seemed to pop up sporadically from various parts of the bakery. Several sweaty consumers heard these loud noises and momentarily stopped shopping. Uneasy expressions appeared as they quickly took their groceries and headed toward the checkout lane. Many in Battletown were superstitious, with strong paranormal beliefs, and none desired to be dragged away by ghosts to the "Den of the Defeated."

Noel sighed at the wave of retreating shoppers before returning her attention to the bakery. The loud sounds had simmered down, but not Noel's rage. She continued to look wildly around the bakery for the strange boy until something unexpected happened.

With a sudden plop, she found herself holding a plastic case of vanilla cupcakes.

JAB
GRAB

A red blur appeared before her, but it was gone before she could react. In its place were red letters on each cupcake that said, *Happy Birthday, Alex!*

Noel turned her head fiercely in all directions, but the bakery was now empty. The boy had disappeared and was probably long gone. Noel was still furious with that boy, but she couldn't help but be a little impressed.

Who was that kid?

There weren't many people who could evade that many of her blows. Cold sweat dripped down her forehead. It had been a while since she'd last broken a sweat fighting with someone. Combat was something that she had an affinity for, so it was rare to find an opponent who required so much energy to deal with.

He got lucky today, but he won't get off without a few broken bones next time.

Suddenly a melodic heartbeat, accompanied by the rhythmic shattering of solid rock with bare hands, reverberated from Noel's pocket. With a frustrated growl, she reached into her pocket as a rich and soothing voice began singing.

I shatter obstacles, just like I shatter rocks.

Crags become craters; mountains become blocks.

I grind relentlessly, day after day.

Victories within my grasp; there's no time to play.

She whipped out her phone, a gray, crudely molded slab of plastic that strongly resembled a misshapen fist. After pushing the two large black buttons on the left and right sides, the hand slowly opened up, revealing a glass screen and several buttons within the palm as the music ceased. A message in flashing red letters on the screen caused her mind to shift focus instantly.

Where are you?! The party can't start till you get here!

Wide-eyed, Noel twisted the hand's ring finger. Immediately, the message was replaced with bright crimson numbers.

Much to her disdain, the hand indicated that it was much later than she thought. Noel had promised that she would be home thirty yosmins ago.

"Crud, I'm late!" she said as she hurried towards the checkout lane. Thankfully most of the remaining customers had already fled the store, so she quickly reached the register.

After scanning her items, she threw a few brilocks on the counter and rushed out of the store. In her haste to leave, Noel completely overlooked the presence of a figure lingering close to the registers. Behind a glorious cardboard cutout of Bricky was a dark-skinned figure with black, half dreads, clad in a white trench coat and wearing a matching white, flat cap. He looked after the departing Noel with great interest. He whipped out a small notepad and pen from his inner coat pocket and began scribbling furiously.

"Huh, so the great Knockout Noel has a sibling? Dan will definitely be interested in that tidbit, and I'm sure that strange boy in the bakery is someone he will want to investigate as well." The White Cap stroked his chin as he watched Noel dash through the parking lot.

"Since Dan told me to keep an eye out for strong fighters, I better prioritize gathering more information about this feisty chick, but I'll keep my eyes open for other juicy things to tell Dan," the White Cap muttered as he quickly left the store to follow Noel from a distance."

...

I hope she's not too upset. Noel thought as she ran through the darkened dirt road towards the only thing that could stir the emotions concealed deeply within her callous heart. Noel wasn't someone known for worrying, but even she was a little nervous as she swiftly approached the warmth that was her home, her haven. It was a small house, barely bigger than a shed, and the very definition of shabby. Its once beautiful white paint was now faded and cracked and reeked of must. A blue tarp covered the top, hiding the roof that had disappeared during a hurricane several years back. Several windows were boarded-up, with only one that appeared to open and close. The wooden steps felt soft and sank slightly when stepped on. Due to its grimy appearance, Noel and her kid sister affectionately referred to it as "The Mud Hut."

She quickly ascended the steps, with each board creaking under her weight. Once reaching the front door, she looked both ways twice. The maniacal laugh of cackling crickets deep within the bushes and trees beyond the dirt road was the only other sound present in the nighttime air. Noel gave a sigh of relief after seeing no signs of activity around her house, by the long-since-extinguished rusty light posts, or by the nearby shady shrine.

Good, I don't see any of those robed Warwolves running around tonight. Those punks, along with the White Caps, had best keep their distance from my sister, Noel thought as she opened the door and entered. After closing the door behind her and locking it, the harsh look in Noel's eyes softened.

It was dark and stuffy inside the Mud Hut, indicating that summer had finally arrived. She quickly set her groceries down on a plastic kiddie table covered with coloring books and various bills as she went to do something about the sweltering heat. The wooden floorboards creaked as she made her way to the window. After using some elbow grease, she pried the stubborn windowpane open and was greeted by a refreshing, cool breeze. Noel sighed in contentment as the brisk wind brushed against her sweating face.

It's good to be back. Noel thought as she looked at the vacant living room. Behind the kiddie picnic table was a busted brown couch, with several loose springs, against the wall. A slight stench came from the trash can in the corner of the room. Noel, in her haste, had forgotten to take that out earlier and silently vowed to do so soon.

The smell of neglected trash didn't really bother her much, but what did cause her to wrinkle her nose was the sickly, sweet scent coming from a small cactus, warmly regarded as Cal, sitting on a small stool next to the couch. Noel was fond of sweet things, but something seemed unnatural about this plant aroma. Honestly, Noel had tried to get rid of it in the past, but this caused her beloved little sister to break out in tears. Since then, Noel had learned to coexist with the funky plant.

As Noel further examined the room, she was surprised by how quiet it was. The little bundle of energy she was expecting was nowhere to be seen. Noel opened her phone. She twisted the index finger and quickly scrolled to see if she had missed any messages but saw nothing new. Noel narrowed her eyes, and a worried expression filled her face as she put her phone away.

Where is Alex?

Chapter 4

Birthday Surprise!

It was then that a small figure cloaked in the shadows be-hind the couch, lunged at Noel. Noel yelped in surprise as this imp-like creature wrapped around her waist and grappled her to the floor. She hit the ground hard, and her vision became blurred. Once it cleared, she recognized the smiling girl who sat on top of her.

"Welcome home, Noel!" the girl on top of Noel said enthu-siastically as she nuzzled her head into Noel's chest.

Noel smiled warmly. "Thanks, Alex. It's good to be back. Now can you get off of me?"

"Pat my head first."

Noel roughly patted the top of her head affectionately.

Alex purred as she squeezed tighter before the two began rolling across the flooring with Alex wrapped inside Noel's arms.

"Eberdar burrito!" Both sisters exclaimed with a happy squeal. After a few moments of relentless rolling, they paused. Their hair, now knotted and messy, resembled the landscape after a tornado touchdown. That didn't matter to either, though, as the sisters' held on to each other with an unshake-able grip.

Noel, flat on her back, took a few deep breaths before raising her legs until they pointed toward the ceiling.

"Ready for part two?" Noel asked with a mischievous grin.

"Yeah! Bring it on, sis!" Alex exclaimed while clinging upside down to Noel's stomach.

Noel shot to her feet like a loaded spring. While they were in midflight, Alex released her grip and leaped several drux into the air. After completing a somersault, she landed in Noel's arms, giggling gleefully.

Noel flashed an amused smile at Alex before setting her back on the ground.

"You're getting stronger, Alex," Noel said while tousling her sister's messy hair.

"Really?" Alex said, beaming. "Am I strong enough to beat you?"

"You're getting there," Noel said with a smile. "Now, how about we break out these sweets and get this party started?"

"Yeah!" Alex exclaimed while throwing a fist bump in the air.

They found themselves sitting around the kiddie table, stuffing their faces with cupcakes and boxes of apple juice while cheerfully chatting away.

"Did you like the cookies I made for you, Noel?" Alex asked after taking a massive bite out of her second cupcake.

"You bet! They were delicious, Alex!" Noel remarked after cramming her third cupcake into her mouth. "You'll have to make them again sometime!"

"Sure!" Alex exclaimed while beaming brightly.

"So, how was school today?"

"In writing class today, they had us write essays about our heroes. My friend Sara wrote about her dad because he is a police officer who catches bad guys and keeps everyone safe. He even caught a guy while he was robbing a bank."

"Oh? So, who did you write about?" Noel asked.

"I wrote about you because you are my hero. Ever since Mom left to buy mammoth milk, you've been working as a boxer. Every night you are out trading blows with other fierce fighters. You're the coolest! I want to be strong just like you someday."

"It's not that big of a deal," Noel said, smiling with a dark look in her eyes. "Besides, someone has to put bread on the table since *that* woman left us."

"Yeah, but once Mom does get back, things can go back to how they were," Alex said happily. Anger burned inside Noel, but she tried her best to hide it. She refused to ruin this moment for Alex.

"Right. So, what is your birthday wish?" Noel asked, trying to change the subject.

"Can I get ten wishes since I'm turning ten?"

Noel laughed. "You can make ten wishes, but only one will come true. You better choose the one you want the most."

"Then I would like to go to Kearce Stadium and watch one of your boxing matches live," Alex said excitedly.

"Absolutely not," Noel said firmly with her arms crossed. "It's dangerous to walk around Battletown at night, especially this area right now. Between the White Caps and Warwolves, I don't want you outside the Mud Hut when it's dark outside. Besides, your bedtime is always around the same time as my matches. Wish for something else."

"Then it would have to be this," Alex said as she embraced Noel. "To be able to spend more time with you during the day. I miss getting to see you after school, and I get sad not being able to see you until night."

Noel returned the embrace. The flames of her anger dimmed, slowly extinguished by a gentle warmth that burned brighter and permeated her entire body. She felt lighter than a balloon as she hugged her now sniffling little sister.

"Hey," Noel said gently, "that wish will come true as soon as this boxing season ends. Then we'll be able to spend a lot more time together."

"Really?" Alex asked excitedly. She extended her left pinky. "Do you promise?"

Noel wrapped her muscular pinky around Alex's and shook it.

"I pinky promise."

"Yeah! I can't wait!" Alex exclaimed as she got up from the kiddie table and began dancing.

"Yeah, now go get your pajamas on," Noel said while glancing at the clock. "It's getting late, and school is in the morning."

"But don't I get to stay up later because I'm ten now?"

"You're already past that time. Now go," Noel said sternly.

"Okay," Alex said dejectedly as she headed to her room. "I'll see you in the morning."

"Goodnight. I'll see you in the morning," Noel said as she sat back down on the bench with her face in her palm. Becoming a boxer at Kearce Stadium provided the sisters a much-needed source of income. Now a new worry was coursing through Noel's head.

How will I provide for us when the boxing season is over? I have to win that finals prize money!

This thought coursed throughout her restless mind for the duration of the night.

The Secret Meeting of Phantoms

Many kadrux away, hidden deep within the shadows of an undisclosed warehouse, several figures wore cadaverous clothing that glowed an ivory hue, causing them to resemble ghostly apparitions. These were none other than the infamous group known as the White Caps.

They sat in fine, ivory wooden chairs around a large circular table crafted from well-varnished maple. Several unlit, white candles, held within metal cages, decorated the table. Each White Cap, with black goggles covering their eyes, stared expectantly at the one empty chair at the table. It was the largest of all the chairs, made from warped ebony wood and painted the color of the darkest night. Engraved in the refined lumber was the image of a mighty fire restrained in a colossal cage of obsidian. These words were carved above the cage: "Within the obscuring shadows, both the strong and the weak are one and the same."

"So, where is the boss?" one of the White Caps, who happened to be named Bryan, asked while tapping his fingers on the table. He wore the typical attire of a White Cap, which consisted of a white trench coat with a light pink collar, lapel, and belt. Underneath, he wore a white suit with matching pants and light blue dress shoes. He wore a flat white cap upon his head, with his most prominent distinguishing characteristic being his dirty-blond goatee, not that it stood out within the warehouse's darkness.

"Must be running late," Rosch, the White Cap sitting beside him, responded. "Maybe he got delayed by something. I'm sure he'll be here soon." Rosch was a dark-skinned man with his hair up in half dreads and a thick mustache resting upon his upper lip. He casually reclined in his chair. His eyelids fluttered as he struggled to keep them open. Being in the darkness for long periods always made him feel drowsy.

"I hope so. I can't stay out too late tonight," Bryan mumbled as he rested his cheek upon his fist on the table. "Kelly has been getting on my case for being out late so many nights. She says if it keeps going on, then she is going to pack up the kids and move back in with her parents."

"Bryan," Rosch said while trying to stifle a yawn, "you knew from the beginning what working for Dan would entail. It's not the type of work for a married man with kids. You should have just listened to us and left Kelly and your kids behind."

"You know I can't do that!" Bryan exclaimed as he shot up from the table. "I may be a criminal mobster who has done many nefarious deeds for Dan, but I'm still a husband and father. I have a responsibility to provide for them, just as I have a responsibility to Dan as one of his many hired hands."

"We'll see how far that gets you," Rosch sneered as he kicked his feet on the table. He pulled a cigarette from his coat pocket and placed it between his teeth. After pulling out a lighter from his pants, he flicked his fingers until a single flame appeared. Everyone else in the room gasped as Rosch brought the flame to his cigarette. After taking a deep breath, Rosch put his lighter on the table. With a crude motion, he pulled out his cigarette and exhale deeply. A giant cloud of smoke oozed out of his mouth as he smirked at Bryan. "Virtue only gets in the way in this field."

"Well, well, I must disagree, Mr. Rosch," a voice with authority spoke. Every White Cap turned his attention to the single black chair at the table, which now held a shadowy figure. Rosch's eyes widened, and his skin became pale as their boss continued to speak. "Virtue is everything here. It's what separates us from the mindless, bloodthirsty beasts outside these walls. Someone who can't grasp that has no place here in my inner circle."

"Forgive me, boss!" Rosch yelled as he quickly brought his shoes off the table and bowed his head. His face was more than a little sweaty. "I misspoke!"

"Rosch, Rosch, let's have a little chat. It's time we discuss your performance and attitude here at work." A low buzzing came from Dan's direction as the flow of sweat from Rosch's pores intensified.

"First, you put your dirty shoes on my clean, antique table. That's incredibly rude. Did your parents never teach you that? Second"--the buzzing coming from Dan continued to intensify-- "you ridiculed Bryan's commitment and virtue, both of which are sacred to a sidven's honor. This honor compels Bryan to act in his family's best interests, enabling his optimal performance for my vision. Lastly..." The same buzzing appeared again, this time right before Rosch. The soft humming resembled the sound of an angry rumble bee. Rosch strained his eyes to see through the shadows. After they finally adjusted, he went slack-jawed as his cigarette fell to the ground. Before him was Dan's gloved hand, stretched out right in front of Rosch's forehead.

"You brought pure, unfiltered, and unrestrained light into my warehouse. You know you are allowed nothing more than the glow from your uniform while inside and in my presence. Light dispels the soothing layers of shadows here and will never be brought into my presence unannounced," Dan said with a dangerous gleam in his eyes.

"Please spare me, Dan! Please!"

The only response Rosch received was the feeling of cold metal tightly grasping his forehead.

"Aarrgh!" Rorshe screamed as he felt several volts surging through his body. His limbs locked up. With glazed eyes, he sat rigidly in his chair. Thin smoke came from his singed eyebrows. He groaned as Dan released his grip. Rosch tried to reach for his smarting forehead, but his spasming arms refused to cooperate. A sour scent wavered in the air as a wet spot appeared in Rosch's slacks. Dan gave a low sigh as he quickly planted himself in his seat and began addressing the White Caps present.

"Moving on, gentlemen, it's time to start this meeting. Rick, how have our operations been running?"

The one called Rick swiftly stood, unfazed by his coworker's singed and soiled appearance. He was a short, plump fellow but quicker than most gave him credit. "Quite swell," Rick responded. "Sales of Jaguar Juice have skyrocketed here in Battletown. We have dozens of trained sellers hitting the streets at night, which has resulted in major profits, thanks in part to your brilliant marketing plan."

"Excellent," Dan said as he nodded in approval. "Keep up the good work. Soon we will move to the next step of production, so ready yourselves. Sanchez, how are things progressing with our ground team?"

Sanchez stood with an air of confidence. He had piercing blue eyes, dirty blonde hair, and a matching finely waxed handlebar mustache.

"Superbly," Sanchez said with a clear, refined voice. "The phantoms under my command have eliminated many of the 'problematic' thugs plaguing Battletown. With your keen insight guiding us the past week, we have disposed of the 'Crazed

Lion Gang of the North,' the 'Brutal Bandits' that terrorized the South, and the "Leg Stealers" causing mayhem in the west of town. Next, we plan on eradicating the Crimson Storm gang, responsible for countless acts of brutal murder within the urban district of Battletown, within the next couple of days."

"Sounds good, Sanchez. Please inform me of the slightest change; warfare is a fickle creature, after all. Bryan, update us on the status of scouting and recruitment."

"Yes, sir!" Bryan slowly rose. His legs had fallen asleep from all the sitting, causing him to stumble slightly. Luckily, he caught himself by extending his arms but was red-faced. Now, of all times, he had to make a fool of himself in front of the boss.

"Recruitment has been booming. Due to Jarek's hard work, many citizens sympathize with our cause, with about twenty-one percent deciding to join our ranks. Scouting has also been going well. There are several interesting sidvens we are keeping tabs on. The other scouts and I have been stockpiling loads of important details regarding each target, such as addresses, friends and family, daily schedules, and personal information. Everything we've noticed has been written down in the note-pads we keep on hand."

"Good," Dan said, flashing a wicked smile. "Information will allow us to achieve our goal. Go ahead and leave your notepads with me. I will review them in great detail shortly. Also, Bryan, grab Rorshe's notepad for me. He ... is not in any position to hand it to me himself."

"S-sure," Bryan stuttered nervously as he walked towards Rorshe's twitching body and pulled the notepad carefully hidden within his colleague's jacket. The notepad was covered in dust, grime, and little plastic candy wrappers. Bryan did his best to brush off the unwanted particles and trash quickly.

Rorshe, you really need to do your laundry more often," Bryan complained before walking up to Dan and handing him the notepad. Rorshe grimaced, but it was unclear whether it was from his pain or lack of tidiness.

"Very good. By the way, who was Rorshe looking into?"

"From what he told me before, it's a female boxer who has recently gained a lot of popularity. She is coldhearted, merciless, and has a formidable knockout punch."

"Really?" Dan said as he gazed into the notepad quickly. After flicking through the pages, he gently placed the notepad on the table and leaned forward in his chair. He looked directly into Bryan's eyes with an intrigued look.

"Please, continue to look into this female boxer for me, Bryan. I expect to know more about this Knockout Noel."

"Yes, sir!" Bryan responded before turning towards his seat, only for a cold, metallic hand to grasp his shoulder.

"And one more thing Bryan," Dan said as he leaned forward. Bryan shuddered slightly as Dan continued to speak in a low whisper. His cool breath felt like a snake slithering across his ear.

"The work you do for me is of great importance. Don't ever think of it as 'nefarious.' We are working towards creating a new foundation for a better tomorrow, but no firm foundation can be established if crumbling remnants of the past remain. Please remember this as you continue working for this town's future."

A low buzz swirled around him. Bryan felt a light chill overcome him, but he steeled his resolve enough to respond.

"Yes, sir. I'll continue to investigate others with potential for recruitment. In addition, I'll keep an extra close eye on Noel and inform you if I find anything else of interest."

"Excellent," Dan muttered with a serpent-like smile. "Now go and share my vision."

Chapter 5

Battletown High

Jab! Jab! Cross! Jab! Jab! Cross! Jab! Cross! Jab! Cross! Jab! Cross! Jab! Cross!

The stadium's built-in training gym offered membership to anyone interested. The gym was a giant room with several black punching bags dangling from the ceiling and offered a wide variety of exercise equipment that facilitated workouts ranging from muscle strengthening to cardio.

All of the various machines were loud and intimidating, but the only sound in the gym was the mighty blows of Noel's fists as they rained down upon her punching bag. The poor sack now resembled a trash can after a late-night cavern bear attack.

Not enough! she thought as she launched a new barrage of punches even more deadly than her last set.

"Noel!" Ajax yelled as he approached with the slow intensity of a hurricane.

"What?!" she yelled back, not even bothering to make eye contact. Once the guns were up, she refused to focus on anything else till her prey was devoured.

"What are you doing?!" he roared.

"I'm training for my next match," she said matter-of-factly as she continued to launch devasting blows upon the tattered remains of the former punching bag. "If I can take my opponent out quicker, then you won't have anything to complain about."

"Oh, I have plenty. For starters, what are you doing here when you should be at school?"

Noel kept swinging, unfazed by the question. "First period is study hall, and the second is P.E. Why would I waste my time in those classes when I could be here? Besides, neither takes attendance seriously and if they ask where I was, I'll tell them that I was in the bathroom taking a dump big enough to shatter the toilet."

"Really," he said sarcastically with crossed arms. "That's your excuse?"

"How else would I explain a shattered toilet in the girl's bathroom?"

The owner slammed his open palm into his face. *Why do I have to put up with this? I'm going to need a few drinks at the Soda Shack after this.*

"Look," he said as he put a hand on her shoulder. "I appreciate your dedication, but you are still a kid. If you keep cutting classes like this, your teachers will become suspicious, and DCF will come after you and your sister. The last thing you want is the Department of Children and Families looking into both you and your sister's personal lives more closely. Between your absent mother and dilapidated house, they'll send you both to foster care quicker than you can knock out an opponent. From the moment the doors are open to when they close, you WILL be at school, and you WILL do what is expected of you. Are we clear?"

Noel paused mid-blow. She turned to face the owner with a dangerous glare, only for him to return it with matching intensity.

"Mind your own business. And don't diss the Mud Hut." Noel grunted as she turned to pick up her gym bag and headed toward the exit.

"Wait," Ajax called. His nose twitched in discomfort.

"What now?!" Noel said with an irritated look.

"Take a shower before you go. You won't make any friends reeking of sweat."

"I don't care about making friends," she muttered as she obediently headed to the female shower room. "The only thing I want is to get stronger."

After a quick shower, she swiftly changed her clothes. On her way out, she spent a minute carefully rearranging her bangs so that they perfectly covered her right temple. Once satisfied, she left the gym and headed to her least favorite place, Battletown High School. The infamous five-story high school could only be described as brutal. All of the different classes were spread apart from each other and hidden within the hazardous maze-like hallways. The flooring was a gray tile with several large, deep holes and greased areas. The walls were narrow spaces with either protruding, retractable spikes or were covered in loading chambers that shot hard, fist-sized leather balls. The classrooms above the first story had no stairs, with only a handful of long ropes for climbing to class. The classrooms below the ground level required students to travel through dark, treacherous tunnels underground where strange animals growled viciously.

Noel didn't bat an eye as she completed the daily grind of journeying from class to class through the many dangers, toils, and snares. Noel found herself snoring through study hall with a brood of snakes slithering all over her. After shaking them off indifferently, she hustled down to physical education, which was held in the gym on the ground level beside the main building, where she swiftly eliminated her foes in a deadly game of dodge-the-ball-if-you-value-your-life.

During this barbaric game, scattered throughout the gym floor, on the walls, and hanging from the ceiling were several stone-colored leather balls covered with metallic spikes. Everyone playing was divided into two teams, and to win, a player had to throw the balls at all of their opponents until they were physically unable to stand or perished, whichever happened first. The wooden vinyl flooring soon became slick with the blood of Noel's defeated classmates. Noel yawned with a bored expression as she quickly hurled spiked leather balls at the last few remaining stragglers, all of whom were on her side. Teammates meant nothing to Noel. She had the strength to win by herself, so she saw no need to rely on others. But they did serve a purpose by providing her extra targets to eliminate as the screams of both ally and foe gradually died with every ball thrown. It wasn't the same as training in Kearce Stadium's indoor gym, but she still appreciated this chance to exercise her arms. Noel knew she needed to pack in as much exercise as possible before the next period started because it would be a while before she could use her arms for physical exertion.

Soon she found herself sitting at an all-too-familiar desk in the back corner of third-period algebra. It was a small classroom that smelled of apple cinnamon. Adorning the ivory walls were several mathematical degrees alongside various cooking utensils and photos of their teacher, Ms. Jilper, standing beside a variety of chefs from around the world, all holding fancy, gourmet dishes. Besides her teaching materials, a wide variety of spice and seasoning containers sat upon her white marble desk.

This is so lame, Noel thought as she slumped over her desk with only a fist supporting her cheek. Her teacher, Ms. Jilper, was in her earlier twenties, with a long, brown braid down to the middle of her back. She wore a long-sleeved, white button-up shirt with matching white dress pants, a yellow belt, and white dress shoes. She was known for her strict teaching style but was very popular because of her kind personality and how form-fitting her clothes were over her generous bust and hips. Many boys kept their eyes glued to her during class for reasons other than their personal interest in mathematics.

Ms. Jilper's method of teaching could only be described as heated. Whenever someone answered a question incorrectly or was caught daydreaming, she would increase the temperature in the classroom to motivate the whole class to try harder. Currently, the heat inside the room was getting really intense. Granted, several of Noel's classmates had bricks for brains, but the class idiots weren't the sole reason that the room temperature was now high enough to induce heatstroke. The group subconscious of the dopey boys in class purposefully chose to answer incorrectly to further their devious agenda. Everyone, including Ms. Jilper, was sweating profusely, with their educator's white shirt now becoming see-through. All of the boys eyed the sight of her now-exposed black undergarments with perverse delight. With their last breaths, Tyrek, Kirk, Doug, and the remaining guys engraved the view into their brains before collapsing from the unbearable heat.

That sure backfired, Noel thought with a bored expression as several other classmates began dropping like flies.

Ms. Jilper, during the entire class, kept harping about quadratic formula this and Pythagorean formula that, completely unfazed by the scorching room. Noel could care less that $a^2 + b^2 = c^2$ because what good did it do? It wasn't like that knowledge unlocked power that she could add to her punches and be used to terrorize her opponents. This kind of stuff just wasn't practical to her, and unless Noel learned how to perform a Pythagorean punch, then algebra could square root itself. She stared at the clock as time slowly dragged on.

"Come on, you lousy clock!" she muttered. "Let this class end already, so I can get the rest of this school day over with! I need to get back to training at the gym!"

After what felt like an eternity, the class bell finally rang, and Noel shot up out of her desk and dashed to the exit.

"Wait just a minute." Ms. Jilper called out to her.

"What?" Noel grunted. She was standing an arm's length away from the exit.

"I didn't dismiss you yet."

"Lady, do your ears work?" Noel responded, clearly frustrated. "The bell rang. Your class is now over, and I'm out of here."

"Oooooooohhhhhh," the other kids murmured as they circled around Noel and Ms. Jilper.

"I don't like your tone, young lady!" Ms. Jilper said, arms crossed in disapproval. "I am your teacher, and you will respect me and my authority!"

"You aren't the boss of me, lady!" Noel snapped. "The only reason this class listens to you is that it's mostly boys, and they're entranced by those udders on your chest!"

"Go to the principal's office! Now!" Ms. Jilper screamed, red-faced, eyes twitching.

"Finally, I can leave!" Noel exclaimed as she headed out the door in a huff.

Who does that lady think she is? she thought as she headed down the hallway towards the principal's office. The journey was more than a tad hazardous. Upon climbing up the rope to the fifth floor, Noel had to crawl through the nearest window and climb up the remainder of the building's wall to reach the top. The jagged structure had several loose bricks, just ready to send someone plunging to their doom.

If that wasn't challenging enough, Battletown High's building had several clusters of rumble bee nests hanging from the top. The muddy-red, ten-drux structures were made of a combination of dirt and blood from previously living creatures who were permanently defeated by the rumble bees that resided within.

The low rumbling sound could always be heard around the upper levels of the building as the yellow and black, six-armed creatures, barely bigger than a small child, were always on the lookout for additional building materials. While climbing up the building, Noel encountered five hideous creatures hovering around.

"Great," Noel muttered as the rumble bees, who finally noticed her, began flying straight towards her. "Looks like I have to deal with these pests now."

The first rumble bee attempted a combination aerial dive/punch, but Noel rammed the back of her fist into the creature with a loud crack. Now with a caved-in face, the rumble bee fell to the ground with a dying buzz. The second tried to deck Noel with a haymaker, only to be caught within Noel's mighty grasp. With a loud snap, she bent the creature's wrist farther than it could extend as it buzzed in pain. Noel mercilessly rammed the rumble bee against the concrete wall without missing a beat. Once the buzzing stopped, she chucked the insect towards another bee. Upon impact, both fell and hit the ground with a thud.

Before the fourth rumble bee could respond, Noel hurled a brick straight at it, knocking it out of the sky with a painful splat.

After seeing all its deceased comrades, the last rumble bee gave an angry buzz as it zoomed towards Noel, who quickly scurried up the building. Hearing the angry rumble bee behind her, Noel climbed nonchalantly as she approached her destination: a rumble bee nest. Noel climbed around the muddy structure until she was directly above. Noel raised her left arm, noticing that the last rumble was directly below. With a tightly clenched fist, she brought her hand down on the base of the nest with a mighty force of strength. The nest tremored briefly before breaking off the building, falling on the last bee, and landing on the ground with a loud crash.

"That was a nice warm-up, at least," Noel said as she finished climbing the roof. Getting to the top was no easy task, but walking across it was just as dangerous. It consisted of several slick shingles; the janitor was paid many brilocks to grease them every morning before school. While she trudged across the roof, she aimed a dangerous glare at the slippery shingles. She dared the tiles to try to make her slip so that she would have an excuse to crush them mercilessly. After the spineless shingles got cold feet, Noel made her way to the small, one-room building on the very top of Battletown High School: the principal's office.

Noel entered the office and sat cross-armed in a cushioned chair, rapidly tapping her foot. Compared to the rest of the building, the principal's office had a calming kind of presence to it. The scent of clean cotton filled the air, with lyricless jazz music playing quietly in the background. The former principal's head crusher and spiked paddle were nowhere to be seen. In their place lay bookshelves crammed with many educational books such as "Teaching vs. Telling," "Positive Affirmation over Violence," and "Opening a Student's Mind Without Using a Spiked Bat."

In front of her lay a huge wooden antique desk polished with varnish. This aged wood was adorned with mementos from around the world. In the center lay a marbled name bar that read "Dr. Fredick Freuaget, Principal." Said principal sat in a swivel chair on the other side. He was a middle-aged man with an educator's body hidden behind a suit and tie. His face was shaved, with his brown, balding hair neatly trimmed. He wore thick-rimmed glasses over his green eyes filled with care and curiosity.

"Ah Noel," Dr. Freuaget said in a friendly manner. "What brings you here to me today?"

"Jilper was being a butthole," Noel muttered. "She made a stink when I tried to leave her class after the bell rang."

"Oh? Please tell me more."

Dr. Freuaget listened quietly as Noel spent the next several yosmins badmouthing Ms. Jilper.

"I just don't get what her problem is?!" Noel ranted. "Why is she such a buzzkill always trying to police her classroom?"

"Outrageous," Dr. Freuaget said. "Who is she to try acting like a teacher?"

"I know, right. She's nothing but some newly certified teacher with a huge pole up her butt."

"Who wants that?"

"She just needs to get off my case. I don't need her telling me what to do."

"So that is what this is about. You're upset about Ms. Jilper trying to enforce the rules of her classroom."

"Yeah, the nerve of Ms. Jilper. Who does that blit think she is anyway?"

"Who do you think she is?"

"The teacher of that useless algebra class."

"And who is in charge of that useless algebra class?"

"Ms. Jilper," Noel muttered.

"And was your behavior appropriate for a teacher who just wanted you to wait to leave until after she dismissed you?"

"No," Noel muttered while looking down. "I ... went a little ... too far."

"I'm glad that you see that now." Dr. Freuaget clapped his hands. "Now, just two things remain, and then we can put all of this behind us. First, you will need to apologize to Ms. Jilper, and then you will need to report to detention after school."

"What!" yelled Noel as she jumped from her seat. "You can't be serious, Dr. Freuaget!"

"Of all of the time we have spent together, Noel, have I ever been anything but serious?" Dr. Freuaget said with eyes as firm as stone. "You will do both requirements today before leaving school grounds."

"But I have to be at the gym today!"

"I already called Ajax, and he agreed that until those two things are done, you will not be spending any time at the gym."

"That is an abuse of power!" Noel roared. She was trembling with fury.

"This," Dr. Freuaget corrected, "is accepting the consequences of your choices. You chose to act rudely towards Ms. Jilper, and now you will accept the consequences of your actions. Do you understand?"

"Whatever," Noel growled, refusing to make eye contact.

"Excellent, now back to class. It's still fourth period, and if you hurry, you can catch the tail-end of the lecture about cell components. You might even enjoy learning about mitochondria and proteins."

"Sure." Noel groaned as she trudged out of the office, with Dr. Freuaget warning her to be on the lookout for the carnivorous chickens that escaped from the cafeteria earlier that morning. Noel simply rolled her eyes with a grunt of acknowledgment.

"Poor child," Dr.Freuaget said with his hands formed into a steeple after Noel left his office.

"Life has not been kind to her. She has already faced many trials at a tender age. The spirits of most sidvens would break at a mere fraction of what she endures. Yet, she keeps pushing forward no matter how overwhelming the obstacle is. Her unyielding spirit and aggressive personality are lacking in today's populace. If only she had been born when our founders walked these bloodstained lands. She is the spitting image of what our blood-thirsty pioneers envisioned when they created the foundation of Battletown. I wish her luck in this life because it won't get any easier."

Chapter 6

Time for Answers

"Ugh, that was a pain," Noel grouched as she sauntered out of Battletown High.

She spent two hinos after school in detention and managed to cough up an apology to Ms. Jilper. Her teacher still seemed slightly miffed about the udders comment, but she accepted Noel's apology. But not before giving Noel an earful about showing her instructors the proper level of respect. Noel gritted her teeth but took the tongue-lashing in silence.

The sun was still high in the sky, but it would be setting soon. Noel quickened her pace. On a normal day, she would hustle over to the gym in Kearce Stadium to train, but there was something that she needed to do first.

After a few moments, she arrived at the parking lot of Jab-en-Grab. With bold strides, Noel entered the store. She had one objective, and her fists tightened in anticipation as she sauntered towards the bakery. An all-too-familiar boy was behind the counter, hard at work flattening dough with a rolling pan. He worked both diligently and silently with rhythmic motions as Noel approached with a frightening expression on her face.

Noel quickened her pace into a dash, but the boy remained unfazed. Whether his unchanging expression was from unawareness or indifference, Noel couldn't say, nor did she really care. Only one thing mattered to her right now.

Time for you to get some! she thought as she leaped over the counter and dove fist-first towards the boy. By chance, the boy just happened to look up, his eyes widening as he saw a fist a finger's width from his face.

"Wha..." was all the boy could say before his body became a blur that Noel passed harmlessly through.

"How..." was all Noel could say before crashing loudly into an aluminum cart with several racks filled with sugary confections. A shower of sprinkled cookies and frosted cupcakes rained down upon her. She groaned while clutching her aching head and looked up to see the boy standing above her with a concerned expression.

"Hey, are you alright?!" the boy asked, offering Noel his hand only to tense up at the fierce glare she shot at him.

"Jennifer Smith?!!"

"Yeah," Noel said as she slowly got back on her feet. Still covered in brightly colored icing and sprinkles, she strolled towards him. She cracked her knuckles with a bitter scowl and the aroma of freshly baked sweets. "I still owe you a good beating."

"Wait!" the boy said, waving his shaking arms. He shivered as he felt beads of sweat pouring down his face. The fierce look in her eyes terrified him to his core. "I decorated those cupcakes for you. We should be good."

"Nah, we ain't good, cake dropper."

Noel edged closer until she was in striking distance. The boy tried desperately to flee, but with his back to the bakery counter and Noel blocking off every other exit.

"I called in two weeks ahead of time to have that cake prepared, and thanks to you, cake dropper, I never got to enjoy my precious cake."

"Look, I can make it up to you," he begged. "Just name your price."

Noel grasped the boy by his collar. She held a fist to his neck with a frightening look radiating a wave of intense burning anger. The boy's skin went clammy, and the uncertainty on his face grew as Noel's merciless grip tightened.

"There is only one thing that I want from you. Now spill!"

"Spill what?" the boy asked with a baffled expression.

"How can you do this?!" she yelled as she punched with enough force to split an antique oak table towards the boy's palate, only for his body to blur. Noel's fist passed through harmlessly, and although she was expecting it, the experience was a tad startling. She opened her palm and felt something akin to the wind push against her hand. It reminded her of when she leaped off a five-story building during her first-grade track and field day at Battletown Elementary. Feeling the air brush against her had been an exhilarating experience, but it paled in comparison to what she was feeling now.

She could barely make out her arms while this living blur tried to flee far from her, but her grip upon his collar was ironclad. She pulled back her hand and tenaciously held onto him, disregarding the vibrations she felt traveling through her arm.

"You might as well give up on running away. Now that I've got a good grip on you, you won't be escaping me. Now, talk, cake dropper. Who are you?"

A deep sigh came from the blurry boy as his velocity quickly decelerated. Somehow his hair had remained neatly combed, and his yellow-rimmed glasses stayed on despite how much his head had just been moving. His body became rigid as he faced Noel with eyes that seemed to dart around the bakery before focusing on her.

"Alright, you win," the boy said, surrendering his arms. "My name is Dex, and I work part-time here at Jab-en-Grab between my high school studies."

"You look pretty scrawny to be in Battletown High," Noel said skeptically as she carefully scrutinized his skinny figure. "The food they serve in the cafeteria has more muscle than you."

"That can't be healthy. Thankfully I'm homeschooled," Dex said with an incredulous look. "The public education system here is barbaric, with primitive standards for preparing children for success in the adult world. Who in their right mind desires an education from such an institution?"

"Weak talk from someone who I can't land a punch on. Speaking of which, how come none of my punches hit you?"

Dex looked at her blankly. "Because I moved my head out of the way whenever you attacked."

"I know," Noel said as her glare intensified. "How do you do it? Are you some kind of ghost or something?"

"Absolutely not. I'm one-hundred-percent flesh and blood. I'm just really good at dodging any attack aimed at me, as long as I can see it. My muscles move faster than most can strike."

"How?" Noel asked as her grip tightened on Dex's collar, and he gave a nervous gulp.

"My reaction time is heightened due to rigorous training from my childhood. If someone tries to strike me, I can move the particles in my body so fast that most solid objects can't hit me." He shook his right arm until it became a blur of energy.

"Whoa," Noel muttered in surprise as she tried touching his right arm, only for her hand to go through with that same windy feeling. "But what about your clothes?"

"They're made of a special material that won't fall off me. I don't want to be naked every time I use my ability. That would be embarrassing," Dex said with a slight blush.

"Yeah, no one would want to see that," Noel said matter-of-factly before narrowing her eyes. "So why do you always dodge? If you can move so quickly, why not use the same technique to throw punches and kicks of the same speed?"

Dex's gaze became downcast as a sorrowful expression covered his face. "I ... don't like hurting others, and I especially don't like getting hurt. My focus is solely on helping others. If I'm in a prickly situation, I only use my ability to evade blows. That's enough for most confrontations, so I just have to avoid anyone who can actually hurt me. Thankfully, only a few people could ever land an honest blow on me. Your punches are impressive, though, Jennifer, frightening even. So, can you let me go now?"

"Not yet," Noel growled as she leaned in until she and Dex were face to face. "Now, tell me more about this training...."

Suddenly, loud shrieks pierced the air of Jab-en-Grab, followed by a chorus of maniacal laughter. Noel quickly shoved Dex against a wall. A bag of flour fell from an overhead shelf and landed on his head.

"Ow!" he grunted as the fine, white powder fluttered around him and covered him from head to toe. He shot an annoyed look, which quickly morphed into concern as Noel glanced outside the bakery with a darkened expression.

"What's going on?" Dex asked warily.

Noel put a hand on the counter and leaped over it with a deft motion. With a nonchalant expression, she sauntered towards the checkout registers.

"Sounds like the Crimson Storm Gang arrived. You better find a place to hide, cake dropper. They're here for blood."

"Then where are you going?" Dex asked with a concerned expression.

Noel kept strolling towards the sound of screams and laughter with clenched fists and narrowed eyes. She glanced at Dex out of her peripheral before returning her focus to the vicious gang up ahead.

"To meet them head-on. I'm also here for blood."

Chapter 7

Crimson Storm

"Yes! Let that river flow!" a sidvan yelled with maniacal glee. He wore a tattered, grimy, white hoodie with matching raggedy sweatpants. A white bandanna with red splatters and a pair of red sunglasses covered his face. The word "Splat" was painted all over his clothing, which reeked of iron. This sidvan was a member of the Crimson Storm gang that terrorized the stores and recreational areas around this part of town. Their trademark was bathing the sites they victimized with red liquids such as ketchup, paint, and the blood of those whose lives they had taken.

He took bold strides across the flooring in the checkout area, now smeared with red paint and ketchup; the brown hair from his mohawk waved wildly. In his hands was a giant crimson Warhammer, whose head was covered in flames. With vivid velocity, he violently swung around his bright hammer. The metal spikes upon his wristbands clanged loudly as many shoppers fell prey to the weapon's scorching steel.

"Enjoy the taste, scrub?!" the sidvan exclaimed as he took another swing with his hammer, which sent another customer sprawling. Blood and teeth flew in the air as this shopper crashed against a checkout counter. The pupils within his swollen, barely-open eyes ricocheted. He was covered in nasty cuts and scrapes, but none as alarming as the ugly, burnt crater that made up what used to be his left jaw.

"My hammer sure did!" the sidvan chuckled with a blood-thirsty grin. He was cheered by the handful of similarly-dressed individuals, all holding chains and bloody weapons. The shoppers present quietly shot daggers at the ruffians before them. Several of the beaten consumers were entangled in spiked metal chains, with the remaining lying still on the cold floor, now splattered with liquid rubies. While gnashing their teeth, those still conscious tried to break free of their bindings using the last of the strength within their badly bruised and battered bodies, but to no avail. Their captors only chuckled with glee as they pulled harder on the chains. Their captees writhed in pain as the spikes dug deeper into their already-bleeding skin.

"And guess what?!" the sidvan yelled as he raised his hammer above the injured sidvan menacingly. "My hammer is still hungry, and when Splat Jr. is hungry, then Daddy Splat will always provide! Any last words, punk, before I splatter you all over the place?!"

The wounded sidven, who was a middle-aged man, struggled to breathe as he focused intently upon Splat. With narrowed eyes, he slowly raised a hand with his middle and ring fingers extended. The members of the Crimson Storm oohed with amusement at the rude hand gesture. They loved the ones that were bold to the very end.

"Nicely done; now die!" Splat yelled as he brought his hammer down. The wounded sidvan didn't flinch. True citizens of Battletown never showed fear of death, even when it stared directly back at them. Death could come at any moment, and if any allowed fear to paralyze them, how could they continue living their daily lives? Death may have been the inevitable curtain that concluded life, but the unconquerable spirit of those within Battletown flowed with a strength that refused to surrender, even in death.

The swollen eyes of this doomed sidven closed with a silent resolve as the flaming warhammer came down. After hearing a loud pop, he opened his eyes to see Splat flying through the air. Splat Jr. cycled viciously in the air before hitting the ground with a loud clang. Next to the fallen warhammer stood a girl with her fist raised. She had a calm expression but a glare in her eyes as she took a defensive stance. Three of the nearest gang members ran towards Noel with daggers in hand.

"Pathetic," Noel muttered as she quickly dodged their crazed strikes. Before they could respond, she counterattacked with swift punches that landed perfectly between the squares of their eyes. The three Crimson Storm members groaned as they hit the ground like the sidvans they'd terrorized prior.

The faces of the remaining members tensed as they quickly detached their chains around those they held captive and circled Noel. Their smirks returned as they whirled their chains overhead, and a menacing shrill filled the air. The Crimson Storm gang launched their chains at Noel with loud, obnoxious howls.

Noel ducked down, jumped from side to side, and jumped up as she evaded the attacks. She dashed towards the closest gang member, but before getting close enough to attack, the remaining members launched chains at her.

I've got to do something quick, or I'll run out of time to get more info out of that cake dropper, Noel thought as she evaded more chain strikes. She had to give them props for their effective teamwork and coordination. They may be kill-happy thugs, but they had their act together when it came to group synergy. She'd have to mix things up a bit.

With a soft clang, Noel caught a chain that whirled close to her face, much to its wielder's shock. With a mighty tug, she yanked the chain with an impressive amount of force that caused the thug to stumble towards her. Before he could respond, Noel's fist sent him sprawling against the floor, unconscious.

That's one done. Now for the rest... she thought before feeling a chain wrap around her extended arm. Noel grabbed the chain with her other hand and yanked it with all her strength, but this wielder was prepared and pulled back with all of his strength. This thug was still being dragged slowly towards Noel, which gave the other gang members an opening to hurl their chains upon Noel. Soon she found two metal chains wrapped around each arm and leg. She grunted heavily and tried to break free, but even she was struggling against the sheer numbers against her.

"Easily now, girl," another thug muttered as he wrapped a chain around Noel's neck and gave it a hard tug. Noel gasped but firmly held her footing as she shot dangerous glares at the Crimson Storm gang. They may have her securely tied up, but they felt no sense of relief or security. The furious glint within those eyes burned a horrendous fire. Just gazing at her pupils made it feel like their flesh was melting off as their sneers turned into fearful expressions. They wanted to run, to flee as far as they could away from this girl, no, this monster.

But they couldn't; they were hardened thugs, after all. They'd taken lives like children take candy from grocery stores. So with iron resolve, they each planted their feet firmly on the ground as Splat slowly approached Noel with heavy steps. He bent down and picked up his flaming warhammer from the scorched tile flooring before returning his attention to Noel.

"Pretty impressive display, kid," Splat muttered as he rubbed his bruised and bloody jaw before stepping closer to have a better look at Noel. "You're something else. I'd ask you to join us, but you're too dangerous, even for us."

With a loud crack, Noel crashed her forehead into Splat's. He yelped in pain as he stepped back without losing his grip on his hammer. Blood trickled down his forehead as his sunglasses fell to the ground, revealing his dazed blue eyes before they quickly refocused on Noel.

Noel gasped for air as the thug holding her neck chain tugged hard. Splat shot a fearsome glare at the said gang member, who, with a surprised look, loosed the chain's hold upon Noel's neck. As she took several deep breaths, Splat looked at her with a calm, almost reverent expression.

"What's your name, girl?"

Noel glared mercilessly at Splat before responding with, "Noel."

"Then, with the greatest respect," Splat said solemnly as he raised his warhammer overhead, "Noel, I send you off to the Den of the Defeated."

The fire in Noel's eyes raged, completely undaunted, as Splat Jr flew towards her. Victory was assured; Splat knew he was about to paint the store with Noel's blood. But something just didn't sit right in his gut. Something about the intense flames burning within her eyes gave him an ominous feeling. He'd looked into the eyes of many people right before taking their lives. Most stared at the impending doom bravely, but these eyes were different. These weren't the fires of someone too tenacious to die.

They were ravishing, eternal flames that devoured everything.

With an unhinged roar, sweating profusely, Splat brought down his hammer.

Chapter 8

Only the Strong Survive

A loud crack echoed throughout the store. Everyone present stared in disbelief as Splat Jr. made contact.

"Huh?" Splat gasped with wide eyes at what appeared to be a ghostly apparition. Before him, blocking his hammer's blow with a rolling pin, was a boy, the color of cotton, who had appeared out of nowhere. A fine, white powder fell from him, filling the air and covering the ground like newly fallen snow. There was a slight tremor in his legs, but his expression was fierce as he held the rolling pin rigidly out in front of him.

"G-ghost?!!" Splat screamed with a slight stutter as his rigid body quickly jumped back. His face paled. With shaky movements, he held out Splat Jr. to ward off the "apparition" before him as he spoke with as much volume as his body could provide. "Dark Spirit, are you here to drag me away to the Dark Den for last week's lunch incident? You won't get my soul without a fight."

"Dude! I'm not a ghost! I was making bread, and a bag of flour spilled over me. I'm just as alive as you are."

"Are you sure?" Splat said with a perplexed look. "You remind me of someone I whacked at the Pizza Palace last month for putting broccoli on my pizza. Ever since, pizza has tasted funky."

"I'm no ghost! Now step away! I won't let you hurt Jennifer!" Dex yelled with a grunt as he struggled to keep the hammer's head away from Noel. Slowly it descended closer to his face.

"Who the blurf is Jennifer?! The one I'm about to end is Noel, the girl behind you. Only a ghost would call someone the wrong name!"

"For the last time, I'm not a ghost! Now leave Noel alone!"

"Fat chance, ghost boy!" Splat said as his grip tightened on Splat Jr. "After I send you back to the Den of the Defeated, Noel will get a first-class ticket there!" Splat said as he swung his hammer toward Dex. The flour-covered boy intercepted the attack with his rolling pin, but the cooking utensil broke in half under the weight of the crushing blow.

"Ha! I've got you now, ghost!" Splat yelled excitedly as he brought down his hammer upon Dex. Bravado morphed into disbelief and fear as Dex took the appearance of some blurry apparition as Splat Jr. passed harmlessly through.

Sweat poured down Splat's face as he rapidly swung his hammer at Dex, not that it had any effect. At this point, Splat was getting more than a little fearful of Dex, and he wasn't alone. The rest of the Crimson Storm gang and many customers were turning pale.

It was a common belief that ghosts not only existed but were escaped souls from the "Den of the Defeated." These apparitions, believed to be shadows of their former selves, desired nothing but to drag away the souls of the living and feast upon their life energy.

The Crimson Storm gang was already on edge with a chained Noel on their hands, but an intangible ghost boy added to the mix was beyond their emotional capacities. With tense expressions on the remaining gang members, their grips loosened on the chains constricting Noel, and they began taking a few steps back. Seeing this moment of weakness, Noel grabbed the chains around her arms. With a grunt, she yanked the chains from the unsuspecting grips of the thugs. Before the Crimson Storm members holding onto her leg and neck chains could react, she swung the chains in her grasp around until they struck the remaining five thugs in their temples with a loud clang. Their eyes rolled back as they fell to the ground.

Noel grunted as she quickly removed the chains wrapped around her limbs. Ignoring the red marks all over her skin from the chains, she focused on Splat, who was sluggishly swinging at Dex.

"I ... refuse to lose ... to a ghost," he panted as he swung desperately but still couldn't get a solid hit. Honestly, at this point, Dex could have stood completely motionless and Splat still wouldn't be able to hit him.

"Hey, leave him alone!" Noel yelled at Splat as she took a fighting stance. "Your fight is with me. If anyone is going to beat that ghost, it'll be me. Now come on!"

Splat slowly turned to face her. After taking a moment to gather his resolve, he raised his warhammer overhead and charged toward Noel with a loud battle cry. Suddenly all of the lights within the store went out simultaneously.

Bang!

Splat ceased his movement. His hammer fell to the ground. With a dazed expression, he put a hand to his chest only to find a stream of crimson flowing out.

"Wha..." was all Splat could say before another loud bang caused him to fall to the ground. His plasma, now pouring from the opening in his forehead, joined the red canvas on the tile floor. Noel quickly turned around as a handful of sidven wearing glowing, white trench coats with matching white caps appeared within the store carrying various rifles.

"Oh no! More ghosts are invading!" A member of the Crimson Storm shrieked while pale-faced and trembling.

With heavy steps, the ghost-like figures quickly approached the downed members of the Crimson Storm gang as they aimed their rifles at the thugs. Several of the shoppers wore tense expressions until they heard the voice of one of the glowing figures speak out to them.

"Have no fear, good citizens! My name is Sanchez, and we are the White Caps," one of the men dressed in white said with a clear, strong voice as he stepped into the center of the checkout area. He had a dirty-blonde handlebar mustache that was finely waxed and wore a pair of dark goggles over his eyes. "We've come to deal with this violent pack of the Crimson Storm gang. You no longer have to worry about this group or any other causing you harm here again because this store is now under the protection of the White Caps."

The shoppers clapped with relieved expressions while the members of the Crimson Storm gang, that were still conscious, tried to flee, but they didn't make it far before the remaining White Caps quickly cut off their escape route by surrounding them.

"Not so fast!" the White Cap said, flashing an intimidating grin. He strongly resembled a wolf with hungry eyes as he returned his attention to the remaining members of the Crimson Storm. "The fight to restore balance is far from over. For too long, the mighty within this town have mercilessly trampled over those they perceive as weak. Brutality is confused with justice, but we'll establish true justice. A justice that doesn't favor those with bigger muscles but is impartial towards all. You low lives have two options, either yield to us or taste the firepower of our rifles. So what will it be, Crimson Storm, submission," he said as a wicked smile stretched across his face, "or death?"

"We'll never surrender!" They bellowed. Fury filled the eyes of the Crimson Storm as they jumped back on their feet and dashed towards the White Caps with fists raised. They didn't make it far before a series of bullets through their chests stilled them.

The shoppers and staff, excluding Noel and Dex, cheered loudly. Nothing brought louder cheers than when the lives of murderous low lives were snuffed out. This lot may have enjoyed brutal bouts, but murder was an extreme that even they drew the line at .... unless it was the life of a murderer coming to an end.

"And there's more where that came from, dear citizens," Sanchez said while planting a foot on the corpse of a Crimson Storm member. "We will continue to clear out the bloodthirsty tyrants of Battletown that suck away the life and livelihood of everyone here just like the disgusting parasites that they are. We'll create a world where the weak are fed choice steaks while the strong beg for table scraps."

"You're out of your mind!" Noel roared as she ambled towards the speaking White Cap with loud steps. "I bust my butt and bloody these knuckles every night to put food on the table, and you phantom phonies think you can just stroll in here and give me food that I didn't earn! I ought to knock you out!'"

Sanchez aimed his rifle at Noel with a cool expression. He carefully analyzed her and was more than a little impressed. Even with a gun pointed at her from a drux away, she stood undaunted with her arms crossed. The glare he faced seemed to be daring him to try pulling the trigger.

Several of the other White Caps aimed their weapons at Noel, but Sanchez shot them disapproving looks as he lowered his weapon.

"You must be the infamous Knockout Noel. It's an honor to meet you in person," Sanchez said with an over-the-top tone of voice that Noel immediately didn't trust. "You display such an intimidating presence during your fights. It is a true testament to the fighting spirit of this town. However, you have so much untapped potential going to waste. You should partner with us. Fighters who ally with us reach new heights of strength that most can't fathom."

"Not interested, Sanchez. You guys don't seem that intimidating if you need to use guns," Noel said as she struck a fighting pose. "I don't need your charity, and I have no desire to work with someone like you. Now leave before I get your fancy mustache bloody. I'm sure there is an abandoned cemetery that you fakes can go haunt."

Sanchez sighed before raising his rifle at Noel once more. "You're strong, Noel, but don't let that blind you to the current situation. A new era is approaching, one where the strong are torn asunder by those labeled as weak. You can stand with us and reap the benefits of a new town order, or you can stubbornly cling to the values of the past and become a barrier we gun down. Join us, Noel, don't throw your life away because of pride."

Noel's glare sharpened. "Make my day."

She detected Sanchez's right eye twitch and noticed the remaining White Caps shudder before they all hardened their expressions. With steady hands, they kept the barrels of their weapons aimed at Noel as they put their fingers over the triggers.

"Wait!" Dex said as he calmly walked forward, now with all of the flour shaken off of him, and holding a cloth bag.

"I agree that the way of life within Battletown is barbaric, but Noel is nothing like the Crimson Storm gang. She fought valiantly to save those being attacked." Dex said while stepping in front of Noel.

Please don't harm her. I'll pay 400₺ brilocks if you peacefully leave without firing your weapons at anyone else here tonight. If you're unsatisfied then I'm sure that others in the crowd would be more than willing to contribute their brilocks as thanks for riding us of that violent gang, so please lower your weapons. Enough blood has been shed in here today."

Sanchez stepped forward and took the bag from Dex before carefully counting the contents. Inside were precisely 400ᖯ brilocks of the smooth rocks. He quickly put the bag within his inner coat pocket before placing a hand on Dex's shoulder with a firm squeeze. "Thank you for the kind donation. You're both bright and cultured, a rare thing within this town. I hope we meet again soon." He said with a pleasant tone. Before Dex could respond, Sanchez turned to address the other White Caps.

"We shall honor this boy's wishes. Go and collect brilocks from anyone else willing to donate. We're going to head out immediately."

"Yes, sir!" the remaining White Caps said as they quickly approached the remaining customers.

"Hang on!" Noel yelled as she approached Sanchez. "I'm not done with you yet!"

"Unfortunately, my business is concluded with you today, Noel. Your safety has been paid for with blood." Sanchez said as he turned to leave the store with the remaining White Caps following closely behind and carrying several bags filled with clanging brilocks. "If you're unhappy, take it up with your spectacled friend over there."

The ivory glow from the White Caps' clothing dimmed until it was completely extinguished. With a loud click, the lights reappeared. Sanchez and the other White Caps were nowhere to be seen.

Dex sighed in relief, but his expression became fearful once again when he saw the furious expression Noel was aiming at him.

"The blurf is your problem, cake dropper! How dare you pay those spinless, gun-wielding, make-believe ghosts. They didn't deserve any of those brilocks, and now they're going to think they can get away with even more! I ought to bust your chops!" she exclaimed and sauntered towards him with a raised fist.

"For starters, how about a thank you," Dex replied sharply with crossed arms. "I just saved your life twice."

Noel paused. The sound of teeth gnashing reverberated from her clenched jaw as her face turned a light scarlet.

"I didn't ask you to!" Noel exclaimed with her chest puffed out. "I don't need anybody's charity! If someone isn't strong enough to survive on their own strength, then they become a meal for the mighty!"

"Noel, that's not what true strength is," Dex said while shaking his head. "All of the powerful people are surrounded by many mighty individuals."

"Says the ghost boy who can dodge any attack," Noel said, pointing directly at Dex. "Tell me, why did you pay the donation when there is no way that their bullets could have harmed you?"

Dex motioned at all of the surrounding shoppers before responding.

"Because everyone else in this store is vulnerable and could have been hit if I tried to resist. It'd be better to just pay the White Caps and have them leave peacefully than fight back and risk more sidvans getting harmed. Money can be remade; lives cannot. I'm sure there are people who would be sad if you had died here today."

Noel became silent and looked away as an image of a sobbing Alex filled her mind. The fire in her eyes didn't dim, but her expression softened. She looked back at Dex, noticing a strange look in his blue eyes. Behind his glasses was a gray glint within those deep pools, brimming with anger and fear. Not for his well-being but for hers as well as everyone else present. A strange sensation overcame her. One she could not put a name to, now floating within her being. Wary of it, she compressed it tightly and hid it deep within herself before addressing Dex with a subdued scowl.

"You're just too scared to use your abilities; that's why you didn't fight back seriously. You must not be from this area, so let me explain something to you, cake dropper," Noel said with a loud huff. With a look of distaste, she put a hand on her hip while pointing a rigid finger at the ground. "Life here in Battletown is hard. Every day you wake up, it's a fight against yourself, others, and life, all trying to shred you to ribbons mercilessly. Either you fight back and win, or you lose and wind up at someone else's mercy. Compassion for the weak will only weigh you down."

"It doesn't have to be, though," Dex said softly as he bent down and offered his hand to the wounded sidvan leaning against the checkout counter. Surprised and hesitant, he slowly accepted Dex's hand as the pastry chef pulled him to his feet. The sidvan looked into Dex's eyes and gave a respectful nod before turning to assist the other shoppers with what appeared to be trace signs of a smile.

Dex returned his gaze to Noel with a gentle smile. "Compassion can be a mighty source of strength as well."

"Spoken like a true sap," Noel muttered as the timer on her phone went off. Her expression tightened as she quickly turned towards the exit, but not before glaring at Dex out of the corner of her eye once more.

"I'll let you off the hook this time, cake dropper, but next time we meet, I will settle the score with you."

"Please, you don't need to trouble yourself," Dex said with a nervous laugh. "As far as I'm concerned, we're good."

"Not by a long shot," Noel muttered as she dashed out of the store and sprinted down the cracked, rocky road with no stops until she arrived at Kearce Stadium. After rushing inside, she was greeted by Ajax.

"Oh squirt, you finally made it," Ajax said in a friendly manner before stopping to point at the cuts and red marks all over her limbs. "You're all banged up and reeking of snickerdoodle. Did the local Girl Scout troop attack you again?"

"No, the Girl Scouts and I have ... an understanding. All of this was from... something else," Noel said with a guarded expression.

"Are you okay? I heard that you had a rough day at school," Ajax said with a touch of concern. He put a well-muscled hand on her shoulder and squeezed it firmly. "You get into a scrap with someone on the way back from detention?"

"Yeah," Noel said as she gently removed his hand and walked away to begin her workout. She tried to push the image of Dex out of her mind as she started doing her push-ups, but the thought of the one person she couldn't land a punch on had burned itself into her memory.

"One day soon," Noel muttered, "I'm going to beat the stuffing out of that boy."

Interlude 2- Hurry Home, Noel

"Rawr!" Alex roared cutely at the giant five-drux-tall teddy bear in the bedroom she shared with Noel. The sound of old springs popping echoed against the sun-bleached white papered walls while Alex galloped across the faded blue blankets covering the discolored and worn ivory mattress.

She crouched in a cat-like position as she prepared to pounce on her old friend that always kept her company when Noel was out boxing at Kearce Stadium.

"I've got you this time, Ricardo!" Alex yelled as she leaped off the bed onto the stuffed bear and began throwing a series of quick punches. The bear continued to recline carelessly in the farthest corner of the bedroom as Alex's attacks bounced off harmlessly.

"You're one tough cookie, Ricardo, but can you handle this? You'll be toast long before Sis returns from her match tonight!" Alex exclaimed as she jumped onto the wall, only to bounce right off and launch a flying kick into Ricardo's fluffy face.

"So soft," Alex moaned happily as her foot sank into Ricardo's face, and the bear tipped over and fell right onto Alex.

"You tricky fiend," Alex muttered, half impressed, "you got me pinned to the ground when I wasn't ready, but if you think this will be enough to keep me pinned for three seconds, then you have another thing coming...." She stopped suddenly. Outside of the Mud Hut, unfamiliar voices could be heard. Alex quickly peeked outside the bedroom window and detected two adult males in the front yard who were approaching her window. Remembering what Noel told her to do in such a situation, she quickly crawled out from underneath Ricardo and dragged him into the room's closet. Alex slammed the door behind her and grasped tightly to the bear. Quietly, Alex peeked through the openings of the closet.

The figures wore alabaster trench coats and hats. Alex wondered fearfully if ghosts from the Den had come for her before remembering her friend Sara had mentioned a group that tried to resemble phantoms by dressing in all white. These "White Caps" were horrible people that even the police had trouble dealing with. They took brilocks from townsfolk, sold bad things, and hurt people in a bad way.

Why are they here, of all places? she wondered as she tried to make out the two.

"Bryan, why are we here right now?" Rosch asked in a confused and slightly dazed manner. The brown grass crunched under their feet as he and his associate carefully crept around Noel's house.

"As I told you already, Rosch, we're scouting out Knockout Noel's house while she is at her boxing match," Bryan said in a frustrated tone, using both hands to clutch his forehead. This had been a reoccurring question he had been asked throughout the night.

"Sorry, Bryan," Rosch said with a strained expression. It took him a lot of effort to organize his thoughts before voicing them. "After our last meeting with the boss, I've been having a hard time remembering things. It's like trying to carry sand in a bag with a hole in it."

"I know, Rosch, and I apologize if I'm getting a little snippy," Bryan replied with a frustrated sigh as he threw his hands down in a "what do you expect from me" position. "Having the exact conversation multiple times throughout the day is exasperating."

"Bryan, why are we here right now?" Rosch asked, their previous conversation forgotten.

"Ugh!" Bryan moaned while facepalming himself. "We are trying to learn more things about Knockout Noel!"

"Why?" Rosch asked with a blank expression. "What's so important about her?"

"Because she is a phenomenal boxer," Bryan stated matter-of-factly as he leaned against the Mud Hut's wall causally. "Her debut boxing match was about three months ago against a veteran boxer named Mini Megan, whom she defeated with a single punch in the first round and continued to assault until Ajax had to forcibly remove her from the ring.

Since then, Megan has disappeared from the public eye while Noel quickly made a name for herself as the definition of merciless. Currently, Noel is undefeated, having bested every boxer she has faced, including Pronto Paula, Rapid-Fire Rebecca, and Mac-en-Clobber. Along with one other female boxer, she has risen through the ranks within her first season and is favored to win the national female boxing championship qualifiers.

With all of the star power she has acquired so far, I could see her as a valuable asset. Due to her sheer fighting prowess and strength, she would be an excellent sidven for the White Caps to partner with. That's why we're here, trying to learn as much as we can about her. We must increase our bargaining power with her when the time comes to deal."

"Ugh!" Rosch said, grasping at his forehead. "That's a lot of words. It's making my head hurt. But why Noel? Why not use other famous celebrities or athletes?"

"It's all about the trends and culture here, Rosch," Bryan said as he reached for a cigarette. He would need something to calm his nerves if he wanted to end this day with his sanity intact. It was bad enough with all of the family problems he was going through with Kelly and the kids, but having to babysit a brain-damaged Rosch was driving him off the deep end. After lighting his cigarette, he took a deep breath before continuing.

"Rosch, what is the most important thing to the people here?"

Rosch scratched his head as the gears in his burnt-out noggin tried their best to start. "Um...brilocks, shiny gemstones, um ... free health insurance?"

"Not even close. The thing the locals love here more than anything else is fighting, and the more brutal, the better. Sidven will gladly pay any price to witness a good fight. Now, what do you call the sidven who are skilled at fighting?"

"Um..." Rosch stammered for a moment before answering, "Someone that you don't want to make angry."

Bryan cracked a smile before responding, "Celebrities, Rosch, and locals take the words of celebrities to heart. Did you know that all of the Noel-themed merchandise at Kearce Stadium sells out almost instantly? Do you know why? Because the sidven of this town are crazy about that blood-thirsty girl. So if we had a local celebrity like Knockout Noel on our side endorsing our products, it would be phenomenal for business. If we want to appeal to the younger population, we need the backing of younger celebrities like her. Don't get me wrong, there are several other sidven that we are looking into recruiting, but the only one we are investigating this thoroughly is Knockout Noel."

"But what makes her so important? It's not like she is the only boxer in town," Rosch said with a perplexed expression as Bryan pointed to his right temple.

"Have you ever seen her right temple?"

"Um... no. Is it made out of gold or something?"

"No, Rosch. Hidden behind her hair is a birthmark shaped like a fist," Bryan said as he bent down and picked up a hardened cluster of dirt with his right hand. "There is a superstition behind those born with such a birthmark. Some say that they were graced by an angel's touch at birth, while others claim that they're cursed by the dark lord, Divo. Only one thing is for certain: those with these birthmarks go down in history as conquerors who annihilate all who oppose them. Someone like that is definitely needed as an ally in our cause here in Battletown."

His right fingers flexed, crushing the dirt cluster as it became a fine dust that fluttered in the air before trickling slowly to the ground. Rosch stared slack-jawed for a moment before offering a response.

"Okay... I think I've got it now," Rosch grunted with a hand to his forehead. His head was killing him from having to think so much at once. "But the boss says that science always prevails against superstition, so why do we even care about some birthmark?"

"Because it's not superstition, Rosch. Many legendary figures that impacted society had similar marks. These rare birthmarks are physical signs of superior genes for strength, resilience, and formidable prowess. Noel is a prime candidate and one we must closely observe if we are to further our agenda of solving the social disparities within Battletown."

"Umm... I guess that makes sense." Rosch said. His pupils darted every which way in his sockets while he scratched his head with a blank expression. He felt like steam was leaving his ears as he tried to understand what Bryan had just said with very little success.

"Good. Now let's get going for now. There are some other things that I want to check out today before it gets too dark. Let's go grab a quick bite to eat first."

"How about at Happy Smacks?" Rosch asked excitedly.

"No! We've eaten there for the past several days, Rosch! We're doing something different tonight!"

"Sorry, Bryan. I forgot," Rosch said glumly.

"It's my bad, Rosch. I'm still having a lot of family troubles, and you're the one I'm taking it out on. I'm sorry," Bryan said, only for Rosch to grasp his shoulder.

"Don't worry, Bryan," Rosch said with a big smile. "I understand, and I'm here for you. If there is anything that I can do, just say the word."

"Thanks, Rosch, I appreciate that," Bryan said, his lips curving into a smile. He put an arm around Rosch's neck. "You know, I like you a lot more with half of your brain fried out."

"Boy, I must have been a real piece of work back then," Rosch muttered.

"Yeah," Bryan chuckled as the two White Caps left the Mud Hut. "Say, why don't we leave for now and get something to eat at Happy Smacks anyways?"

"Why?" Rosch asked with a blank expression.

"... Let's just go," Bryan said while dragging Rosch away.

Once the familiar silence returned, Alex slowly opened the closet door and peeked her head out. Seeing that the coast was clear, she returned to the window and noticed that the two White Caps were nowhere to be seen. Alex gave a sigh of relief. She couldn't make out everything that the White Caps had said, just something about Noel being famous and then going to eat at Happy Smacks. *Maybe they saw her while she was eating there,* she thought as she pulled Ricardo out of the closet and placed him back in his corner before plunging herself into his extra-soft stomach. Her tiny arms gripped the bear tightly as tears flowed from her eyes.

"Noel, I wish you were here with me now," she moaned unhappily into Ricardo's fur.

"All of these scary things always happen when you're gone."

After bawling for a few movements, she sat up and wiped the tears from her eyes. "Okay, Alex, no more crying. Noel has put me in charge of the Mud Hut whenever she is away, so I have to be strong to protect it from anything, even the White Caps!"

She turned to patrol the rest of the Mud Hut before pausing to look back out the window. She gazed hard out the window in the direction of Kearce Stadium with both hands held over her chest.

"Noel, please come home soon."

Chapter 9

A Glimpse of Unparalleled Strength

"Folks, Noel has found herself in a tight spot!" Jesse B yelled into his microphone.

No dip, buddy, Noel thought as she shielded her face. It wasn't rocket science to understand that she was in a bit of a dilemma. With arms like two firm pillars, she found herself fending off merciless blows. Like rapid machine-gun fire, her opponent was tearing through Noel's defenses.

Her foe was Dana, a fiery redhead with pale skin and emerald eyes. Slightly shorter than Noel, her hair was tied up in a long ponytail with a green scrunchie that swayed from side to side as she hustled towards Noel. She wore a dark green and garnet sports bra with matching shorts. Dana was known as the demon of close quarters. Within arm's reach, she was an absolute terror to fight. Even Noel, renowned for her merciless offense, was forced to defend against the vicious onslaught. Dangerous Dana tirelessly launched mighty blows leaving no openings for Noel.

"Looks like Dana's infamous 'Demon Hail' is being called down upon Noel!" Jesse said with a finger pointed at Dana. "The same dreaded arm work that hits fast and hard like a brutal hailstorm. Using it, she made quick work of Swift Sally, Muscular Michelle, and Thick-Skinned Theodosia! Will Noel be the one who is knocked out this time?! We'll find out here tonight at Kearce Stadium!"

I've got to create some distance. Noel jumped back, only for Dangerous Dana to press forward.

Crat! Noel grumbled internally. *She isn't giving me a chance to create distance. I'll have to make it myself.*

"Give it up, Noel!" Dana yelled while staying within striking range of Noel. "Nothing can stop me once I've focused on something! Not even Divo's blessing can save you!"

"How about when you tried to see *Attack of the Head Smasher* at the movie theater with Mac-en-Clobber?" Noel asked sarcastically.

Dana's face turned a bright crimson. Her eyes widened, and her jaw dropped like a crumbling bridge. The velocity of her punches shifted as they quickly lost their rhythm but continued to pelt Noel haphazardly.

"That's a low blow, Noel!" Dana yelled with furrowed brows. Her mouth contorted into a frustrated frown. "It's not my fault Mac got caught smuggling spaghetti into the theater."

"Remember what happened when security tried to confiscate it?"

Dana's face turned brighter while giving Noel a menacing glare. "Don't you even..."

Noel smirked. "It ended up splattered all over you, 'Spaghetti Girl.'"

"Drop it, will ya!" Dana bellowed as she squeezed her eyes shut as the crowd began chanting, "Spaghetti Girl" throughout the stadium. Dana put her dark green gloves behind her head as her blush spread to her ears. "I've been trying to forget that day ever since!"

Noticing Dana's shift in focus, Noel retreated further into the ring until she could feel the cables behind her. She pulled herself back, feeling the tension of the elastic cables as they stretched away from the ring. With a loud whoosh, the cables launched Noel into Dana. Noel's glove hit the middle of Dana's forehead with the intensity of a freight train. With a loud thud, Dana fell flat on her back. She tried to sit up with a pained expression before collapsing with both eyes rolled back.

The crowd roared with excitement.

"KO! It looks like Knockout Noel has once again lived up to her name!" Jesse shouted in the microphone. "She has claimed another victory and will be moving to round three of the qualifiers, but I have only one question after seeing tonight's superb win. Is there anyone Knockout Noel can't take out in one punch?"

Noel sauntered off the stage and approached the locker room, ignoring the crowd's cheer.

There is one, but his days are numbered.

After taking a cool shower, Noel returned to the girl's locker room. She quickly changed into a sleeveless t-shirt and ripped sweatpants before throwing on her burgundy hoodie. After glancing at the time on her phone, she hustled out of the changing room.

I don't have much time before I need to get back to the Mud Hut and see Alex. I need to make this quick, Noel thought as she entered the built-in gym. A couple of sidven were working out on the machinery and free weights, including Dana, who had changed into a sleeveless green t-shirt with gray sweatpants. Her hair, damp from her post-fight shower, was in a dark green scrunchy with a pink adhesive bandage on the middle of her forehead. Seeing her victorious foe enter the room, she paused mid-squat. While bearing more than double her body weight on her shoulders, she shot a glare that Noel disregarded.

Several of the other gymnites present pointed at her while whispering. Noel thought she heard someone mutter "demon spawn" and "she only won because she was kissed on the forehead by a demon as a baby" under their breath. Noel's fists clenched tightly as she shot a dangerous glare at the whispering gymnites, causing them to avert their gazes and return to their exercise regiments.

After taking a deep breath and readjusting her right bangs, Noel turned towards the farthest corner of the gym, where a computer stood up on a sturdy oak table. It was often used to play workout music, but it was readily available if any gym members/fighters needed to look up information.

Noel sat on the metal, foldable chair in front of the table. With a serious expression, she began typing on the keyboard with slow, powerful strokes until she reached the Harbor webpage. Harbor was the official site where all video footage was uploaded for all official boxing matches nationwide. It was commonly used as a tool for recruiters to scout promising young fighters for the pro league, but it was used most frequently by other fighters to study their competition.

After logging in, Noel scrolled through the recent uploads. There were several fights that she wanted to watch, but she knew she didn't have nearly enough time right now for all of them.

I must return to the Mud Hut soon, so I'll just watch one tonight. Let's see, Right Hook Rheyna vs Pronto Paula, Bionic Bianca vs Monstrous Meg, Vicious Vicky vs Everlasting Edna, and ...

Noel paused. Her eyes widened as they lingered on one link in particular. Before wasting another moment, she clicked on the link that read: Unbelievable Fight!!! Invincible Inaya vs Brutal Bonnie.

Noel grunted as the video that popped up wasn't Inaya's match against Bonnie, but the interview she had given post-match outside the ring and just a couple of drux away from the inner audience members sitting in foldable metal chairs. Click-bait at its finest, yet Noel continued to watch. Usually, Noel could care less about these kinds of things, but this wasn't just any female boxer.

Everyone who kept up with female boxing knew about Invincible Inaya. She was the current national female boxing champion with a strength so great it seemed surreal. During her five-year reign, Inaya was undefeated, with most of her matches concluded after landing the first punch. Footage of her fights was hard to come by since nearly all ended before any videographer could hit the record button.

Noel was dead-set on winning the national championship qualifiers and earning the national title, so she would have to face her one day. Inaya had a fearsome reputation, but Noel wasn't impressed with the girl she saw being interviewed. Inaya's skin was a beautiful tan with a slim face and high cheekbones that seemed to exude an exotic glow in the stadium's lighting. She wore a spotless white-and-pink sports bra with matching athletic shorts and shoes. Her long, wavy, chestnut-brown hair went down her hourglass figure and reached her glutes. Confidence flowed from her as she spoke with a cheerful, almost musical voice. Everyone, including the reporter, seemed to lose themselves in Inaya's presence during the interview, but Noel was more than a little skeptical. Inaya's breathtaking appearance and pleasant mannerisms were far from menacing, and Noel was beginning to doubt that this girl was the national champion.

This chick looks more like a model or a pageant queen. Maybe it's some look-alike? Noel thought when a loud, deep voice drowned out Inaya's interview. The boxer that Inaya had just defeated, a massive girl with cream-colored skin and short black hair up in a top knot, staggered towards Inaya with heavy steps. She had a nasty fist-shaped bruise under her right eye and wore a dark blue, sleeveless, soaked-in-sweat undershirt with matching dark-blue-and-red athletic shorts and shoes.

"Inaya!" Brutal Bonnie bellowed. "I'm not done with you yet!"

Inaya continued answering the reporter's questions, completely disregarding her enraged foe. With an angry roar, Bonnie grabbed the nearest audience member and hurled him at Inaya. With a small smile, Inaya effortlessly caught the sidvan and gently stood beside the dazed spectator before taking a moment to readjust her hair. Bonnie gnashed her teeth together as she grabbed the empty chair beside her and quickly folded it.

"How dare you ignore me!" the beefy boxer screeched as she charged Inaya with the metal chair in her massive hands. "Now die!" she yelled, bringing the chair down with a mighty clang. The reporter had a shocked look in his eyes, but the beefy boxer just seemed confused. The chair should have smashed Inaya, but she disappeared right before it hit.

"Where'd you go?!" Bonnie roared with a confused expression. She looked from side to side but couldn't find a trace of her opponent.

That was when she heard a voice behind her that made her jump.

"Goodness, Brutal Bonnie," Inaya said nonchalantly with both hands on her hips, "you just don't know when to quit."

In a split second, before the chair would've hit, Inaya effortlessly dodged and circled behind her enraged foe. Inaya's calm expression never left as she made her way back to the shocked reporter.

"You're out of your league, Bonnie; now run along before I have to put you out to pasture. I've kept this interviewer waiting long enough," Inaya said pleasantly while waving her hand.

But the look in her eyes glinted a definite warning, one that was completely disregarded.

"Not a chance!" Bonnie yelled as she raised the chair and dashed towards Inaya once more.

With loud whirls, Bonnie wildly swung the chair at Inaya, only for the national champion to become a living blur. Suddenly Bonnie coughed up blood as she hit the ground, the victim of Inaya's relaxed left hand. Noel rubbed her eyes before continuing to stare at the video with an astounded expression. It had happened so fast that her mind had a hard time believing what she saw. Inaya swiftly struck Bonnie's neck before Bonnie or anyone else present could respond. The unbelievable part was that Inaya's arm hadn't even appeared to move at all, but Noel could make out a tiny blur of movement from Inaya before Bonnie went down.

"Holy crat!" Noel muttered in awe. She'd fought in plenty of scraps during her fifteen years of existence, but not even Noel knew how she could beat someone like that. The short-tempered teen turned her focus back to the interview.

"Inaya, that was incredible!" the reporter exclaimed as several bulky referees moved Bonnie's unconscious body off-camera. "How did you get so strong!"

Inaya looked directly into the camera as the cameraman focused on her smiling face. Noel felt almost as if Inaya was staring straight at her. "Hard work, diligence, and practice. A lot of practice."

Practice, huh? Noel thought deeply. What kind of practice could she do that would let her beat someone as unstoppable as invincible Inaya? Noel could punch a training bag until her knuckles were wet with the blood of her unyielding determination, but it wouldn't bring her any closer to landing a blow on someone who was practically untouchable. What could she possibly do to train for her future fight against Inaya?

Then an idea came to her.

Chapter 10

Unfriendly Challenge

There was an intense aura within Jab-en-Grab that evening as Noel trudged through the front door.

The few late-night shoppers became fearful at the sight of the intimidating atmosphere surrounding the young lady, with every shopper fleeing in terror the moment Noel passed them. The whole store seemed to wait with bated breath as she approached the bakery. A loud crash reverberated throughout the store as she brought her fist down on the counter, completely shattering the call bell.

"Coming!" a voice said, hidden from view behind the counter. An all-too-familiar boy hustled to the counter only to turn pale at the sight of Noel.

"Jennifer Smith, I mean, Noel?!!"

"Yeah, cupcake, now get out from the counter. We have business to take care of."

"Look," Dex said, panicking, "I don't have an ice cream cake, but I can slide you some cookies."

Noel leaned against the glass counter and, in a menacing tone, scoffed at the offer. "Naw, I'm not here for sweets. I'm here for you. Now are you coming out, or am I going in?"

A middle-aged man in a store uniform nervously approached them. Sweat drizzled down his balding head with a noticeable shake in his legs.

"Um, young lady, is there something I can help you with?" he asked.

"No," Noel grunted flatly. "My business is with that boy. Get lost."

"With pleasure!" the man exclaimed as he hurried away, but not before turning towards Dex with strict, uncompromising eyes. "Dexter! Go and help this young lady out!"

Dex groaned but bowed his head in resignation as he met Noel on the other side of the counter.

"What did you want from me?" he asked reluctantly.

"We're going to the parking lot," Noel stated, signaling Dexter to follow her. "I'll explain the rest outside."

Noel exited Jab-en-Grab with Dexter following closely behind. Dark clouds covered the charcoal sky outside. Thunder rumbled in the distance; beads of rain fell gracefully upon them with soft finger-like impacts. The only source of illumination came from the single parking lot light pole, and even that was flickering. Aside from a couple of cars, the parking lot was empty. Dexter had an uneasy feeling about being alone here with this girl.

"So ... you needed me for something?" he said as he shivered involuntarily. Now turning into a moderate drizzle, the placid rain soaked his store uniform. Red dye from his Jab-en-Grab shirt leaked into his white apron, turning it a pretty pink.

Noel bent over and picked up a small rock. Her drenched hoodie and sweatpants clung to her slim figure. She now resembled a cat who had just escaped from a body of water. She swiftly pulled the hoodie off and over her head and tied it around her waist, revealing her sopping sleeveless chocolate undershirt. Three words in bright yellow letters declared a bold message: Victory Is Mine.

Dexter felt his fear rise as she casually began tossing the stone in the air only to catch it effortlessly, unfazed by the bone-chilling rain and roaring thunder overhead.

"Yeah," she said nonchalantly as she strolled towards him, still throwing her rock into the air. "I have a problem that needs fixing."

"T-that's awful!" Dexter said, backing up. "Let me go get someone; they can help you take care of it."

"Nah. The only thing I need is you," Noel said, eyes narrowed with a determined expression as she stood within arm's reach of him.

Dexter galloped back further. Noel noticed a slight blush coming from this boy. His cheeks seemed to glow like burning embers, but she had no idea what could be causing it. She just pegged him as the skittish type.

"I'm flattered, but maybe we should start things a little slower. Maybe a movie or dinner at Happy Smacks."

"Not my pace," Noel countered as she closed the gap. Thunder rumbled with every step until she was within hitting range of Dex.

With a loud crack, lightning tore through the nighttime sky. Swift fingers of radiance shredded the dark clouds while the falling rain reflected the intense illumination. The screech of shrill high winds resembled the dying wails of wounded warriors right before the finishing blow, yet this weather paled in comparison to the look within Noel's eyes.

Noel enclosed the rock within her fist, and she slammed it into an open palm while gazing intently at Dex. "The only thing I want to do is hit you hard all night long. You'll be too sore to walk after I'm done with you."

Oh my gosh, it's happening again!!! What am I going to do!!! Dex screamed internally. He felt his heart racing like a deer trying to escape a forest fire. He forced himself to take a few deep breaths. After his pulse slowed, he responded with a cautious smile.

"How about we head back inside the store instead?" he said with a nervous chuckle while gesturing towards Jab-en-Grab's front entrance. "The rain is freezing, and that lightning in the sky looks serious. I'm sure we can come to some agreement over a warm glass of hot chocolate. Surely it wouldn't be in your best interests if we both got sick from this nasty weather," Dexter pleaded with both shaking arms grasping his shoulders. Perspiration was falling from his face, not that it was noticeable because of the frigid rain.

Regardless of the weather, he had no desire to go anywhere with this barbaric girl. He had heard stories from his mother that aggressive girls went after boys like him, and apparently, she wasn't wrong. Still, he had no intentions of winding up as the prey of Noel or any other girl ever again, so he would do anything to escape, even if it meant making a deal with a destructive force of nature.

As if on cue, the store's manager appeared from inside the store just to put up a sign saying that Jab-en-Grab was now closed.

Why manager?! Dex wailed internally. *Jab-en-Grab never closes!*

Noel, who had completely disregarded the store manager's antics, kept her gaze locked upon Dex. Her thoughts focused on what he had said, with two words, in particular, echoing within her mind.

"An agreement?" Noel repeated with a pensive look in her eyes. Her scowl slowly morphed into a small smile. "No, we're going to have a challenge, and the winner gets to decide the loser's fate."

"Hold on," Dexter said, looking confused, "what do you mean decide the loser's fa...?"

"Here is the challenge," Noel said, interrupting Dexter while pointing at him. "You have to stay in that spot, and for ten zins, I will try to hit you. If I make contact once, I win, but if I can't land a solid hit, you win." She threw her rock high in the air. "We'll start when the rock lands in my palm."

"How about we just call it a day and be friends? I can give you a complimentary cupcake," Dexter said. Time seemed to drag, giving the rock the illusion of slowly gliding down toward this savage girl's palm. Once it landed, Dexter felt the terror in his heart multiply.

"Nah!" Noel yelled as she hurled the rock straight towards Dexter's face, but it passed right through him, almost as if he were some apparition.

"You know something like that won't hit m..." Dexter started before being interrupted by a loud beeping. Dexter turned his head only to see that the rock had busted the windshield of a fancy-looking Rock Rumbler, causing the alarm to shriek to life. Dexter was slack-jawed in horror.

"That the manager's new ri..." Dex moaned before he felt a terrible pain in his stomach, causing him to groan. Dexter felt a fist crash into his gut before another collided with his cheek. With a yelp, he hit the pavement hard as his glasses flew from his face and landed on the ground with a loud clang. The world was spinning, and reality seemed to change suddenly. He saw colors he had never seen before, smelled things that weren't in this parking lot and could swear that he heard a bell ring three times.

"Hitting me when I wasn't looking was a low blow," Dex moaned as he put a hand over his now-bruised cheek only to discover that his glasses were no longer on his face. He patted around the ground until he found his glasses. As he slid them on, he was surprised by what he saw. Dexter clutched his aching head. His cranium must have banged the asphalt hard because as he sat there sluggish from the pain, he saw Noel standing above him.

The dark clouds dispersed, the thunder and lightning ceasing as if on cue, revealing several brilliant stars within the slumbering sky. These sparkling diamonds surrounded the bright moon as light from the gemstones of night shined down upon the breathtaking girl before him.

Noel had an air of sovereignty. Her tan skin glistened in the enchanting starlight showering down upon her. Her short hair, braided like two half-crowns of obsidian over the left side of her head, shimmered beautifully in the heavenly glow. The gold hoop earrings she wore on her ear lobes glinted. The wind, now a light breeze, gently blew her right bangs away from her forehead, showcasing her fist-shaped birthmark. Her usually defiant, brown eyes, now a jewel-like amber hue, gleamed with intensity in the dazzling light. She wore a fierce expression, both fists clenched and down by her sides like she had just won a brutal brawl effortlessly.

Dexter was awestruck before remembering his promise.

"So, what do you want from me?" he groaned.

Noel didn't hesitate to respond. She flashed a smug smile before answering.

"You, Dexter, will become my new punching bag."

Victory
is
Mine

Chapter 11

Healing Hands Hospital

"What?" Dexter asked, dumbfounded. Surely, he must have misheard her. There was no way she actually wanted him to be her punching bag.

"You heard me," Noel said, arms crossed. "Until I've won nationals, you will be my punching bag. I plan to punch you every day until the champion's belt rests on my waist."

"You're crazy!" Dex yelled as he jumped back on his feet. He swayed slightly, still off-balance from Noel's ferocious assault. "Just use an actual punching bag."

"No. I won't get stronger hitting regular bags," she declared as she stepped towards him and grabbed his shoulder. Noel's resolute eyes met Dex's gaze as she continued. "I need something more challenging to hit to improve my skill as a boxer."

Dex was silent for a moment. His facial expressions shifted rapidly from fearful to concerned to melancholy before finally lingering on uncertainty.

"Why do you want to get stronger?" he asked, glancing at her forehead before returning his gaze to her eyes as she scowled.

"That's none of your business!" Noel snapped. She released her grip on Dex and pulled out her phone. "Now give me your number. I'll text you when and where we will be meeting."

Hesitantly, Dexter gave his number to Noel before heading back inside Jab-en Grab for closing. Noel gazed at the number on her phone with a determined look. She left the store's parking lot as she made her way through the darkened, rocky path back home, seeming to disappear like the flickering light.

I finally have a way to beat her.

It wasn't until the early morning of the following day that Noel and Dexter again crossed paths. As light pierced the sky's obsidian cloak, they found themselves on an empty "dodge the ball if you value your life" court in Paslow Park. The concrete court was unlevel, with cracks and potholes scattered throughout. Surrounding the outer perimeter of the court was a trench filled with many vertical, pointed sticks sharp enough to pierce bone easily. Thankfully, no living creatures had fallen in this morning, so the air was void of the scent of rancid flesh and the loss of life. Granted, most true residents wouldn't bat an eye to the fallen within the trench. To them, anyone who succumbed to such a gruesome fate deserved to perish. Life only belonged to those mighty enough to overcome any obstacle that it provided.

"Ugh," Dexter said, trying to stifle a yawn. His gray hoodie was comfortable and kept him warm during these cool mornings here in Battletown, making it a staple piece of clothing. On the front was an image of a cartoon character shaped like a combination of a carrot and broccoli with the words "Carroccoli clobbering" underneath the character. It was from a popular show called *Food Fighters,* where people battled each other with various food-shaped creatures. Alex was really into the show and always made Noel watch it with her every Saturday morning.

"I came here just like you wanted me to, so what did you have in mind?"

Dexter's head swerved to the right to avoid the fatal fist that lay a fingernail's length away from his cheek.

"Just this," was Noel's only response before launching a barrage of punches. Dexter's body became like a ghost: visible to the eyes but impossible to touch. It was like trying to strike a beam of light as Dexter moved, completely unscathed by the fury of the blows.

Blurf! I can't land a punch on him! I've got to mix things up a bit, Noel thought as she jumped forward with a powerful punch.

Dex carefully kept his eyes trained on Noel as he dodged by backing up and kept retreating as she pressed forward with many quick punches. Dex narrowed his eyes, trying to figure out what Noel was planning. While phasing through several jabs, he stroked his chin and carefully analyzed her movements. There was no doubting the intensity of her blows; an average opponent would have tasted the concrete after the first punch. However, when the straightforward approach failed, this chick was a pro at performing the unexpected.

"Just what..." he started to say as his foot snagged in a pothole. He stumbled backward, his arms flinging wildly as Noel appeared in front of him, fist raised.

"I've got you!" she yelled, throwing a mighty punch toward the midair boy. Noel's fist approached Dex's body fast, but not fast enough. Dex's arms quickly palmed the ground and swerved his body a hair's width from the devastating blow. Noel's face promptly morphed from smug satisfaction to shock and finally to frustration.

"Eat this, cake dropper!" She hurled punches left and right, only for Dex to dodge by swerving from side to side and unlodging his foot from the pothole. Dex quickly rolled to his side and jumped back to his feet. Noel growled and dashed towards him, fists raised, and hurled punch after punch. This went on for many hinos, and through sheer tenacity and rage, Noel kept training with no intention of stopping.

Noel felt the burn within her muscles. Her lungs felt like they had been replaced with lead. Noel panted heavily as her punches slowed drastically. Beads of sweat drizzled down her face, and her arms and legs trembled slightly as she tried to hide her fatigue from Dexter.

"How about we take a break?" Dexter asked, not overlooking the speed decline in Noel's fists.

"No," Noel answered resolutely. "I'm not done with you yet."

She continued throwing punches, with Dexter inevitably dodging every single one. It wasn't until the sun was over them that Noel took a knee. Her breathing was short and rapid, like an angry beast. Her arms shook as they felt heavy as lead, not that she cared. She had too much to lose if she stopped here.

Dexter saw that her body could no longer maintain the regiment, but the fire in her eyes burned bright. Dexter flinched slightly even though he knew she could do nothing to hurt him in this state. Yet a strange sensation flew through his body, warning him that Noel was still very dangerous. Swallowing his remaining hesitation, he approached Noel.

"Noel, it's time to take a break. You need to rest."

"No... I can still... keep going."

"If you don't rest, then this training will have the opposite effect. You need to stop!"

"No... I don't quit. I keep fighting until I win."

"Why is winning so important?! Why would you drive yourself to exhaustion just to win a few boxing matches? Your health is far more important!"

"Shut up!" she bellowed as she mustered all of her remaining strength to stand. "I have to win all of my matches and qualify for nationals to provide for my sister!" She took shaky steps towards Dexter. "I have to win so that I can keep her safe!

Losing isn't an option, so I don't care what I have to sacrifice. I will do anything to gain the strength I need, and nothing, not this body, my opponents, or you, will keep me from getting stronger." She staggered as she took a wild swing at Dexter, that was nowhere close to connecting, and stumbled before falling to the ground. Dex ran towards her with a worried expression while calling her name. His voice reached out for her desperately but failed as her world became swallowed in a sea of black.

Eventually, the sea of black disappeared, and Noel found herself in a bed with white sheets. She was in a room with light brown wallpaper, white tile floors, a beautifully varnished wood cabinet in the far corner, and a giant window that showed the outside world. It was open, letting the bright sun and pleasant breeze inside the room. It was a beautiful day, and just as Noel started to enjoy it, she felt a presence beside her.

"You finally woke up."

Noel turned her head only to see Dexter sitting in a chair beside her bed. "Are you feeling better?" He leaned forward, his face filled with concern while observing Noel's dazed expression. As much as he would love to call it quits early and head back to his warm bed, he had no intention of leaving this exercise-crazed girl alone when she was unconscious.

"Yeah," Noel said as she yawned, "I guess all I needed was a little res..." She stopped. Her eyes widened in silent horror as she glanced down and realized she was no longer wearing her street clothes. Instead, she was wearing a gown with a wristband that had her name on it. Sweat began to bead on her face as she grabbed Dexter by the collar.

"Dexter, where did you take me?" she said in a slightly lower tone.

"Well, I was concerned, so I brought you to the hos," Dexter began before a man in a white coat entered the room. He was an older man with puffy gray hair that was balding on top.

"Hello there, Noel! I'm Dr. Fistmore," the man said in a professional manner. "I came by to..."

"Get out!" Noel snarled, glaring at the doctor. As he was about to say something in response, Noel stated, "I'm choosing the Tahalix Clause." The doctor briskly ambled out of the room without uttering a word closing the door behind him.

"You seriously took me to the hospital?! What is your problem?!" she said, glaring daggers at Dexter.

"You passed out after your nonstop training. Did you expect me to leave you on the court?"

The harshness dimmed from her eyes as she released him from her grasp. "Yeah, thanks... Now we need to leave. Right now."

"Wait, you have to be discharged first. Leaving AMA is really frowned upon."

"Do you know how much it costs to stay at a hospital? I can't afford to be here until they discharge me. Besides, I just declared the Tahalix Clause," she said, jumping out of bed. "We need to leave now before they get here."

"What are you talking about? Dexter asked with a bewildered expression. "Who is coming?"

The door crashed into the wall with a loud clang, and two burly men sauntered into the room. They were wearing neutral white polos, which matched their tan khaki pants, both of which clung tightly to their muscular bodies. They were a little under five drux, and a chill ran down Dex's spine.

"Department of Finances," they both said in unison. They stood blocking the door while staring at Noel without a single emotion on their faces. They both wore rectangular name badges; according to them, these two men were called Smash and Trash. Smash was light-skinned with a bald head and a bigger build. Trash had the same skin type but was a little taller with his short, black hair in a side part pompadour with a chin strap beard.

The man named Smash stepped forward and spoke. "Noel Smith, I was told you planned to use the Tahalix Clause. Can you confirm that you intend to pay using your fists instead of financial assets?"

"Duh!" Noel said, stepping forward and giving the two men the stink eye. "You think that I can afford to pay for my time here? I'd have to choose between paying the bill and having groceries for the next several months."

Trash stepped forward next. "I understand. Here, sign this," he said while handing Noel a document with a pen. "This is the Tahalix Clause form. Once it is signed, the Tahalix Claus will legally take effect."

Noel slowly signed her name while Dexter rapidly read over the fine print.

"Noel, are you crazy! You can't seriously be planning to fight these two in a battle to get out of paying! If you lose, the consequences will be dire. Not only will you have to pay for today, but you'll have to pay for any additional medical attention that you'll need after this. Once you sign this, they are legally free to beat you within an inch of your life. If things go poorly, you may require time in the ICU."

"I've got it worked out," she said under her breath. "I just won't lose. Besides, I put a different name on the form. If I lose, I could always defeat them in a legal battle." Dexter put a hand to his forehead as Noel handed the signed document to Trash. He pulled a pair of navy glasses from his breast pocket and thoroughly analyzed the document. After a moment, his glasses shimmered. He frowned and motioned for Smash to come over and look at the paper. Smash whipped out a beryl monocle from his pocket and put it over his left eye as he looked over the form. Smash's monocle shimmered, and Smash frowned as well.

"This signature is wrong," they both said in unison. "Jennifer Smith is not your legal name, and falsely identifying yourself on a legal document is a crime punishable by the law. Law enforcement may need to be contacted...."

"Wait! Hold on just a minute!" Noel said frantically. Getting law enforcement involved was the last thing she needed right now. "Jennifer Smith isn't my legal name, but it's the name I go by frequently. It was a simple slip-up."

"Oh," both said together.

"Then here is another form for the Tahalix Clause," Trash said, handing Noel another form. "Be sure to use your **legal** name on it. There have been several cases of sidvens purposefully putting the wrong name on these forms and massive legal battles occurring as a result. This document is meant to protect both sides legally."

"Yeah, right," Noel muttered before returning the newly signed documents to Trash. After briefly examining it, he nodded in approval.

"The signature here is correct. Now we may proceed with the Tahalix Clause," he said before carefully folding the paper and putting it in his pocket. Both men removed their eyewear as they squared off against Noel. Trash gave Dex an expectant look as he pointed toward the door.

"I'm going to have to ask you to leave the room. This financial discussion concerns Noel's stay here at Healing Hands Hospital, and you are not on the list of those authorized to participate."

"Really?" Dex said sarcastically. "Beating up underaged girls for financial profit is acceptable, but me sticking around during this 'meeting' is somehow crossing a line? This feels more like an abuse of power."

"I'm afraid you're sorely mistaken, glasses boy," Trash said, glaring slightly. "This falls within our legal practice as allowed by the 'Degree of Brutality.' We are above board as long as I have this signed Tahalix Clause. Now, you must leave this instant!"

Trash pointed a rigid finger towards the exit.

"If you refuse to leave, then you will be considered an interloper, and we will be allowed legally to use lethal force to remove you from the hospital grounds," Smash said as he stepped forward with his beefy arms crossed. The throbbing veins on those arms were more than a little intimidating, but Dex refused to leave. He could tell that these guys meant business, but the look in his eyes conveyed one message very clearly to everyone else in the room. He wasn't going any-where.

Noel looked irritated as she cleared her throat, and Dex turned to face her.

"Dude," Noel said gruffly as she focused her eyes on Trash and Smash, "I can handle things here. You can wait for me outside. This won't take long."

A chill went up Dex's spine as he gazed at the blazing embers within her eyes. Most would call those the eyes of a monster seeking to rip others to shreds, and while Dex didn't nec-essarily deny that, there was also something nostalgic about these flames. This scorching fire was fueled partially by anger but seemed to burn intensely from a hidden passion. Some-thing deep down fueled Noel with an unyielding, unmerciful, and uninhibited strength. It was for that reason Dex stepped in front of Smash with a resolute expression on his face.

I can't let her fight alone. Noel's strength is frightening, but until she has tempered it, she runs the risk of being devoured by it.

Smash's eyes twitched as he breathed in loudly through his nose. "Fine. Have it your way, glasses boy, but don't start beg-ging for mercy after you and Noel end up bedbound. Trash, you deal with Noel, and I'll teach this boy a painful lesson about why you never mess around with the Department of Finances."

"Fine, but don't tire yourself out. We have five more residents we need to see after we've finished this dispute," Trash replied before returning his attention to Noel. "Now it is time to collect your payment. I hope you're ready," Trash said as he struck a fighting pose with clenched fists raised.

"Bring it on," Noel said, glaring into Trash's eyes. "I won't lose to you."

Chapter 12

The Fight for Noel's Finances

Trash rushed over, swinging his arms in a multitude of mighty blows. His fists hit with the intensity of a raging rhino; thankfully, they were easy to read. As Trash threw constant right and left hooks, Noel sidestepped, always staying out of reach. After several punches, Trash slightly overextended his reach. Sensing the shift in balance, Noel slithered within striking range and sent her fist straight into Trash's face. His nose warped to the left with a loud snap. Trash grunted in pain; blood dribbled down his nose. Noel was about to throw another punch at Trash's nose, but a pair of arms appeared and wrapped themselves around her. It was Noel's turn to grunt in pain as the arms squeezed her tighter and tighter.

"Not bad for the famous Knockout Noel," Trash said as he continued to crush her within his arms, "but you're a boxer. You might as well give up. Holds are something you're not familiar with in boxing."

"We'll ... see about that," she grunted as she threw her face into his chest, her teeth digging deeply into his skin. Immediately Trash cried out in pain as he released Noel from his grasp, only for Noel to launch a series of blows into his face and stomach. Trash bellowed in pain as he pushed Noel away. He wobbled slightly from side to side with a look of anger in his eyes.

"Smash, get over here! I might need some help with this one!"

"What's the problem, Trash?" Noel said, flashing a cocky smile. "Are you afraid that you can't handle me by yourself?"

"Quiet, girl!" he yelled. "You've just gotten a few lucky hits in. Don't let it go to your head."

"Sorry, but that is your problem, Trash! My hands are full over here!" Smash grunted. He was more than a little busy himself. Smash was hurling his brick-sized fists at Dex, but nothing was connecting. Smash began panting heavily after a few yosmins of failed attempts to knock out the living blur right before him, but Dex nimbly dodged every single attack. Terror was forming within Smash's eyes.

"Are you blurfing kidding me!" Trash exclaimed. "That scrawny glasses kid should be an easy win. A strong breeze could blow him over!"

"You'd think, but I can't land a single blow! Every attack just passed through him! I think he may be some kind of apparition!" Smash said fearfully as his fists moved in desperation. "The souls of those we've bled dry financially are finally coming for us!"

"Smash, how many times do I have to tell you that all that ghost superstition is nothing but hogwash! Now stop screwing around and finish him off already... Ahh!" Trash yelled as Noel sent her fist crashing into his jaw. Trash hit the ground hard, and after watching his body remain still for a few moments, she turned her attention to Dexter's fight with Smash. Smash threw a fury of punches, but none came close to hitting Dexter. Finally, Smash put his hands on his knees as he bent over, breathing heavily.

"Have mercy on me, apparition!" Smash bellowed as he fell to his knees and bowed before Dex. "Please don't devour my soul!"

"Oh, blurfing blat blits!" Trash groaned in an exasperated tone. He struggled to get on his knees before his arms gave out, and he hit the ground with a thud. "You're a grown man; now get over your childish fears and crush that kid!"

"Hey, if you want to get dragged off to the Den, then be my guest, but I plan on living past today, Trash!"

"I'm no ghost, Smash," Dex said, interrupting the conversation. "I'm just a regular sidvan who doesn't like pain, but if you want to do your good deed for the day, let Noel and me go. That's the best way to start atoning for the long list of cruelties you've committed in the name of the financial department. Otherwise, I'll have to fight you a little more seriously, Smash."

Smash reached into his pocket and put his monocle over his eye. After the blue glass twinkled, he put it back in his pocket. With a determined expression, he slowly got back on his feet and struck an intimidating fighting pose.

"Sorry, ghost boy, but I have a job to execute here. As much as I don't want to go to the Den at the end of my life, I can't just allow potential payers to walk away. This building can't sustain itself financially if it doesn't receive brilocks from clients. Failing to receive payments would result in bankruptcy for Healing Hands Hospital, and then everyone would have to travel out of town to receive urgent medical attention."

Dex stood there wide-eyed and carefully analyzed Smash's words before glancing at Noel, who stood above Trash's unconscious body with her left fist tightly clenching onto something.

"Noel, are you sure we can't just pay your bill instead? I'm willing to pitch in if it means we don't cause the economic collapse of this building."

"Not a chance!" Noel yelled as she crossed her arms with a look of defiance on her face. "Whether I'm talking to a White Cap, someone from finances, or the blurfing president himself, the answer is still the same. No, you aren't getting my money! You'll have to settle for broken bones and bloody noses!"

"Thought so," Dex sighed before taking up his fighting stance. "Guess that means we're fighting this one out then. May the best, and hopefully least morally corrupt, sidvan win, Smash."

"Right back at you, ghost boy," Smash muttered respectfully before charging straight at him and leaping several drux into the air. With a loud cry, Smash brought down his fist where Dex had been standing, only for Dex to dodge.

"Not bad!" Dexter yelled before taking a deep breath and a moment to readjust his glasses. It irked him how they always had to reposition whenever he dodged an attack. He would go without them if they weren't necessary for his vision. "I like your determination. If I were your ghostly judge, I'd give you an acquittal."

"Thanks, that means alo…" Smash said before freezing in place. Slowly his hands moved to his crotch, which was in excruciating pain, only to find a foot firmly planted against his crushed boys.

"I hope having kids wasn't on your bucket list," Noel said before crashing her fist into the back of his head. Smash groaned lightly as his eyes rolled in his sockets. He crumpled into the ground face first with a loud thud. "Yeah, that guy won't be smashing anytime soon."

"A little excessive, don't you think?" Dexter asked. Despite the situation, he couldn't help but feel a little concerned for the two financial department members that lay at their feet.

"It would have been us otherwise. Here, the ultimate authority belongs to the mighty. The winner gets to determine the fate of the defeated. That is how things work in society. Now let's beat it."

Dexter's face tensed at her words, but he followed behind her. A blush formed on his face as Noel headed towards the door. He was so distracted by what lay before him that he failed to notice the presence behind him.

"Not ... so fast ...Noel."

Noel heard a yelp behind her. She turned to see Trash back on his feet, tightly grasping Dexter's wrists. With a loud grunt, he twisted Dex's arms behind the boy's back in a double chicken wing hold.

"End of the line, Noel! Now you will pay for your stay here, or your friend will have his arms broken! So what's it going to be?!" Trash yelled. To emphasize the point, he further bent Dexter's arms backwards. Dexter groaned as he struggled to break free.

Noel calmly approached Trash with slow, purposeful steps. "Trash, do you know how we get our nicknames at Kearce Stadium? Every boxer is given a word that is added to their name, and it is that one word that describes their prowess in battle and embodies the kind of strength they possess. Tell me, Trash, what do you think it means when someone is given the word 'knockout?' Let me tell you. It means that no matter who I'm against or what the situation is, there is only one out-come for any who oppose me. So tell me, Trash, how do you want your beating: well done or medium rare?"

"Nice bluff, girl," Trash scoffed in disbelief, "but there is nothing you can do to save your friend."

"You sure about that?" Noel said calmly as she opened her left hand and revealed a folded paper.

Trash's face instantly changed into an expression of horror. "What!? How did you get your dirty hands on the Tahalix Clause form?!" He pushed Dexter to the ground and searched his pants pockets, only to come up empty-handed.

"I took it from you after you hit the ground. Funny how this one sheet of paper is the only thing protecting you legally from several counts of assault and battery. Shame if something bad happened to this important piece of paper. Oops," Noel said as she ripped the paper in front of Trash. His face morphed from pure terror to red-faced with animosity. He charged at Noel with both hands intertwined and raised overhead to attack, but the calm look never left Noel's eyes. When he was within Noel's reach, she clenched her fist and hurtled it into Trash's already-broken nose. Trash gave a weak scream as the skull around the nose collapsed. Trash hit the ground again, but he showed no signs of getting up again.

"Looks like you'll need to find a new job. Maybe you can get one with the dump truck. They're great at picking up trash."

She turned her attention back to Dexter. "Come on, let's get out of here."

"Yeah," Dexter replied, looking really uncomfortable, "but do you plan on leaving here dressed like that?" He pointed to her hospital gown, and she noticed that it wasn't tied in the back. Her backside was completely exposed. Thankfully, they'd kept her undergarments on her when she was changed, but the greenish-blue floral-patterned gown clashed with her blood-red bra and panties.

"Yeah. This gown is tacky, and it keeps falling down my shoulders. Either I'm changing, or the one who designed this gown is getting a fist to the jaw."

"Your clothes are in the cabinet. Once you're dressed, we should hurry up and go," Dexter said, trying to redirect her from the poor soul who crafted her gown. "I'm sure you're eager to get back home. Today sure has been tiring, huh?"

Noel turned her head and glanced at him with a wild look.

"What are you talking about? That was just a warm-up. The real workout begins the moment we leave this building."

Dex looked at her like she had grown a second head.

"You can't be serious, Noel! The whole reason you came here in the first place is because you overexerted yourself! Do you really want to have to come back here?!"

"It's your fault for overreacting," Noel said with an annoyed grunt.

"Overreacting! You passed out from excessive training!"

"Next time, just dump cold water on me. That'll do more than a trip to the hospital ever could," Noel replied nonchalantly as she began to walk away before stopping at the hospital exit to turn her head. She glanced at Dex from the corner of her eye as she swung the door open. "Now let's go. We don't have a moment to waste."

Dexter hung his head but followed after her as he groaned. "Fine, but can we get something to eat first?"

Chapter 13

Happy Smack's Chat

"Okay, I think it's time we talk training," Dexter said. The two had decided to get lunch at one of the popular fast-food chains within Battletown and the surrounding areas, Happy Smacks. They specialized in making meals out of beef, chicken, and fish. The food wasn't the healthiest option out there, and the service was nothing to write home about, but they were abundant in the holy trinity when it came to what people desired in food (good tasting, quick, and cheap). Dexter had ordered a baked fish salad with water, while Noel ordered a triple happy stacker cheese and bacon burger combo with fervor fries and a large cup of Crackling Cola. She had also ordered a Happy Smackers meal off the child's menu because she thought Alex would enjoy it. Alex **loved** collecting the toys from each meal, and the thought of seeing her smile after receiving her meal warmed Noel's heart.

Noel and Dexter sat in a green booth surrounded by other green and orange booths and tables, each filled with cheerful families, chattering groups of friends, or lonesome individuals here to enjoy lunch in solitude. The room's walls were painted a bright yellow, but it had many large windows that allowed a pleasant view of the chaos of the outside world while enjoying a greasy five-patty burger with a milkshake so thick they required thorough chewing before being swallowed. The secret behind the Happy Smacker menu's huge success was the immense levels of grease used for everything. The food, the drinks, the napkins, the toilet paper, everything was soaked with grease. Even the air gave off the strong aroma of fryer grease, which could be smelled from over a kadrux away.

Dex felt himself wanting to gag from this insane level of grease wafting through the air that he breathed. He was afraid that being inside this eatery another five minutes would give him a heart attack, while Noel continued to gobble down her food indifferently.

Seriously, everyone here is so afraid of this 'Den of the Defeated,' but no one bats an eye about this place. The saturated foods served here could kill someone way quicker than a ghost.

Noel, too, was baffled. She didn't get why Dex seemed so tense at Happy Smacks. The famous saying here was, "If the food doesn't kill you, then keep eating until it does! Every bite is a battle, and until you lose, it is your duty to keep fighting!" Unsurprisingly, these words had a remarkable impact on Noel, as she chose to eat here regularly.

"Why? I already know that I'm going to spend my spare time beating the living crat out of you. I don't see why we need to discuss that," Noel said as she shoveled some piping hot, golden-brown fries into her mouth.

"Because," Dexter emphasized, "training is more than physical exercise. It's about making wise life choices that will complement your physical training and make you the best Knockout Noel that you can be."

"So what, you want me to start flushing the toilet after every use, washing my hands before every meal, and brushing my teeth three times a day? That sounds like a waste of time and brilocks to me. It would be better spent bruising my knuckles in a real scrap."

"First off, those are all things you should already be doing. Ew. Second, the changes I'm talking about are more closely intertwined with your physical performance. Like your diet, for example."

"What about it?"

"Look at what's on your plate," Dex said as his face crinkled. "You have a giant greasy burger. Sure, you're getting protein, but all of that grease will clog up your arteries. You have a pile of overly saturated fries with enough salt to dry out your body. Then there is your soda, which is nothing more than sugary carbonation that will hinder your performance with boxing."

Are you seriously dissing my lunch?" Noel said, rolling her eyes. "It's my food; lay off."

"It's more than just your lunch. You frequently stock up on junk food at Jab-en-Grabs almost every night. Your evening meals normally consist of fatty ribs and pastries from the deli."

"Hey!" Noel exclaimed with a glare in her eyes. She took a big bite out of her burger before menacingly pointing a finger at Dexter. "You need to back off. You're starting to bug me."

"Seriously, I've never seen you eat or buy a single healthy source of nourishment ever," Dex said with dismay as he watched Noel sloppily consume the rest of her burger. It was like watching a wild beast from the prairie devour some poor animal it had just caught. "What would your mother think if she saw this?"

"I couldn't care less if that woman has a problem with my diet," Noel grumbled while shoveling the rest of her fries into her mouth. "It's my body, so I get to choose what I eat, when, and how much. And nobody who values their life will tell me otherwise."

Dexter chose to overlook that she was talking with food in her mouth. In all actuality, there was one thing he was impressed about right now regarding Noel. The fact that she could shovel enormous amounts of food into her stomach and still come off looking so skinny.

Where does she put it all? Maybe everything she eats gets burned away from her never-ending training? Dex pondered to himself as his thoughts shifted back to the unhealthy state of Noel's diet.

"You're only hindering your performance with boxing. Hey," Dexter said with a slight pause before continuing, "Why were you pushing yourself so hard during our practice earlier? I remember you said something about providing for your sister, but I don't see why you must push yourself to exhaustion. You are already powerful and talented. A normal workout ought to be enough to prepare you for the national qualifying boxing match and beyond."

"No," Noel replied. "I will not be strong enough if I resume my normal routine. I need you to get stronger."

"Dude, I just saw you deck two grown men. What do you need even more strength for?"

Noel was silent for a moment before responding. "Does the name 'Invincible Inaya' ring any bells?"

"N-nope, never heard of her. Who is she?" he replied with a bit of a squeak. Noel might have imagined it, but she almost thought she saw his eye twitch. *Weird.*

"Invincible Inaya is the current five-year reigning national female boxing champion. She is the 'Heavenly Hurricane' and possesses unparalleled speed, strength, and reaction time. Most of her punches are so fast that they can't be viewed even when replayed on the slowest camcorder setting. And the power behind those fists is unlike anything I've ever seen. Inaya makes Dana's 'Demon Hail' look like a harmless sprinkle. Honestly, my chances of beating her are very slim."

"Then why worry about beating her?" Dexter asked. "You could make it to the championship round and become the runner-up. The prize money is still an impressive amount."

"No," Noel said defiantly. "I haven't worked my butt off just to come in second place. Nothing is worse than that. I will beat her, and if I have to endure nightmare-inducing training to get there, then so be it. I have too much riding on this; I have to go all out."

Noel slammed her fist against the table, and a large crack appeared under it as Dex sighed.

"I'm not sure you realize exactly what you're signing up for, Noel," Dex said with a serious expression. "To train enough to punch me is one thing, but defeating Inaya is on a completely different level. That is a long, arduous journey where only a few successfully make the distance because the strength level gap is staggering. I've seen others with similar goals try to obtain this kind of power, with their relentless pursuit destroying them in the process."

"What are you getting at?" Noel asked as she leaned closer, and her voice deepened. "You think I'm not strong enough?"

She grabbed Dex's collar and pulled him up until they were face to face. Although he knew full well that Noel couldn't land a fair punch on him, something about the fire burning in her gaze served as both a source of fear and captivation for him.

He knew the bright light that burned in those eyes filled with ambition was like a ship sailing at sea without a rudder and map. Without direction, Noel could spend a lifetime traveling and never reach her desired destination. Yet she showed no fear even to adversity and never hesitated to ram through any obstacle obstructing her path.

Noel's grip tightened as she spoke clearly with a ferocious tone.

"Let me tell you just like I told Trash. I am Knockout Noel, and I will beat anyone who stands in my way for the national title. Even Invincible Inaya herself will taste defeat after she crosses blows with me, and you are the key to her demise!"

Noel exclaimed as she stood from the booth while clutching Dex's now-wrinkled collar.

She stepped out from the booth while dragging Dex simultaneously. With swift motions, she grappled him until she was behind him with one hand tightly clamped around his neck and the other holding his left arm behind his back in a chicken wing. Dex winced in pain, trying to break free, but to no avail.

"See," Noel growled in a low tone as she leaned her mouth towards his ear. "You think that just because I can't hit you, I can't hurt you, cake dropper, but you're wrong. I've been paying close attention to you, and I've noticed three weak spots with your dodging abilities."

Dex squirmed uncomfortably as his face turned bright red. This was the closest he had been to someone of the opposite gender, and he was having a hard time processing everything. Between Noel's hot breath tickling his ear and her body pressing into his back, he could feel his body temperature rising. If this lasted much longer, he was afraid he might start melting.

To make matters worse, everyone else in Happy Smacks was staring at them. Most of the ladies giggled as their big eyes sparkled with absolute joy at the sight of Noel and Dex's interaction.

"Those two are so precious! Young couples sure are bold these days." The ladies squealed with delight as they watched with eager anticipation.

Conversely, the men either rolled their eyes or gave low chuckles as they caught sight of Dex within Noel's vicious headlock.

"Yep, there is no escaping for that poor glasses boy now. His days of freedom have been cut short. It's always tragic to happen at such a young age."

All the children present pointed and laughed while making kissing faces.

Ignoring Dex's flustered demeanor and the reactions of the other sidven around them, Noel spoke in Dex's ear with a low voice.

"First, your ability only works if you are paying close attention. If you're looking away, then you won't be able to dodge, as I proved when I threw a rock at your manager's Rock Rumbler."

"He was so irate about that," Dex muttered before being silenced by Noel's arm squeezing his throat.

"Second, you can't dodge things that aren't intended to hurt you, meaning that even if I can't punch you, I just have to grab ahold of you. Third, your dodging ability doesn't work if someone is already holding onto you. Keeping that in mind, and with some careful planning, I could defeat you in battle. So, tell me, cake dropper, do you still doubt my resolve?"

The only response Noel received was Dex rapidly tapping his shoulder with his free hand as his face turned violet. Noel loosened the hold around Dex's neck as he quickly inhaled many mouthfuls of air.

As the color returned to his face, a small smile started to form, much to his own surprise.

I must be out of my mind, and yet ...

"I never doubted you, Noel," Dex said with a squeak. "It's just that the strength you're aiming for is not reachable ... on your own. You will need help, my help. With my assistance, you'll reach that level by conditioning your body just like mine. Stick with it, and you'll be a Knockout Noel who can even topple Invincible Inaya."

Noel narrowed her eyes and craned her neck to get a better look at Dex's face. She stared intently at him. The boy twitched as her stare seemed to penetrate him. After a few uncomfortable moments, she broke the silence with a single word.

"Why?"

"Because it'll make you stronger."

"No. Why are you helping me? What's in it for you? No one does anything for nothing."

"I..." Dexter said before pausing for a moment. His cheeks appeared slightly flushed as he mustered the bravest face he could. "I just want to assist you, and if you let me, I can help you acquire an unrivaled strength. However, the only way that this will work is if you trust me."

"How am I supposed to do that?"

"For starters, you can let me go and trust that I won't run away. Can you do that?" Dex asked sincerely, without a trace of patronization. He felt the arm around his neck unwrap itself from his neck as he gave a sigh of relief, a warm presence grace his cheek. He gasped as Noel's hand clutched his face and firmly turned it until their noses nearly touched.

Noel gazed deeply into Dexter's eyes, searching for something to help her understand him better. To Noel, he seemed nervous, not out of fear or deceit, but for some other reason. She wondered if she could trust someone she couldn't readily land a finishing blow on. It would probably be safer to stay uninvolved than take a chance, but at the same time, what other options were there? And which could bring in the same level of results? Meaning that she only had one real choice to qualify for the national boxing tournament and defeat Invincible Inaya.

"Alright," Noel said as she released Dex and stepped back. Dex put a hand to his cheek as he slowly turned towards her. His face was still red as he felt the remaining warmth from Noel's touch. His dazed expression transformed into an eager smile as he stuck out his other hand.

"I'm honored to have your trust, Noel."

Noel momentarily gawked at Dex's outstretched arm before slowly reaching out with her own. She clasped his hand firmly and was a tad surprised that his grip was no slouch either.

"I'm looking forward to working with you."

"Cool," Noel said as she let go of Dex's hand. "So, what is the name of this style of training?"

Dexter readjusted his glasses as he leaned forward. The lighting from the store's ceiling created a glare within the lenses of Dexter's glasses, hiding his eyes behind a wall of white light as he spoke in a serious tone.

"It's known as Podge, but you can refer to it as the living punching bag style. During my childhood, my parents often sent me up to the snow-covered mountains of Vorav. For many months, while my father wrote articles regarding sidvan conditioning to frigid temperatures, I was forced to train in an obscure martial arts style. Every day I spent training in the freezing cold from dawn until dusk wearing nothing but thin pants. Over time, my reflexes quickened as dodging dangerous attacks was painfully engraved into my muscle memory. The training is rigorous, but if you are consistent, then it can be learned. Are you still with me?"

The entire eatery fell silent. Everyone, from the families sitting throughout the store to the customers waiting in line to place their orders and even the employees behind the counter, leaned forward with bated breath as they waited to hear Noel's response.

Noel's expression hardened as she put her hands on her hips.

"So, when do we begin?"

Chapter 14

Mind's Eye

"Uhh, how long do we have to do this?" Noel groaned with a drawn-out sigh as she sat crisscross on the hard ground within Paslow Park. She stifled a yawn. Her eyes stared longingly at the "dodge the ball if you value your life" court, with one of her fists supporting her chin while a group of teenagers occupied the court. The scent of blood was strong in the air as spiked leather balls whizzed loudly and zoomed mercilessly across the court. She witnessed the shrieks of the defeated as the sound of bones breaking became audible upon impact from the deadly balls. This continued until only the passionate, victorious outcry of the last, sweat-soaked sidvan resounded, to which Noel gave a small, envious smile.

At least that kid is doing something worthwhile, unlike me.

Both Noel and Dex sat underneath a large crimson tree. The thick branches covered in mahogany, teardrop-shaped leaves cast a generous shadow over them, shielding them from the late afternoon sun.

"Until you've focused your mind on your surroundings," Dex said between deep breaths with both eyes closed. Sitting crisscross with both hands on his lap, he resembled a stone statue. "It's an important part of Podge training."

"How is some dumb breathing technique with my eyes closed supposed to help with anything? I get more out of doing push-ups and punches than role-playing as some golem. I only care about my breathing technique when I'm on the toilet after downing something spicy."

"Thank you for that lovely imagery," Dex said wryly with a wrinkled nose before glancing at Noel with one eye, who was now lying flat on her back, staring into the blue sky filled with many uniquely shaped white clouds. Her arms were crossed, and she had a dissatisfied look.

Dex opened his mouth to say something when he suddenly paused as an idea popped into his head.

"Noel, describe the clouds you're looking at."

"Look at them yourself, cake dropper," Noel muttered.

"Humor me for a moment, Noel," Dex said as he closed his eyes again.

"Fine," Noel sighed before pointing towards the sky. "That white one up above looks like a right-handed boxing glove, that one looks like a piece to some board game, and that one looks like a giant beast. Now that one looks like..."

"Now try closing your eyes and describing them," Dex said, quickly cutting her off.

"You can't be serious!" Noel exclaimed while sitting up. "That's impossible!"

"Just try it," Dex said softly.

Noel rolled her eyes before lying back down and closing her eyes. However, with her lids now shut, she could see nothing except the back of her eyelids.

"Take a few deep breaths, in ... and out," Dex murmured rhythmically. "Now, try to focus on the sky."

Noel took a few deep breaths that strongly resembled frustrated sighs. Her eyelids clenched tightly while her expression grimaced. A few beads of sweat began rolling down her now red-face. After a few moments, her eyes flew open as she began gasping for air.

"I told you that it was impossible! Stop wasting my time with this blip!" she yelled as she rapidly sat up and grabbed Dex by the collar of his shirt. Her fist shook, but Dex continued to sit; eyes closed and completely unfazed.

"Hey, stop ignoring me!" Noel roared as she shook Dex violently. He remained expressionless for several moments before pointing to the sky above.

"There is the cloud you said looked like a game piece," Dex said calmly.

"Wha..." was all Noel could say before Dex began swiftly pointing towards several other clouds in the sky.

"The boxing glove, the giant beast, that one looks like a marionette, that one a snake, and that one in the distance looks like an oddly shaped orange."

Noel's eyes followed his finger's movements with amazement before returning her gaze to Dex.

"But your eyes are closed; how are you doing that? Are you squinting?" Noel asked with narrowed eyes and an accusatory pointed finger.

Dex opened his eyes and gave a small smile. "Podge is more than just dodging and throwing punches, Noel. It's about sensing the world around you and feeling its inner workings. You become one with it, and it is always with you. When combined with physical training, your strength will reach new levels as your heightened focus bolsters your senses. Podge will always tell you everything you need to know about any opponent or obstacle if you take the time to master it."

"Is that so?" Noel said skeptically, arms crossed. "And what does it tell you about me right now?"

After taking a few deep breaths, Dex closed his eyes briefly and opened them to gaze deeply into Noel's eyes.

"Your hands are calloused from all the time spent training with a punching bag, yet tender enough to gently hold your little sister. She is the reason your heart keeps beating. You desire to protect her more than anything, but I can see your desire to be the strongest growing every day like a fog covering your heart. I see it spreading into your arteries like the greasy fat from fast food. It's fighting for control of your very being with your fear for your sister's safety and the intense anger you feel towards your mother," Dex said, pausing for a moment before resuming with a slightly fearful expression. "Also, I better stop; otherwise, you'll do more than glare a hole through me."

"I'm glad you picked up on that," Noel muttered with an angry glint in her eyes before sighing. "That was impressive, Dex ... most of it, anyway."

They stood there silently for a moment before Noel broke the silence. "Hey, can you do that again, but on something else this time?"

Dex grinned from ear to ear. "Of course!"

Chapter 15

Song of the White Caps

"How about I tell you a little bit more about the Bloodroot tree we're sitting under?" Dex said as he placed a hand on the crimson tree. "It appears isolated from the remainder of the park, but actually, it is connected to...." Dex started to say before being drowned out by a deep, melodic voice.

We stand in the shadows of this land without light.
In our glowing crusade to make all things right.
We'll put down the monsters who call this place home.
We'll take back our land filled with hope and shalom.

"Who is that?" Dex pointed at the dark-skinned sidvan passionately strumming a guitar while standing on the "dodge the ball if you value your life" court, wearing colorful clothing so bright it was as if a rainbow had vomited all over him. He sang beautifully, belting out powerful, heart-felt lines while overflowing with confidence and vigor. A handful of sidvans gathered around him, including the teenagers who had just been playing on the court, with curious expressions.

We are the White Caps; we fight for the weak.
Slaying the mighty with deadly technique.
We long for a land overflowing with peace.
Where justice prevails, and evil will cease.

"That's just some local musician. I think his name is Jarek," Noel said nonchalantly. "He goes around Battletown singing various songs. Normally they're about famous fights or popular fighters, but lately, he has been singing more about the White Caps. Honestly, I haven't been paying him much attention lately."

Blood-thirsty beasts, beware; you are done.
For the dawn of the White Caps is only begun.
We'll halt the destruction and violence you leave.
For where you find pride, we only find grief.

"You mean he's singing a song that's painting those murderous White Caps in a positive light!?" Dex yelled, anger appearing in his eyes. "Why is no one going down there to stop him!"

We are the White Caps; we fight for the weak.
Slaying the mighty with deadly technique.
We long for a land overflowing with peace.
Where justice prevails, and evil will cease.

"All he is doing a singing a bunch of stupid songs, cake dropper. As long as he's keeping his distance from my sister and me, I don't care how he spends his free time. Besides, his music is weak. I could beat that guy into submission whenever I wanted to."

So come join the White Caps and fight the good fight.
The night may be hazy, but victory's in sight.
We'll end the mighty, blast them straight to the den.
Ceasing their rampage, granting peace without end.

"I don't think it's going to be that simple, Noel, look," Dex said as he pointed at Jarek, who was now surrounded by a decent-sized crowd who were merrily singing along to the chorus with loud booming voices.

We are the White Caps; we fight for the weak.
Slaying the mighty with deadly technique.
We long for a land overflowing with peace.
Where justice prevails, and evil will cease.

"It's more than a simple melody with words, Noel," Dex said with a severe expression. "This is a battle for the soul of Battletown."

"Right," Noel said with a roll of her eyes and a sarcastic tone. "And my new dream is to be a famous Food Fighter coach after watching *Food Fighters* because the show's theme music is just that good."

"For starters, yes, it absolutely is!" Dex said with a gleam in his eyes. "The opening still awakes a fire within my soul even after thirteen seasons and makes me want to coach my cheese-covered vegetable team 'nice and gouda,' and that's my point, Noel. Music touches both the culture and very souls of sidvan kind. Songs immortalize celebrities, important events, and influential groups. If pro-White Cap messages spread, they'll continue to amass supporters."

So pick up your arms, and fight for this land.

The soul of this nation is all in our hands.

"Dex, you're just paranoid. Even if a few chumps in Paslow Park like that junk, it won't change anything. They're just babbling nonsense. Everyone will forget all about it soon. Now enough talking about music, we need to set up our next training session. I have plans tomorrow on Openday, and my match against Right-Hook Rheyna is the day after. How about we meet up the day after at Paslow Park, once school is finished ?"

"Yeah, that should be fine. I'm off that day...." Dex said before being interrupted once more by Jarek's singing voice.

> She's the dazzling girl,
> You never want to meet.
> With just one punch or smile,
> She'll knock you off your feet.
> Inaya, Inaya, impossible to denya.
> Inaya, Inaya, succeeds with a trya.

"I guess Jarek still remembers a few nonpolitical songs, but I never guessed that he would sing one about Inaya. She must have gotten popular if they already have songs about her," Dex stated while glancing at Noel's expression as it shifted quickly from calm to tense.

"Yeah," Noel muttered while she listened carefully to the words Jarek was singing.

> Our graceful champ can break the sky.
> Her strength is unthinkable.
> Her ethereal form untouchable.
> That's why she's called invincible.
> Inaya, Inaya, soaring through the skya,
> Inaya, Inaya, hidden from the eyea.
> Inaya, Inaya, cannot be defieda.

Inaya, Inaya, her fist says goodnighta.

"I've changed my mind; let's meet up early tomorrow morning. I need the extra practice," Noel said quickly.

"Come on, really?! Didn't you say you had plans? Besides, I don't want to wake up early on one of the few days I have to sleep in," Dex grumbled.

"Suck it up," Noel said coarsely, her arms firmly crossed. "That's nothing compared to what I have to do."

An unhappy feeling flooded her body as she thought about how Alex would react. She could already feel her heart tying itself into a knot.

How am I going to break this news to her?

Chapter 16

Unhappy Alex

Noel and Alex were snuggled next to each other on the brown couch in their living room, happily enjoying juice boxes and the leftovers from Happy Smacks while watching programs on the television. After a satisfying episode of *Food Fighters*, while wrapped in the warm embrace of an old blue blanket, Noel causally broke the news that she would be gone for most of the next day. She thought this would be the best way to relay the information, but Alex was far from pleased.

"What do you mean you'll be gone most of tomorrow?!" Alex whined as she knocked the blanket off of her shoulders. "Tomorrow is Openday! You're always off on Openday!"

Openday was the beginning of the week. It was considered a day to rest and restore everything weary and worn within the body. Every sidven had many battles they had to fight every week, and the purpose of Openday was to give everyone a day to rest before beginning their weekly warfare against life. Schools and several businesses were always closed on this day. This included the boxing stadium, so usually, Noel stayed home and entertained Alex on every Openday.

"Openday is supposed to be our day to spend time together! You told me before that it was the one day that we would have the whole day to be together, and now you're saying that you're going to be gone for most of it!" she yelled with her arms crossed and brows furrowed. "I'm very mad at you for breaking your promise!"

"Alex …" Noel said with a warm, soothing voice, "I'll be back later in the afternoon. I have some special training at Paslow Park, and then we'll spend the rest of the day doing whatever you want."

"Nooooooo! I don't want to lose my one full day with you!" she sobbed, throwing her arms around Noel. Noel's shirt, now soaked from the flow of tears, as Alex clung on tightly. Noel firmly hugged her in return. The sisters stood locked in a warm embrace as time seemed to stand still. Finally, Noel removed Alex from her waist and took a knee as she looked Alex in the eyes.

"I promise I will make it up to you somehow and that soon we will spend more time together. Okay?"

Alex was silent for a moment. She sniffled before muttering a halfhearted "Okay."

"Still love me?" Noel asked, arms extended.

Without hesitating, Alex locked her arms around Noel's neck and kissed Noel on the cheek before leaning towards Noel's ear and whispering, "Yeah, dummy."

Noel chuckled as she ruffled Alex's hair, with Alex purring in happiness. After a moment, Alex broke free and asked something she had been wondering about.

"Why do you have to go train at the park tomorrow? Why can't you do it here? I can always help you, you know?"

Noel paused for a moment. She didn't want to tell her little sister that she had difficulty concentrating on training if she was present. After carefully choosing her words, she responded.

"A special training that will help me throw faster and stronger punches. I have to get a lot stronger if I'm going to become the new national boxing champion."

"But, you're already the strongest person that I know. If you ask me, the only ones who need to train are all the girls you beat up," Alex grumbled skeptically while crossing her arms.

"Thanks, Alex!" Noel said happily. Her kid sister's unshakable faith always warmed her to her core and made her want to strive even more to be the unstoppable force of strength Alex saw her as. However, she had to be realistic if she were to defeat Invincible Inaya. Noel continued to stroke Alex's hair while firmly holding her with her other arm.

"Your love gives me strength, but I still have a lot of training to do before I'm strong enough to claim the title of national female boxing champion. That's why I'm going to the park tomorrow. Someone was going to meet up with me and help me train."

"Who's that?"

Noel hesitated for a moment. "A boy who I met recently named Dex."

"Whaaaat! You met a boy?!" Alex yelled as her mouth swung open like an unlocked gate. A strange fog clouded her mind as she tried to process what she had just heard.

Her short-tempered sister, with terrible manners and who beat up every guy who got too friendly with her, was going to meet a boy at the park. This could only mean one thing.

"Is he your boyfriend?"

"Nope," Noel said dismissively with a wave of her hand. "He's just my personal punching bag. I threw a rock at him before knocking him to the ground. He has been my lacky ever since."

"Whoa!" Alex exclaimed, wide-eyed. "So, he is your boyfriend, after all."

A vein bulged on Noel's forehead as her left eye twitched. A forced smile emerged on her face as the temperature seemed to rise around her.

"No, Alex," Noel said. For one of the few times out of the ring, she was on the defensive. "I wouldn't date that weak-kneed cake dropper if my life depended on it. I'm only keeping him around to throw punches at him."

Alex giggled. "You like him. Girls only throw rocks at boys that they like. What's he like? Is he cute? There are a few boys at school that I want to throw rocks at myself."

"Alright, enough of this silliness," Noel said, cutting her off. Things would only get out of hand if she didn't end this conversation. "You will not be throwing rocks at any boy until you're older. Now, I will call Sara's mom and ask if you can go over to their house tomorrow. If it's okay, you need to make sure you have anything ready that you'll take with you."

"Aww, but I want to meet Dex," Alex complained.

"Absolutely not! Now go get your stuff together!" Noel said firmly.

"Fine." Alex groaned as she got up and went to her room, but she stopped before leaving. Slowly she turned to face Noel with a downcast expression.

"Sis, if Sara is busy, are you going to make me stay home alone again? Men in white coats have been coming around the house a lot lately, and..." Alex's lips quivered. "I don't want to be here alone if they return."

A look of alarm filled Noel's eyes as she jumped up and dashed towards Alex before crouching down beside her. Noel cupped her sister's face with her hands and looked deeply into her chocolate eyes.

"Are you okay? Did they see you?" Noel asked quickly as her heart raced until she felt a familiar set of tiny fingers grasping her face.

"I'm okay," Alex said, and Noel gave a visible sigh of relief. "They never saw me, but two of them have been in the front yard several times looking around. It scares me."

"Then why didn't you tell me earlier? Their recent visit would have been their last time walking with both legs," Noel said angrily.

"Because since Mom left, you have been doing everything to care for me. I didn't want you to worry."

Noel raised a hand as her eyes narrowed.

"Dummy!" Noel yelled as she bopped Alex on the head with her free hand. Alex whimpered as she brought her hands up to her smarting head. Tears filled her eyes, but she stared in shock at Noel as her sister's eyes glistened, and she quickly embraced her.

"Don't ever hide that kind of information from me again, Alex!" Noel said with a pained tone as she spoke into Alex's ear. "I'm your big sister, and worrying about you is my job. Let me know if you feel scared or unsafe, and I will protect you. The only ones that should be afraid are those who mean you harm, especially when I get my hands on them. Do you understand?"

"Yes, sis," Alex sobbed before wiping her eyes with a sniffle. With serpent-like quickness, her arms slivered around Noel. "I won't hide anything from you again."

"Good," Noel said as she wiped her eyes with her forearm. They stood there for a moment, wrapped in the warm embrace, before Noel released Alex and stood.

"If Sara is busy, then you won't be leaving my side for a moment. Do you understand?"

An excited gleam appeared in Alex's eyes as a mischievous smile began to surface.

"Does that mean...?" Alex started to say before Noel cut her off.

"Get moving, Alex," Noel said with a waving motion. "I'll let you know for sure in a few moments after I'm done talking to Sara's mom about what the final plan will be for tomorrow."

"K!" Alex said merrily, and she skipped out of the room with a happy tune escaping her lips.

Noel sighed in frustration as she picked up the phone and dialed the number for Sara's house.

Hopefully, Sara will be free to hang out with Alex tomorrow.

It would be a busy day training with Dexter to learn this Podge's punching-bag fighting style, and she couldn't afford any distractions.

But Alex's safety took priority, and she would never allow her sister to be in harm's way more than required for someone living in Battletown. Clearly, she was going to have to have a little chat with White Caps that had been visiting the Mud Hut, but that would have to be a job for another day. Right now, she had to focus on her plans for tomorrow, so with a determined expression, she pulled her phone out of her back pocket and began dialing. After a few moments, someone picked up.

"Yes?"

"Hey, Kelly, it's Noel. I had something that I needed to ask you."

Interlude
3- Sinister
Stipulations

It was later at night. A girl wearing a hoodie made her way down the darkened streets. She loomed menacingly, being seven drux tall. Only one streetlight flickered on and off as she pulled up into the empty parking lot of the Jab-en-Grab. While she leaned against the shopping cart bin, she pulled up her sleeve and checked her watch. After pressing the illumination button, the time flashed brightly across the screen.

"Where is he?" the girl mumbled as she tapped her foot, looking from side to side. She was wearing a pair of black goggles with red lenses as she scoured the vast lot only to find that no one else was present. "He's supposed to be here."

She stood in the parking lot with the only sound coming from the low buzz of the streetlight. Suddenly, the flickering of light ceased, and the sound of silence flooded the entire lot.

"Well, well," a voice called out from the darkness. This figure made his way across the lot, carrying a baby-blue brief-case with six men huddled closely around him, all wearing white caps with white coats. He wore a short white jacket with a ruffled, light-pink shirt, navy ascot and light-pink pants. A white fedora with a baby blue ribbon sat upon his short red hair. On every one of his ivory fingers sat an expensive ring with a yellow gemstone. His baby-blue dress shoes clicked as he approached. "Looking for me, were you? I hope you weren't waiting too long. The lights always go out in this lot at 2:75 every morning and won't come back on for another six yosmins."

"Like I care, Dan," the girl growled in annoyance. "Did you bring the juice?"

The one known as Dan smirked as he opened his case and pulled out two vials: one halfway filled with a red liquid and the other half filled with green juice.

"You mean these?"

"Yeah, those!" The girl quickly reached for the vials, only for Dan to yank them away.

"Not so fast, Meg. You know how things work here. You pay the price; then you get the juice."

"Then take my money!" Meg exclaimed as she grabbed a small bag filled with brilocks from within her hoodie and handed them to Dan, only for him to shake his head.

"I'm afraid that money is the least of our worries. You see, our agreement with you is a little different. Asides from your financial assets, we also require that you demonstrate the power of our Jaguar Juice through your improved performance at the stadium."

"You doubt my skills as a boxer, even after crushing both Livid Lucy and Bionic Bianca?" the girl shouted as she raised her right arm. With a fierce battle cry, she brought her fist down on the shopping cart pin as it bent around her hand as if it were made of putty. "You see, with Jaguar Juice in my system, no one can beat me! Now give it to me!"

She swiped for the vials as Dan leaped back, only for his six men to surround Meg, each holding an assault rifle aimed directly at her.

"Hold your fire!" Dan said with a raised hand as he approached Megan. "Your level of strength is amazing, but let me remind you that even you can't compete with the speed of a bullet. It is in your best interests to cooperate with us."

Megan glared intensely but lowered her arms as Dan stepped forward and placed the vials in her hand. Megan stared back with a dumbfounded expression as Dan explained.

"That is for your good work so far. You've become quite the force to be reckoned with in female boxing, which has created a financial boom for us. However, another upcoming star is among the ranks, and her outstanding performance is drawing attention away from you. That will cause complications with our long-term plans, so using our Jaguar Juice, you must crush Knockout Noel and prove that you are the strongest of the rookie boxers."

"Then I'll crush her!" Megan exclaimed before leaving the parking lot. "It'll be my pleasure to end that blit finally. She'll have to share a hospital bed with Lucy and Bianca after I'm through with her."

"Boss," one of Dan's hitmen said as Dan pulled out a cigarette and lighter from his pocket, "are you sure about setting her up against Knockout Noel? That chick is the scrappiest girl I've seen in a while. She won't go down easy."

"I know," Dan said, lighting his cigarette and placing it between his lips. A great billow of gray smoke emerged from his mouth as a wicked smile crept onto his face.

"That's what I'm counting on."

Chapter 17

Podge Training

It was a couple of hinos later in the day. It was dim and muggy outside as the sun slowly made its way through the sleeping sky.

Lucky sky, Dexter thought as he trudged towards the park. He was absolutely not a morning person, and every fiber of his being fought him as he crawled, sloth-like, out of bed. Dex left for the park after throwing on his gray Food Fighters hoodie with matching gray sweatpants. He knew that Noel would be furious if he showed up late. He wasn't concerned about getting physically hurt since she couldn't land an honest punch on him, but the cold stare in her eyes was terrifying when she was angry, and he had no desire to be caught in the line of fire. Much to his surprise, Dex found himself alone at the park upon arrival. He stood beside the wooden park sign that read, in splotched, crimson letters, "Paslow Park, the park of everyday pain and enjoyment. The birthplace of the mighty, where weakness is replaced with strength."

After waiting a few moments, the soft shuffle of footsteps resonated as they slowly drew closer to Dex. He turned and witnessed two figures approaching. The taller of the two was wearing an old maroon hoodie that was all too familiar.

"What are you looking at, cake dropper?" Noel snarled.

"Nothing really, but ... um, who is that behind you?" Dexter asked, pointing at the little girl behind Noel.

"Hi!" the little girl said as she greeted Dex cheerfully. She was wearing a pretty pink zip-up jacket with fluffy white trim and covered in sparkles. "I'm Alex. I'm Noel's sister. You must be Dex. I like your hoodie! I love *Food Fighters*!"

"Me too!" Dexter agreed eagerly. Noel rolled her eyes as the two began passionately discussing the show. "The different *Food Fighter* creatures are so cool, and their battle graphics are amazing!"

"I like all of the cute ones like Mac-en-Doodle and Pastrypuff. They have the cutest battle cries. Pastry Pummeling!" Alex roared as she took a playful fighting stance.

"Nice, but that's nothing compared to Carroccli's famous 'Carroccoli clobbering!' Dexter roared lightheartedly as he took a mock battle stance.

Alex laughed giddily before saying, "I like you, Dex! I'm glad that you're Noel's boyfriend."

"Wha ... no ... I mean, we just met not too long ago, and ..." Dexter stuttered with a face redder than a tomato.

"Knock it off, Alex." Noel sighed before glaring at Dexter. "And you, get your head in the game!" she yelled before aiming a right uppercut at his face. Dexter easily dodged it, but the motion helped clear up his fluster.

"I brought my kid sister with me. She was going to go to a friend's house, but that friend had a sudden change in plans. So, she'll be playing in the park while we train. Are we clear?"

"Yeah," he said, and after taking a deep breath, he took off his duffle bag and began digging through it until he found what he was looking for. He stood and handed her a small box.

"What are these?" she asked as she opened the box. Inside were four curious, blue leather objects with yellow straps attached. They appeared to be some kind of strap-on weights with noticeable skiffs but were otherwise in good condition.

"Voravian weights from my personal collection," Dex said while pulling out one of the weights. An excited gleam appeared in Dex's eyes as he continued to speak. "They're filled with tiny beads made of voras, a special metal found exclusively in the Vorav mountains. The metal has a unique property of temporarily gaining density from active motion and is commonly used for Podge training sessions. Every beginner of Podge spends most of their initial training using them. You will wear them on your wrists and ankles during your training today. We'll start in the sandbox. I should mention that these weights won't come off unless I-"

"Yeah, sure, just put them on," Noel said, interrupting him. She quickly pulled off her hoodie and stood before Dex, wearing only her brown "Victory is Mine" undershirt with matching brown sweatpants. She held out her arms expectantly as Dex sighed before silently attaching the weights to Noel's wrists and ankles.

The biggest smile blossomed on Alex's face as she made a heart with her tiny hands. She couldn't get enough of watching these two together. Seeing her big sister finally interact with a boy was like a dream come true for Alex. Noel now was like a princess from a love story who'd finally met her Prince Charming and, after facing many dangers together, would ride out on the blazing sunset fertilizing the land with the corpses of their foes. The princess would then dictate the prince's every word and action for the rest of his natural life and for all eternity in the afterlife, like every ideal happily ever after!

That would be so romantic! Alex thought as she sighed happily.

Noticing Alex's silly expression out of the corner of her eye, Noel raised an eyebrow. She had no idea what Alex could find so amusing about the cake dropper putting weights on her. Brutal acts of violence and incredible feats of strength captivated Noel when she was a child. Seeing someone throw a car overhead or wrestle a murderous beast was entertainment, but watching someone put equipment on another was a snooze fest.

Kids these days are just into the weirdest things, Noel thought to herself before shaking her head. She needed to concentrate, but she found it difficult to focus, with Alex staring at her and Dex like they were curious creatures at the zoo.

"Alex, you can go play, and in just a little bit, we'll have a break for lunch."

"Can I watch for a little bit first? I promise I won't get in the way," Alex asked with a big smile and expecting eyes that seemed to shine like diamonds in the light.

"Yeah, sure," Noel mumbled as she turned her face away. She had the most challenging time telling her kid sister no when her eyes sparkled. They packed a punch deadly enough to get Noel on the ropes.

"Thanks!" Alex said as she embraced Noel in a sudden hug. Noel was taken aback but warmly returned the embrace with a smile. "Now, back up. I'm about to get serious."

"Okay!" Alex said, and she retreated as Noel and Dexter stepped into the sandbox. Dexter had a small smile on his face as they opposed each other.

"What's so funny, cake dropper?" Noel asked, slightly agitated, fists raised in an offensive stance.

"Nothing. I've just never seen such a tender look in your eyes before. You really care about your sister."

"Shut up!" Noel yelled as she threw a jab toward Dexter's face, which he dodged.

Jab! Jab! Cross! Jab! Left Uppercut! Right Uppercut! Left Hook! Right Hook! Cross! Cross! Left Hook! Right Uppercut! Jab! Jab! Right Hook! Noel launched a series of precise but slow blows aimed at Dexter, but nothing hit.

"Ugh!" Noel grunted. Her arms ached from the additional weight, with her legs not faring much better against the soft, sand foundation. Despite this, she kept relentlessly firing punches at Dexter.

"Not bad, but that is only the warm-up. We're about to kick things up a notch," Dexter said as he sidestepped Noel's punch and dashed to the side of the box. He quickly squatted and pressed a button on the outside of the sandbox. Suddenly the sand started to shift and cycled through the box.

"Whaa!" Noel said as she wobbled, nearly losing her balance. She quickly moved her feet as she put maximum effort into maintaining her balance against the shifting sands.

"Exercising on the sand is a great way to work on leg strength, but exercising on shifting sands is even better. Now you'll have to focus more on maintaining your balance while fighting, so try your best!"

"Eat this!" Noel exclaimed as she hopped after Dexter, continuing to throw a barrage of weighted punches while Dexter dodged them effortlessly. Beads of sweat dribbled from her forehead while her clothes clung to her damp skin.

"Keep an eye on my movements!" Dex yelled while dodging all of Noel's punches. "The basic principle for Podge-styled offensive strikes is to attack where your opponent will move to next. Don't waste energy striking where they are currently at, or you will never hit them."

"Give me enough time, and I'll find a way to land a blow no matter what, you four-eyed know-it-all!" Noel bellowed while attacking mercilessly. Her arms and legs felt as heavy as stone. The heat from the blistering sun wasn't doing her any favors.

Noticing her level of fatigue, Dexter retreated to the far end of the sandbox and put his hands in his pockets. He pulled something from his pockets while jumping from leg to leg to maintain his position. From what Noel saw, it appeared to be a pair of wristbands made from a pink fabric that Dexter slid on his arms.

"All right, one more exercise, then we'll take a break, Noel."

"If that's all you got left in you. What's the exercise, continuing to run away from me?"

"Not this time," Dexter said, striking an intimidating fighting pose. "Now, you have to hold me off for five yosmins."

"Bring it on," Noel declared as she and Dexter charged each other. Before Noel had a chance to react, Dexter struck first. Noel gasped as Dex's fist drove right into her stomach; she felt bile rising in her throat but forced it down with a swallow. Her legs wanted to buckle, but Noel willed them to stay upright as she jumped back.

I've got to create some distance. As soon as Dex lets his guard down, I'll strike, Noel thought, with her arms ready to attack at a moment's notice.

Dex wasn't having any of that. He reappeared beside Noel with a loud whoosh and launched a mighty blow that Noel barely managed to block.

"For defensive measures using Podge, you have to be able to read your opponent's movement to predict their attacks and deploy the appropriate counterattack. Like this!"

She couldn't see it but felt the impact against her shoulder as she nearly lost her balance. Then a second and third blow followed, each hitting a shoulder with the same level of deadly precision. She felt her muscles grow heavier with every one of Dex's punches. She jumped back and threw her guard as Dexter quickly closed the gap. He appeared to have several arms as each blur began firing dozens of punches. All Noel could do was block as she tried to fend off the fierce blows while struggling to keep her balance against the relentless sand. If she fell into the hungry gaze of the sandbox's eye, she would be a sitting duck.

"Come on, Noel!" Alex cheered from outside the sandbox. "You can do it! Beat Dex!"

A scorching heat radiated deep within her soul and blazed within her eyes. This new warmth seeped into her exhausted muscles and gave her a sudden pool of strength. Tapping into it, she blocked his attacks and started throwing punches back at him. Both began circling each other in a rhythmic pattern of punching and blocking/dodging. It almost gave the appearance of dancing. Finally, Dexter caught both of Noel's hands within his own. "That's time. Let's rest."

It took a moment for clarity to return to Noel's eyes. After she refocused on her surrounding, a strange warmth enveloped her hands after realizing her fists couldn't move, ensnarled within Dexter's clutch. She glared before yanking her hands away and hopping out of the sandbox. She fell off-balance and immediately took a knee as the world spun around her upon landing on solid ground.

"Noel!" Alex screamed, alarmed as she rushed towards Noel. "Noel, are you all right?!"

"She'll be fine," Dexter said as he hopped out of the sandbox and clicked the button with the back of his heel. "She just overexerted herself from our training. She'll be good to go after she has rested a bit."

"Really?" Alex half sobbed. "You're sure that she'll be all right?"

"Yeah, you heard him," Noel said with a tired smile as she pulled Alex into a one-armed hug. "I'll be fine after I've caught my breath."

"Thank goodness!" Alex sighed as she wrapped her arms around Noel and nuzzled her head into her chest.

Noel relished the warmth that was now both around and inside her. She turned to face Dexter, who was staring at them awkwardly.

"So, cake dropper, why don't we take a break for lunch? What are we eating?"

Chapter 18

Monstrous Encounter

"These are some delicious turkey and cheese sandwiches!" Alex exclaimed while munching happily.

They were sitting at one of the picnic tables in the park. While eating the sandwiches Dexter had packed, all three carefully avoided the spikes on both sides of the table. Originally these tables were designed for arm wrestling competitions where the loser lost more than his honor. Nowadays, most people use them for eating and watching their children play.

"I'm glad you like them." Dexter beamed. "The turkey is a healthier source of protein, and the provolone cheese provides calcium. Also, the whole grain bread is an excellent source of fiber to clean out the body."

"Enough about nutrition! We have something more important to talk about!" Noel demanded.

"Yeah!" Alex agreed. "Like your dance in the sandbox. It was so romantic!"

"No," Noel said, glaring disapprovingly at the blush forming on Dexter's face, with Alex giggling in the background. "I meant your fighting prowess during that. You've only ever dodged before, but back there, that was the first time I have ever felt so overwhelmed fighting someone close to my age. It was almost like I was fighting a completely different person."

"Um…" Dexter looked nervous by the turn of the conversation. After pausing for a moment to carefully choose his words, he continued. "That isn't my actual skill with hand-to-hand combat." He picked up his arm and began tapping on the pink wristband that he was still wearing. "This is a strength band. It absorbs previous wearers' strength and fighting techniques and transfers a portion of that essence to the current wearer."

"Whoa! So it was like Noel was fighting a lot of people at once?" Alex asked, amazed.

"In a way, sort of. Soul bands are another item that originated deep within the Vorav mountains. On the highest point of the tallest mountain lies a towering tree unlike any other, called Jeynam, It's covered with lustrous, violet bark that shimmers like a crown jewel. Hanging from its massive branches are sparkling, silk-like strings of satin. Every Podge practitioner must journey through the harsh conditions of the mountain's peak to reach Jeynam and pluck one of its shining strings, which is later crafted into a strength band."

Dex shivered unconsciously from recalling the frigid mountains known for brutal snowstorms, vicious wildlife, and the unyielding passion of those who practice Podge within the Usmon temple. He returned his gaze to his pink wristbands.

"Strength bands serve as a symbol and piece of the journey one takes while learning Podge and are considered sacred. They are never to be stolen but can be given away freely to whoever the wearer wishes. The soul bands I'm wearing were given to me," he said as he returned his gaze to Noel and Alex, who listened intently, disregarding their half-eaten sandwiches.

"The one who gave these wristbands to me was the only one to ever wear them before me. Words fail to describe how exceptionally strong this sidvan, AKA my sparring partner, is.

She was on a completely different level, and every day her fists, hungry for the taste of blood and violence, satiated themselves by pummeling me. She was strong enough to pound a mountain into her own likeness. In fact, if Noel were to wear these, she would have no problem hitting me. That is the level of strength that these bands provide."

Noel's eyes narrowed as she scowled at the pink bands before returning her gaze back to Dexter with a heavy frown.

"Don't **ever** suggest that. Strength only means something if it is gained through hard work. It's worthless if it is earned from cheating with devices or other shortcuts. I will gain the strength to strike you, but I will gain it from pushing my body to its limits," she growled as she picked up her sandwich and took a big bite out of it. She hated the idea of the strength band and what its use allowed.

That device is a cheat! Sidvens wouldn't even have to train anymore. They could survive just by leaching off of someone else's strength instead of mustering their own. I don't like it! But, … it has provided me with a new way to train. Still, though … I hope the White Caps or any of the other vicious gangs don't get their hands on something like this. Noel thought to herself before shaking her head. She couldn't allow herself to get distracted.

"Now, less talking and more eating. We'll continue our training once we're done," Noel commanded.

"Okay," Dexter and Alex said in unison as they turned their attention back to their sandwiches.

After eating, Noel and Dexter resumed training inside the sandbox while Alex went to play on the bloody merry-go-round. After more intense sparring, Noel's arms and legs soon felt even heavier than before. She felt even slower when she threw her punches and strongly desired to remove the weights on her legs and ankles. She didn't understand the point of using weights when all she had to do was punch him, but here she was, drenched in sweat while throwing punches at the speed of molasses, with Dexter effortlessly dodging them. Of course, he would still have effortlessly avoided them even if she weren't wearing them, which made her wonder what the point of wearing them was in the first place.

Finally, after another strenuous round, her body forced her to take a knee while she gasped for air. Noel glared at Dexter, who stood unfazed right before her.

"This is so stupid. It's hard enough trying to hit you without a handicap," Noel complained as she shook the weights on her wrists. "All these things are doing is slowing me down, and my goal is to punch faster."

"Which is why we're doing this," Dexter said as he offered Noel his hand, which Noel ignored as she stood back up.

"The purpose of this," Dexter continued, "is to strengthen the muscles in your arms like your biceps, triceps, and latissimus dorsi. You need to strengthen those muscles to throw stronger and quicker punches."

"I'm going to latissimus dorsi your face once I take these weights off," Noel grumbled as she forced her heavy arms back into their usual fighting stance. Dexter was about to return to his pose when his left eye twitched.

"Sorry," he said as, for the first time, he broke out in a sweat and began speed-walking towards the restroom, "but nature is calling. I'll be back in just a bit."

"Whatever," Noel said as she sat on the ground and took a few deep breaths with her eyes closed.

That was when she heard a shriek. "Noel, help!" Her eyes popped open to behold Alex huddled like a turtle in the center of the bloody merry-go-round while tightly clenching onto the metal handles for dear life. Alex screamed in terror as she whirled in a vicious cycle trapped within the carousel. A hulking figure wearing a blood-red hoodie stood over the spinning carousel. With mighty heaves from her massive hands, she caused the device to move faster and faster while somehow avoiding the sharp blades attached to the ends of the metal handles.

Noel stormed to the carousel in a rage. She'd recognize that bulky figure anywhere. "The blurf are you doing to my sister, Meg!"

"Same as I'm going to do to you!" Monstrous Meg bellowed as she gave the bloody merry-go-round one final fling before turning to face Noel. Alex continued screaming, clinging desperately to the metal handles, but she started sliding closer to the edge. "I'm about to mess your blip up!"

Noel lunged at Meg. The Kearce Stadium official guidelines prohibited fights between boxers outside of the ring. Ajax had repeatedly told Noel in particular, that any conflicts needed to be brought to his attention before in-fighting broke out.

"Listen up, Noel!" Ajax had yelled with a stern glare after she'd tried lunging at Right Hook Rheyna when the prissy fighter referred to her boxing attire as 'cliché.' "If you brats have problems, then duke 'em out in the ring like a true citizen of Battletown."

All of that went out the window the moment Noel heard Alex scream.

Noel threw a punch right toward Meg's jaw, but it was much too slow. The weight on her wrists and her exhaustion from training had significantly slowed the velocity of her fists. Noel growled as her foe caught her punch and effortlessly threw her to the ground. She barely had time to recover before a shadow swiftly covered her. Noel quickly rolled to the side as a giant foot crashed down where she had been, leaving a colossal boot print.

"Not so fast!" Meg yelled as she picked up her other foot and sent it crashing down on Noel. Noel rolled out of the way by the skin of her teeth, only to be caught between the girl's legs.

"Now you're mine!"

Monstrous Meg towered over Noel viciously like a fearsome beast facing its cornered prey, and Noel could swear that she had grown taller since they had clashed in Jab-en-Grab. The behemoth of a girl dropped to her knees as she whammed Noel with bomb-like punches. Noel barely had enough time to put up her guard before receiving the monstrous onslaught. Every blow caused her arms to reverberate back into her face mercilessly. Time became painstakingly slow. She could see every punch as it slowly crashed into her guard and sent it flying into her face. Sounds had been replaced with a dull ringing as the light began to dim. The strength of Noel's arms was waning rapidly as the life was beaten out of her.

After one mighty blow, Noel's head hit the ground with a loud crack as the rocks underneath her shattered. The world was spinning, and she could no longer make sense of where she was or what was happening. Everything was a blur of white and black as her eyes rolled around in their sockets. The situation felt hopeless, and Noel was slowly released into the dark void surrounding her. Her consciousness faded like the light when the day became night. Her eyes focused on the carousel during a single moment of clarity. Noel caught sight of Alex crying in fear as she dangled from the edge of the metal handles, slowly losing her grip. Strength instantly flowed into Noel's body, stoked by the flames of her rage and fear as her brown pupils dilated and became amber. She had no fear of the giant girl above her throwing punches but was afraid that her one and only sister was in danger. This fear channeled a ferocious strength far more incredible than her usual brawn. With a mighty motion, she threw out her arms, blocking and interrupting the girl's ruthless onslaught. With wide eyes, Meg's mouth dropped at this surprising showcasing of strength from someone she had just spent several moments bashing into the ground.

Before her foe could respond, Noel channeled the strength flowing through her into her legs and kicked Meg with all her might, which sent the giant girl flying several drux away.

"Alex!" Noel yelled as she quickly jumped to her feet and ran towards the carousel. She grabbed onto the metal handle and was instantly whirled off her feet.

"Noel, help me!" Alex cried.

"I'm coming, Alex! Hang on!" Noel exclaimed. She winced slightly as the sharp blades on the handles dug into her skin, but she ignored it as she slowly crawled towards Alex. Once she reached Alex, she wrapped one arm around her while holding onto the metal handle with the other.

"Alex, I need you to let go!"

"No! I'll fall!"

"Alex." Noel leaned into her ear as she whispered, "You're going to be okay. You're safe in my arms; now let go."

Alex released her bloody grip from the handles and wrapped her arms tightly around Noel as her older sister let go of the carousel. Alex screamed as the two went flying, only to hit the ground hard while intertwined and rolled several drux away.

Alex opened her eyes only to see the gentle look on her older sister's bloody face. Noel smiled while patting Alex's head.

"You're safe now."

Alex sniffled, ducked her head into Noel's shirt, and started crying. Noel sighed and hugged her tighter as the front of her shirt became soaked in salty tears. The sudden blur of motion caused Noel, still intertwined with Alex, to roll several drux away.

"E-eberdar burrito?" Alex asked, confused.

"Get behind me!" Noel yelled as she quickly jumped to her feet, standing between Alex and the giant girl trudging towards them.

"You got lucky just now, Noel, but no more!" the girl bellowed. "Now I'm going to end you, and then the name everyone will remember will be Monstrous Meg!"

Meg ran towards Noel in full rage. Noel tried to strike her defensive stance, but she could barely get her arms out in front of her. She grimaced as she squinted with one eye, trying to brace herself one last time. As Meg got close with fists raised, an all-too-familiar figure appeared in front of Noel.

"Hey! Leave Noel alone!" Dexter yelled at Meg with outstretched hands. "Beating her in this underhanded method means nothing. If you want to fight her, do it in the ring fair and square!"

"Shut up, nerd!" Meg screamed as she threw a punch at Dexter, only for him to dodge it. Enraged, Meg threw punch after punch in a continuous motion similar to water leaving a faucet. After a few moments of failing to make contact, Meg stopped. She turned white-faced and clutched at her chest with ragged breathing.

"What ... the ... blurf ... are you!" Meg asked between pants. Her back was arched with both knees bent.

"Just someone who believes in making wise life choices and doesn't like bullies," Dex said calmly. He met Meg's rabid glare with firm eyes before closing them and taking a deep breath. "Your blood smells awful, your heart rate is abnormal, and your lungs are damaged. You need to stop what you're doing right now. It won't be worth it in the end."

"Shut up!" Meg yelled as she charged, fist raised. Her face was contorted in a grimace, her other hand gripping her chest.

Dex sighed before digging into his pockets and quickly putting the pink wristbands back on. With narrowed eyes, he stood still as a statue as Meg promptly closed the gap between them. At the drop of a hat, Dex launched a clenched fist.

Meg couldn't see it, but a sudden feeling of dread overcame her. Instinctively, she halted in her tracks and felt Dex's fist grazing her neck. She stepped back, put a hand to her neck, and found a smoking scrape that stung more than it should have.

Dex brought back his fist as he struck his fighting pose. "Now leave, or you will have to take me on."

Meg's eyes, filled with pure hatred, bore into Dex. Her shoulders squared up as she looked down at him momentarily before responding.

"Forget it! No one can win against a ghost," she growled under her breath before turning to send a simmering stare at Noel. "Besides, I could crush you anytime that I wanted."

Noel glared back, undaunted by the giant girl with an intense fire burning in her eyes, her pupils now a dark red.

"Next time I see you, you're dead."

"Please, I'll bury you alive, followed by your sister and Glasses the ghost," Meg grunted before walking away with heavy steps. After her colossal figure could no longer be seen, Dexter immediately faced Noel.

"Are you alright?"

Blood was dribbling down her face, oozing out of her hands, and as she spat, giant wads of it came out. Her brown undershirt had been severely shredded during the ordeal, with her crimson bra now noticeable. The letters on her shirt that survived now spelled out only one word: victim. She gave Dexter a cold glare that sent shivers up his spine.

"Do I look okay?"

"Right ... how about we get you to the ..."

"If you end that sentence with 'hospital,' I swear that you will feel even worse than I look," Noel threatened as she beckoned Alex to follow her. "Come on, Alex. We're going home."

"You can't be serious!" Dexter exclaimed, following after them. "You both are injured and you, Noel, are seriously injured! You both need immediate medical attention!"

"No!" Noel yelled. "I have everything that we need back at the house. I can treat Alex, and all I need is some rest."

"Then I'm coming as well!" Dexter insisted. "I won't leave after you both have been hurt!"

"Get lost, cake dropper! I don't need a punching bag right now!"

"Noel," Alex pleaded with big eyes, looking up to meet her sister's gaze. Her lip quivered as she clutched the front of Noel's shirt. Dirt and blood covered the scattered mess of her short, leaf-strewn hair. With a soft voice, she beseeched her older sister while tugging at the tattered remains of Noel's sleeveless undershirt. "Don't be mean to Dex. Please, let's go home."

Noel's eyes softened, turning back into a warm, comforting brown. She sighed before picking up Alex and carrying her in her arms. Noel left Dexter standing in the park and began making her way back home, only for her to stop suddenly and face him.

"Well? Are you coming or what, cake dropper?"

Chapter 19

Oh, Blurf

After a short walk down the dirt road, they arrived at an all-too-familiar shabby house. In the light of the early afternoon sun, the Mud Hut stood proudly. The blue tarp on the roof waved at them as the mild wind blew as if welcoming their arrival.

Noel gave a sigh of relief while Dex wore a look of apprehension at the dilapidated house. As Noel swiftly climbed the creaky stairs, Dex followed closely behind. With every step, Dex's expression tightened.

"Noel, are you sure it's safe to enter this building? Its foundation feels unsteady."

"Will you just can it!" Noel hissed through clenched teeth. "You're going to wake up, Alex."

Noel turned her attention to her sister, who now slumbered peacefully in her arms. A gentle expression took over Noel's face as she gazed upon her kid sister before stopping at the front door.

Seeing Noel's arms full from carrying Alex, Dex stepped around to open the door. But, before he could, Noel kicked it open. She went inside, and Dexter followed closely behind with a look of mild annoyance.

"Did you really need to kick it open? I could have opened it for you."

"Did I ask for your opinion, cake dropper?" Noel snapped as she gently laid Alex on their worn couch in the living area. It was dark brown with a hideous floral design that looked like it belonged in some grandmother's house. Cushioning and springs were noticeably exposed, but Noel had carefully placed Alex on an undamaged section.

"You kicked the door off of its hinges!" Dexter said while closely examining it. "I really think that you should treat this place with more respect. Also, how long has it been since you took out the trash? The pile is bigger than the container."

"You don't even live here, so lay off!" Noel growled while heading to the corner of the room to retrieve a small case.

"Noel..." Alex mumbled, rubbing her eyes as she slowly woke up. "Are you still here?"

"Yeah, now let me see your hands." Alex obediently did as she was told. Noel picked up her hands and carefully examined them. There were several cuts on her palms; thankfully, they weren't very deep. Noel opened the case and took out a bottle of rubbing alcohol, a box of No-Wo brand adhesive bandages, and a couple of cotton balls.

"Alex," Noel said, dabbing a cotton ball in alcohol, "I need you to stay very still. I'm going to clean your cuts."

Alex's eyes widened, but she took a big gulp as she nodded in compliance.

Noel rubbed the moist cotton ball over Alex's cuts. Alex whimpered as the alcohol worked its magic. Finally, after all of Alex's cuts were disinfected, Noel pulled out a couple of small bandages and began sticking them over her sister's cuts.

"How does that feel?" Noel asked after putting on the last No-Wo bandage.

"Better," Alex said. She winced as she flexed her hands. They still hurt like she had been stung by several short and stubby rumble bees. Alex hated the three-drux-tall, six-armed creatures. They were short-tempered and vicious, not unlike her older sister. Noel, though, was far kinder and more caring, to her at least. Her sister's warm, calloused hand gently ruffled Alex's dirty hair. A familiar happiness flooded her chest as Alex gave a content sigh. No one was more important to her than her big sister Noel.

"Good. Now go back to your room and rest for a little," Noel commanded as she tenderly pulled Alex to her feet and nudged her toward her room. "I'll be there soon to check on you."

"Alright. Bye, Dex!" Alex said, turning towards Dexter with a wave before leaving the room. Once she was gone, Dexter approached Noel with a serious expression.

"What?!" Noel remarked as she crossed her arms. "You gonna complain more about the giant pile of trash in the corner or maybe the dishes that have been in the sink for a couple of weeks?"

Dexter shook his head. He put a hand on Noel's shoulder, meeting her gaze while speaking softly.

"It's your turn next."

"Excuse me?" Noel asked. She smacked off Dex's hand. Her whole body ached, but she desperately tried to hide the intense pain. With an outstretched arm, she pointed a rigid finger toward the front door. "I don't need your help, cake dropper. Beat it!"

Much to Noel's surprise, Dex didn't budge. Instead, he raised an eyebrow.

"You're even more banged up than your little sister. Now take a seat," Dexter said, gesturing towards the couch.

"I can take care of myself. I always have. Besides, if I get seriously hurt, I can always eat that rank cactus," Noel responded gruffly. She took an unsteady step away from Dex only to stumble over Cal's stool. Noel muttered a few choice words as Cal's thorns lodged into her left hand. Noel detested the plant's mere scent, but the pain from its jagged thorns piercing her calloused skin was worse. Cal secreted a unique toxin that had healing properties but burned intensely when applied to the skin. Noel's face contorted into a grimace; it felt like expired, piping-hot honey had been injected into her skin. She tried removing Cal's prickly remnants with her right hand but experienced another problem she could no longer ignore.

"Noel," Dexter said with a patient yet firm tone, "your hands are shaking."

Noel looked at both of her trembling hands in annoyance. Training with Dex, fighting Monstrous Meg, and carrying Alex home had taken a more significant toll on her body than she cared to admit. Honestly, Noel was running on fumes. Reluctantly, she planted herself on the couch.

Dexter's hand became a blur as he removed the thorns with bird-like motions. Once they were all removed, Dex reached into the case and pulled out some supplies. After dabbing a cotton ball in alcohol, he cleaned the cuts on Noel's hands.

Dexter, despite his deep concern, was impressed. Noel's hands were rough and calloused, and the blades from the carousel had barely left scratches on her hands. Her face, though, was another story. Her face was badly bruised, especially around her left cheek and forehead, with dried blood around the corners of her mouth and dribbling down her nose.

"I'm going to clean your face next," Dexter said, with Noel grunting in acknowledgment.

Noel winced as the sting of the alcohol cleansed her skin, but the glare never left her eyes.

"This is your fault," Noel said.

"I assure you that the alcohol would burn no matter who put it on."

"No. I mean with Monstrous Meg. I would have beaten her if I hadn't been wearing these weights and tired from training.

Training with you is supposed to make me stronger, but if I'm losing to people weaker than me, then what good is it?"

Dexter sighed while continuing to clean Noel's face. "What if Meg attacked you after training at the gym? Would it have been the gym owner's fault if you had lost then?"

"No! Because then I wouldn't have lost. I know my routine, and I know my limits. Switching to your routine caused me not only to lose against someone weaker, but Alex was hurt too!"

"You ever think it's because you're pushing yourself too hard? The time I spent training in the mountains was the most extreme physical activity I'd ever done in my life, and yet it's nowhere near as insane as your workout regimen. I had time to rest, but you are always pushing your body to its limits. The only thing that follows long-term overexertion is burnout."

"I don't have the luxury to take it easy, cake dropper!" Noel yelled as she slammed a fist into the couch. "If I'm to defeat Invincible Inaya, I have to get much stronger! I have to train harder, or I won't reach her level! Any moment not spent train-ing is a moment wasted, and I don't have time to spare! We can't all be untouchable ghost boys!"

"Noel," Dexter said patiently while putting a No-Wo on Noel's forehead, "there is always a price to pay for strength. Oftentimes you find yourself at a side road that leads to strength, but there is always a toll booth blocking the way. This leads to the question: do you pay the toll to reach a new desti-nation, or do you keep going down the same path, knowing full well where it ends? Podge is more than just a form of martial arts. It's a way of living that dribbles down into every aspect of your life. It's choosing self-control over mindless violence because a calm and collected mind is far more dangerous than one fixated on death and destruction."

"Enough with all of the stupid wordplay! You and all the adults around me always say a bunch of words that don't make sense. You talk about life like it is some complicated puzzle, but the answer has always been simple for me." She threw out a fist at Dexter, which even a normal sidvan could have dodged. "I just use these fists and pulverize whatever problem stands before me."

"Yeah, I hear you, Noel," Dexter said in a soothing voice as he put one last No-Wo over her nose, "but remember if you live your life that way, then you be like a yolk chipping away at its shell. Without rest and guidance, you will end up broken and hollow."

"Are you done?" Noel asked curtly. "If so, then get out. You're really getting on my last nerves."

A look of concern crossed Dexter's face before his expression hardened. "Fine. Just let me take those weights off you first. They won't come off unless I ..."

"Just go! I don't need your help!" Noel roared. Anger flared in her eyes as she glared daggers at Dexter. Dexter sighed and left, gently closing the unhinged door the best that he could.

"I can't stand that boy," Noel bellowed as she stormed towards the fridge. "Who does he think that he is?"

She opened the fridge and reached for the plastic jug of mammoth milk. As she pulled it out, her arm shook violently. The milk seemed to weigh more than a concrete slab as it slowly sank to the ground in her grip. Frustrated, she slammed the milk on the kiddie table and turned her attention to the weights on her wrists and ankles. She grabbed the Velcro straps around her wrists and tugged on them, but they refused to budge. Noel growled as she began twisting and pulling at the straps with increased ferocity. When that failed, she tried pulling her hands out to no avail. Then Noel tried biting them off, but her teeth started hurting after a while. Quickly she released them, knowing she couldn't afford a trip to the dentist. Noel stormed back to the fridge and opened the door. She stuck her hand inside and slammed the door on her wrist, thus trapping the weight on her arm. She grunted as she tried to pull her hand out of the wrist weight. It didn't work.

Enraged, Noel thrust her free fist into the fridge, leaving the latest of many fist prints. After taking a few deep breaths, Noel recalled Dexter's words.

"These weights won't come off unless I ..."

"Oh, blurf," Noel muttered as she gazed upon the weights on her wrists and ankles and came to a shocking realization.

"I can't take these things off."

Chapter 20

A Late Night Offer

This is just great, Noel muttered internally. She was in the middle of another boxing match at the stadium against Right-Hook Rheyna. She was the same height and build as Noel, with long brown hair tied up in a bun on the back of her head with her purple bangs loosely dangling over her forehead. Rheyna wore a black and violet sports bra with matching athletic shorts. Covering her purple gloves were drawings, most noticeably a smiling mask on her right glove and a frowning mask on her right. Rheyna was a fearsome opponent known for delivering a devastating right hook strong enough to shatter jaws. Noel had her arms up as Rheyna threw a series of rapid hook punches. It was only the second round, but Noel was already at a disadvantage.

"I do not believe it, folks!" Jesse B yelled into his microphone. "Knockout Noel is struggling to keep up with Right-Hook Rheyna! Word on the street is that Noel has taken up a new workout regimen since her defeat of Dangerous Dana, but so far, I'm less than impressed. Noel, who is normally quick enough to overpower fighters such as Rapid-Fire Rebecca and Pronto Paula, is now at the mercy of Rheyna's right hand! Will Noel be able to turn the tables, or will Rheyna's right hook claim another victim? Tonight, that question will be answered here at the Battletown Stadium!"

Noel's arms shook slightly as she barely maintained her guard against the vicious onslaught. Luckily, the density of the wrist and ankle weights always reset early every morning. With minimal use of her arms and legs during the day, she could keep the burden as low as possible. She had thrown a few punches so far, but the weights still on her wrists, now hidden underneath her boxing gloves, severely slowed down her punches, resulting in her being quickly drowned out by Rheyna. She could feel the weights grow heavier upon her with every movement. Out of pride, she had refused to see Dexter to have them removed, and now she was paying the price for it.

I've got to think of something. I can't just play defense all night; my arms are already reaching their limits.

"That all you got, Noel?!" Rheyna bellowed between blows. "I'm disappointed. My rival is supposed to match me in strength and speed, but all you've done is play defensively. This has been going on since you started hanging around that Glasses the ghost boy. I've heard others talk about him. You need to ditch him; he's no good for you."

"Rheyna, are you serious right now?!" Noel grunted while blocking a flurry of Rhenya's left jabs. "We are fighting in round three of the national qualifiers; save your breath and fight me already!"

"I just don't think it's good for your image to be seen with someone who comes off as a spiritual apparition that feeds off of the souls of the living," Rheyna said between punches while Noel blocked. "Someone like that will only bring you down in more ways than one."

"Rheyna, you don't know what's going on, so butt out already," Noel yelled as she leaped back into the ring's cables. "Who I hang out with outside this ring has nothing to do with you, so stop telling me how to live my life! This isn't like one of those screenplays you write where you control everything happening."

After pulling back against the thick, elastic cables, she felt her body whiz through the air as she hurtled towards Rheyna. The purple-haired girl side-stepped. With a grunt, Noel crashed into the opposing ring cables. Rheyna stood with both gloved hands on her hips, her right foot tapping impatiently, as Noel rose to her feet slowly.

"See! This is exactly what I'm talking about! Your performance in the ring has been sluggish since you've been hanging around this 'Smex' character. How do you plan to prevail when you're not in peak form?"

"First, his name is Dex, not Smex! Second, what's it to you, Rheyna? I don't have to be serious to beat you!" Noel barked back as the crowd laughed at their bickering.

"You're embarrassing me!" Rheyna snapped back with a whiney tone while motioning toward the crowd's roaring laughter. "This is an important match where I clash with my mighty rival, the crowd favorite, and manage to pull a narrow victory and rise through the ranks until I stand before Invincible Inaya herself. But how can I face her proudly for the title if my rival, my great motivator for boxing, is fighting at less than one hundred and ten percent? This moment is vital for my rise to fame and your personal development as a character. That's why you need to take this more seriously and ..."

Rheyna kept vocalizing her thoughts regarding their "rivalry" while hammering away mercilessly at Noel's defenses. Rheyna had basically preached the same message to her while they were changing in the locker room. At this point, Noel was actively tuning out most of what Rhenya was saying. *Will this chick ever shut up?! She talks more than Dex and Jesse combined!*

"The flames of our rivalry have burned bright ever since we first crossed fists upon this very stage. Life for me changed forever from that point on. I had someone in my life strong enough to provide the challenge I needed to reach my maximal potential. My potent right hook is matched only by the intensity of your knockout punch. Now you will once more have a taste of the fruits of my labor plucked by my right hand," Rheyna yelled as she began throwing intense right hooks at Noel.

Noel's arms were screaming, and with every touch of Rheyna's right hand, their screams grew louder.

Keeping track of Rheyna's punch count, she ducked down as her opponent threw out a right hook. Noel sidestepped and counteracted with a jab-cross combo. Rheyna threw up her left arm, which blocked Noel's first punch, but the right found its mark on Rheyna's face. Rheyna grunted but threw out a powerful cross. Noel saw the punch coming, but her arms were too slow to block as the blow landed on Noel's cheek. She stumbled back on her lead legs, ignoring the stinging in her cheek until she felt the red corner behind her. Rheyna dashed towards Noel and began building momentum as she hurled a nasty sequence of punches. Luckily, Noel had thrown her arms up to guard against the current flow of nonstop punches, but now she was back in the same situation.

Ugh! Now what?! A picture of Alex appeared in her mind. A wave of familiar anger burned through her exhausted arms. *I can't afford to lose.*

"I won't lose, not to you!" Noel bellowed as Rheyna flinched in surprise. Noel drove a gloved uppercut straight into Rheyna's gut. Rheyna's eye's bulged as her face turned pale. She instantly put her gloves over her mouth as a foul-smelling liquid oozed out and formed a puddle of nastiness on the ring floor. Noel launched another punch into Rheyna's forehead.

"Not bad, my rival," Rheyna muttered before hitting the ground, landing in the puddle with a splash.

Not a shred of sympathy could be detected within Noel's icy eyes as she stared at Rheyna's unconscious body before walking away to the crowd's rowdy applause.

"There you have it, folks!" Jesse B screamed into his microphone while gripping it tightly. "It wasn't pretty or elegant, but Knockout Noel pulled through with an equally brutal KO in the end! However ..." Jesse said, his voice sobering, "Noel's performance tonight was more than a little lacking in her usual prowess. Noel needs to rethink this ghostly Smex training that Rheyna was talking about and stop it immediately. She will not be as lucky during her next match in the semifinals."

Jesse B ducked his head quickly as Noel hurled one of Rheyna's puke-covered gloves towards the announcer, who nimbly dodged it. "Even that was a lot slower than usual," Jesse B said with a disappointed shake of his head.

"Yeah, I know," Noel grumbled as she trudged towards the locker room. "I'm going to have to do something about this."

After quickly showering and changing clothes, she left the stadium and went to the Jab-en-Grab. She strolled inside. Every customer eyed her with concern as she passed the registers. She went to the bakery but, after a few minutes, began pacing around the area in a huff. The manager, noticing Noel stomping, timidly approached her.

"I-Is there anything I can help you with, Ms. Smith?" the manager asked nervously, his legs shaking slightly. He hadn't forgotten what had happened to his car the last time she came to the store.

"Dexter. Where is he?" Noel growled.

"Oh, you mean our new celebrity, Glasses, the ghost boy?" the manager said with a high pitch snicker that graded Noel's eardrums.

Noel grabbed him by the collar and pulled him down to eye level before growling, "You know that's not his name. Now where is he?"

The manager's cackling instantly ceased as his expression became immensely fearful. "Dexter is, um, off tonight."

"Then where **can** I find him?"

"If he's not out harvesting souls, then he must be..." the manager started to say before Noel lifted him higher off the ground. Pure terror flooded his face as he peered into the burning embers of Noel's eyes. He might have been imagining things, but he could swear that he felt a strange presence grabbing ahold of him from within her glare. An intense pressure squeezed his innermost being in an unyielding, fiery stranglehold that left him gasping for air while his voice caught in his throat. "A-at his home ... probably."

"And **where** is that?" Noel questioned as her glare intensified.

"I- I- I don't know. Please don't hurt me! Or my car!" the manager wailed, eyes wide with fear. His legs trembled terribly, with sweat profusely dribbling down his whole body.

"You're useless," Noel muttered, casting him aside and storming out of the store. She ambled across the parking lot and took an angry seat on the shopping cart bin while whipping out her phone. Noel only had three contacts and had no trouble finding the one number she needed. It was the only one in the C section, and she typed a quick text message.

Cakedropper, we need to talk. Meet me tomorrow morning in the park.

Noel's thumb paused over the send button before turning it off and putting her phone away as she stared into the darkness of night. The flickering light of the streetlamp offered brief views of what lay concealed in the shadows. Noel found herself lost in thought, trying to determine her next course of action. She knew that she couldn't continue with the way things were currently, so Noel took a deep breath as she mentally prepared herself for what she would have to do next.

That was when the flickering light went out completely. Noel looked from side to side, but it was pitch-black, and she couldn't see anything. She did, however, hear a sound. It was a consistent thumping from a distance, and from what she could tell as her eyes slowly adjusted, it was seven pairs of feet slowly approaching her. Suddenly six figures wearing glowing white trench coats appeared before her, all led by one person.

"Well, well, if it isn't the infamous Knockout Noel," the seventh of the figures, and the only one not wearing a glowing trench coat, said with a pleasant tone as he slithered closer. "Enjoying the nighttime sky?"

"What's it to you?!" Noel snarled back.

"Easy, girl." The figure raised his arms in resignation. "I just came bearing a gift. I happened to hear that you were roughed up by a beastly fighter named Meg a couple of days ago in the park."

"Where did you hear that?" Noel said, focusing entirely on the figure as she made her way towards him. "Who are you?"

The figure took off his fedora and gave a mock bow. "I'm Dan, and I make it my business to stay informed."

He gave an all-knowing smile as he reached into the inner coat pocket of his milky jacket. With a deft motion, he pulled out a business card. After taking a few steps forward, the other six followed closely behind until he stood within arm's reach of Noel. He handed the card to her, and she gave him a skeptical look. "I'm a businessman specializing in delivering solutions to all life's problems."

"Hey, I recognize those footsteps," Noel said with a low voice as she clenched her fists. "Some of you are the White Caps that terrorized Jab-en-Grab. Did that Sanchez guy send you to cause me more problems? If so, I hope you all brought body bags because no one is here to save you from me this time!"

"My, aren't you the feisty one," Dan said with a small chuckle. "Your fearsome reputation truly precedes you, but no, Mr. Sacheez didn't send me. I sent him with several of my other men to have a ... friendly little discussion with that violent Crimson Storm gang. And now, a large percentage of that bloodthirsty gang has been put down because of our efforts. Now the townsfolk can rest a little easier."

"Your men took hundreds of brilocks from several of the bystanders at Jab-en-Grab the other night!"

Dan shrugged. "They chose to donate; no one was forced to do anything. Making the world a better place isn't cheap. Everyone must pitch in if we're to make any lasting change within society."

"Drop the act, will you! You're nothing but bullies, so beat it before I beat you and your friends into the ground!" Noel yelled as she struck a fighting pose. With a burst of velocity, she shot toward Dan.

Dan smiled as he snapped his fingers. The glow from the other six White Caps extinguished as their heavy footsteps shuffled around the lot.

Even blinded in the dark, she could still sense a general idea of her surroundings, which she claimed was all thanks to the years she'd spent walking these streets at night. As she approached Dan, she could tell that his six hired hands behind him readied their rifles as they aimed carefully at her, but not before she threw a punch directly at Dan's face. After Dan was down, she planned to take out the six remaining White Caps individually, using the darkness to provide coverage.

That was the plan, but it was quickly derailed.

"Wha...?" Noel said as her eyes widened. Her punch had failed to land.

Noel knew she couldn't have missed. Dan had been standing there moments prior, but now his presence was gone as if he had just disappeared, only to be replaced with a low, menacing buzz.

"Not bad, Noel, but," Dan said sinisterly, now beside her, "I have little patience for poor manners."

A hand tightly grabbed her outstretched arm with serpent-like quickness.

"Aaahhh!" Noel yelped in pain as she felt a strong current of electricity flow through her arm.

Her arm spasmed before falling limply as Dan released his grip. With a grunt, Noel staggered backwards. Her legs trembled, but she refused to let them buckle. With a grimace, she shot the most menacing glare she could manage and swung with her good arm in Dan's direction, but she only hit air as his presence disappeared again.

His quick footsteps skulked silently through the shadows as he causally walked around until he stood in front of her.

"Don't worry, I used a smaller amplitude, so you'll regain the use of your arm in a couple of hinos. Now, I need a moment of your undivided attention. To clarify, I'm not here to fight or collect charitable donations from you, Noel. I'm here to help you with your little wrist and ankle weight problem."

"I don't know what you're talking about," Noel grunted as she clutched her numb left arm.

"Come now, Noel, I'm not blind, and neither are your viewers. We saw how much you struggled against Right-Hook Rheyna, a fighter ranked lower than you. You pulled through because you are a spectacular fighter, but the chances of you pulling that off a second time are slim to none. Luckily, I have just the solution for you." He opened his briefcase and pulled out a little vial.

"You should find this to your liking," he said, tossing the vial at her.

Noel caught it with her good hand but continued to glare menacingly at Dan.

"I'm not interested in any strength-enhancing chemicals like that Jaguar Juice crat or any of the other junk that you guys peddle on the streets."

"I wouldn't dream of selling you Jaguar Juice, Noel," Dan said with a coy expression. "I created Jaguar Juice to give the weak a chance to be on equal footing with the strong. Someone like you has no business taking it. What I just gave you is called Gorilla Goo. It looks like glue and tastes ten times worse, but after you drink it, your arms and legs will no longer feel tired. Give it a try."

The streetlight briefly turned on, allowing Noel to glimpse Dan's face briefly. There was something in his eyes that she didn't trust. It felt like the gaze of a predatory lying in wait. "What's the catch? No one gives stuff like this away for free around these parts."

Dan shrugged. "I just wanted to give you a free sample in hopes that we may have business together in the future."

"I don't need your help. Get lost!" Noel growled.

"Fine," Dan said while taking a giant step back. "You're free to trust in me and use the Gorilla Goo to return to your prior state of fighting prowess, or you can simply throw it away. But can you really trust this new training that has devasted your performance? Failing to trust me could very well mean forsaking your shot at making it into the national female boxing championship, something that you have worked very hard towards. Just think, the fame and fortune all gone because you chose to listen to the wrong people. The decision is yours, Noel."

Dan turned to walk away, his party trailing behind. He paused momentarily and turned to gaze at Noel from the corner of his eye before walking away.

"If you decide that you want my assistance, then feel free to contact me."

Suddenly the light from the streetlamp flickered back on. Noel looked around the parking lot, but Dan and his cronies were nowhere to be seen. She stared at the vial in her hand. It had a pretty, cursive letter design on it and a white liquid that sloshed around inside the bottle. She stood deep in thought for a while before hearing a familiar beeping on her phone. She whipped it out to find a new text from Alex asking where she was. She put away her cellphone and pocketed the little vial along with Dan's business card. She still had time to decide, but right now, her main priority was getting to Alex. She ambled down the shadow-covered path unafraid. To reach the one place she felt warmth, there was no path she wouldn't travel down, no matter how dark.

Chapter 21

Crossroad

"Ugh!" Noel grunted in frustration.

It was early in the morning with birds chirping a joyful song about the wonders of the new day, not that Noel heard any of it. The only noise she heard was the gentle creaking of the metal links of a punching bag as it swung back and forth in a mesmerizing rhythm.

Alex had plans with Sara and had gone over to play, so Noel went to the gym to train. She found herself taking all her frustrations out on the poor, defenseless black bag before her, and boy did she have **a lot** of frustration. Thankfully, she had regained complete control of her left arm and was putting it to full use. The bag seemed to groan with every punch, but the intensity gradually dimmed as the wrist weights grew heavier the longer Noel worked. Eventually, Noel's arms fell to her sides in resignation. After less than thirty yosmins, Noel plopped to the ground, deciding to take a break and rest her arms.

She reached for her crimson bottle beside her feet. After taking a small sip, she set the bottle back down and got up for another round with the punching bag. After lasting half as long as usual, she stared angrily at the bag dangling in front of her as her arms became limp noodles hanging off her shoulders.

"No!" she yelled while lashing the bag with limp arms. She felt like a toddler flailing helplessly, and the thought infuriated her.

"This isn't going to work! If I don't do something, then I will lose during the next round!"

She looked towards a bench, on which lay her phone and, beside it, the small vial she got from Dan. She approached the bench slowly. Her eyes darted between the two objects gazing intently at both. Podge or Gorilla Goo? Dex or Dan? New and unfamiliar training vs. the tried and true? Deep within her prideful heart, Noel knew that she had to make an important decision on who to trust right now, which, quite frankly, she was not happy about. Life always became more complicated the more involved she was with others, and Noel was no fan of that.

But, Noel thought, *if I fail here, then I lose my chance to qualify for the national title and will be left without a way to make money until next season. I can't afford to lose, not when I've come this close!*

She reached for the Gorilla Goo, but her phone rang as she grasped the bottle. Noel looked at the caller ID, and Dex's number appeared. Noel hesitated, remembering Dex's words: "I just want to assist, and if you let me, I know I can help you acquire an unrivaled strength."

"Sorry, cake dropper," she muttered before uncapping the vial, "but I've made it this far on my own strength, and I won't allow myself to lose because of your stupid training."

Noel poured the entire bottle's contents down her throat, and with one big gulp, it was gone. Noel walked back to the punching bag, not feeling much different, but took a jab at it. It swung up and hit the ceiling with a thud before swaying back down like a pendulum. Noel's arms no longer felt tired, like it was still the pre-workout!

She began throwing punches like a madman with a small grin as the poor bag became subjected to her reinvigorated beating. Finally, after sand poured out like an hourglass, the deflated bag declared defeat. Noel stood before it with a look of pride on her face. She clenched her fists. She felt like she had the strength to easily fight another ten people and maybe even land a solid hit on Dexter. The thought filled her with a weird sense of euphoria.

"Time to message the cake dropper," she said, picking up her phone and shooting him a quick text.

"It's time to show him what I've got."

Later that morning, Dexter found himself sitting on the bench back at Paslow Park. He had successfully avoided the spikes, but the old wood had splintered underneath him. He shifted uncomfortably as the bench prickled his shorts, but that was the least of his worries.

"Where is she?" he muttered as he scanned the park. It had been days since Dex had last heard from Noel. If he were honest, he was more than a little upset, but that didn't mean he wasn't concerned. He had tried calling several times, but she'd never responded until earlier today. In a brief text, she told him to meet her a little before lunch at Paslow. Dexter had left immediately, but now, she was nowhere to be seen, even after almost a hin.

Burning brightly in the sky, the sun beamed intense rays of heat directly down upon the park. The giddy screams of children as they bloodied their knuckles fighting on the giant spinning tires filled the air. The goal was to last the longest on the tire while knocking everyone else off or breaking their bones (whichever happened first, except in the case of refusing to submit). Submission played a huge role in every matter within Battletown. In every conflict, power struggle, or change within society, there were always sides fighting for control and those fighting to defend it. These forces fought a brutal battle that didn't end until one side resigned or died. While atrocious from outside appearances, this kind of culture bred a resilient mindset that was focused on what was important, with the tenacity to fight till the bitter end to make all goals, no matter how impossible, a reality.

So what is going on inside Noel's head? Dex wondered. *She was clearly determined to qualify for the national female boxing championship, so why haven't I heard from her? She is not the type to give up. On the contrary, she only seems to get stronger with each encounter. Maybe she has been doing some other form of training?* That was when he sensed a presence behind him. He turned only to see a fist fly toward his face. Dex quickly rolled out of the way as his attacker struck a menacing pose. This was expected, but what surprised him was the surprisingly calm look on his attacker's face. She launched a series of carefully executed rapid punches, yet despite all of the exertion, there was not a trace of fatigue on her face. She was even still wearing the weights that he had put on her wrists and ankles, but it was like she was just wearing regular jewelry from the way her arms were zooming towards him. Granted, he was effortlessly dodging them, but she wasn't tiring. If this were to continue, it would end up becoming a battle of sheer endurance, and in this battle, Dex wasn't sure who would run out of steam first. It was Dex's foot slipping under a patch of wet mud that caused him to stumble. After he fell and landed on his rump, his female opponent launched a punch straight at him but halted it a hair's breadth away from his face.

"Well, you seem lively today, Noel."

"Yeah," she said nonchalantly, "I feel great. I feel strong enough to take on the whole world."

"I can see that," Dex said as he got up. He brushed some of the mud off his pants. "Where have you been? I haven't heard from you in days. I've been worried."

"That's not your concern. In fact, you don't have to be concerned at all anymore. I called here today to tell you that I no longer need you. I found a new way to get strong without drawbacks, so there won't be any more problems with the qualifier."

"Really?" Dex said skeptically with a raised eyebrow. "So, what is this new method that you've found?"

Noel pulled out the vial from her pocket and held it in front of Dex's face. "This is called Gorilla Goo, and after I drink it, my body instantly feels refreshed even after an intense workout. All I need to do is keep taking this, and I'll be guaranteed a victory in the qualifier. Then I will have more time to train for nationals."

"And where did you even get that stuff from?" Dex asked with a tense expression.

"From Sanchez's boss, a guy named Dan. I met him a couple of nights ago, and he gave me this vial ..." Noel started before being interrupted.

"You're doing business with a White Cap?! Are you out of your mind, Noel!" Dex yelled. "Those guys are dangerous! Anyone caught up with them always ends up deep in trouble!"

"Hey! I can handle myself!" Noel yelled. "I know what I'm doing!"

"No, you don't!" Dex said, grabbing Noel's shoulders tightly. "You think that garbage that you're drinking will make you strong?! That's rubbish! At best, you're moving sideways. If that junk is in any way related to the dreadful Jaguar Juice, then it's only going to wreck your body. Give up the Goo and return to training in Podge's style, because you will never get any stronger otherwise!"

"No, and that's final!" Noel screamed, pushing Dex away. "I don't need you! I can do this by myself!"

"No, you can't! You need help!"

"I'll help break your bones!" Noel roared as she charged Dex and hurled punches at him while sidestepping around him. Without breaking a sweat, he evaded all of her fervent attacks. Soon Noel's arms became lethargic and shook while she struggled to keep her fists up against the weights as their density snowballed. Sweat poured down her face, resembling a waterfall. Her legs trembled like gelatin, but she willed them to stay standing.

Dexter, with a sorrowful look, just shook his head. "You couldn't land a fair punch on me before, and if you keep this up, then you'll never be able to land one on me ever in the future. You're better than this, Noel. Don't take the easy route. It will not lead you down the path that you want to go. I've seen others give in to temptation instead of remaining diligent with their training. Do you really want to wind up like those broken, empty husks?"

"Man, shut up! I'll become the national female boxing champion, and I'll do it without your stupid training. We're done! End of story! Goodbye and good riddance, Dex! You'll have to deal with knowing that when I win, I'll win with my own strength!" Noel said, walking away while trying to hide her fatigue.

"At least let me take those weights off of you. You've worn them far too long already, and your muscles must be exhausted." Dex reached for her arm, only for Noel to pull away.

"Don't touch me!" she yelled as she glared at him before storming off. "I told you that I don't need your help, or anybody's help."

"Then why do you need Dan?" Noel stopped in her tracks. "Noel, if you truly want to win using only your own strength, then why do you need Dan or the Gorilla Goo?" Noel stood silently, refusing to face Dex. Her fists were trembling.

"Noel, you say you don't need me. You say that you don't need anyone's help, but that's not true. Whether you like it or not, the only paths left from here involve other people. That Gorilla Goo is something you can only get from the White Caps, and Podge's style is something you can only learn from me. Regardless of the path you choose, you'll always end up needing someone's help. Studying Podge can help you reach a new level of strength, while that Goo is nothing more than a crutch that'll barely keep you on your feet. You still need help, but do you think Dan is so benevolent? Do you honestly believe he'll keep giving you free vials of Gorilla Goo? The first may have been free, but there will be serious strings attached if you get any further involved with him. Are you sure this is what you want? Are you sure this is the way to go about it?"

Noel walked away, not bothering to look back or acknowledge Dex's questions. She pulled out her phone and dialed the number on Dan's business card.

"Noel," Dex said sorrowfully, "the price you will have to pay will be far greater than you imagine."

Chapter 22

Unexpected Conditions

"Ah, Noel, I'm so happy that you could grace me with your presence today," Dan said, gripping the tip of his fedora as he gave her a mock bow.

They stood in the back alleyway behind Bob's boxing glove manufacturing warehouse. It was a massive building with a rounded shape that loosely resembled a boxing glove. It was currently colored black, but Bob chose to have it repainted another color every year just to mix it up. It was closely connected to several other buildings, resulting in a closed-in alleyway that trapped the shadows within.

"Yeah. You got a thing for shadows or something?"

"I just feel a little more at ease encased in shadows. Sunlight is ... uncomfortable to me, but you said you had business to discuss, so I came out to meet you during the disgusting daytime."

"Yeah, I don't care," Noel said without a shred of sympathy. "I just want more of that Gorilla Goo. I used up the bottle you gave me, and I need more before my next match."

"But of course!" Dan said, clasping his hands together. "Anything for you!"

"Great! Now hand me a bottle."

"Not so fast," Dan said, reaching behind him and pulling a stack of papers from the dark abyss. "Before I can give you anything, we need to review a few terms and stipulations in this contract regarding your distribution of Gorilla Goo."

"I ain't signing nothing," Noel grunted. "I'll just pay using brilocks."

"I'm afraid that won't work," Dan said. "I'm a man who strongly believes in diversifying his assets. Receiving solely monetary payments for services rendered just screams of unwise business practices."

"Look, just take my money! I ain't signing any contract!"

"Then we have nothing to talk about here," Dan said before turning to walk into the darkness.

"You ain't going anywhere; now give me that Gorilla Goo!" Noel yelled, grabbing Dan's shoulder.

Suddenly Noel found herself surrounded by six huge figures wearing glowing white jackets. Each was holding an intimidating rifle pointed directly at her.

"As you can clearly see," Dan said, shaking off her hand and facing her with a smug smile, "you are in no position to make demands. If you want to deal with me, you must act in a befitting manner, or you will find yourself with ... very limited options."

Noel eyed all of the people surrounding her. She didn't like her odds in this situation. While Noel possessed the ability to pull out a KO in even the direst of situations, that only applied to winnable fights. One wrong move here, and she would quickly be gunned down.

"Not very sportsmanlike," Noel remarked. "You know the people here believe in facing others using only the strength of their fists."

"A virtuous sentiment. However, as I said, I'm a businessman, and I prioritize prudence over virtue. Success comes for those well-grounded to the cruelty of reality, not those with the moral high ground. So, do we have a deal?"

Noel stared at the outstretched hand and the stack of papers within its grasp before sighing.

"What are the terms?" she asked.

...

"Noel, you're back!"

Noel had barely stepped through the front door before Alex tackled her to the ground. Noel smiled as she warmly embraced the creature clinging tightly around her waist.

"Yeah, I'm back," Noel said as Alex snuggled closer before suddenly stiffening as she began wildly sniffing Noel.

"Where have you been?" Alex asked with a suspicious look on her face.

"I just came back from training with Dexter."

"No, that's not it," Alex said, shaking her head with disgust. "I smell something else on you. I never smelled anything like it before, but it's disgusting! It's like a combination of your sweaty gym shorts, dog doody, and the dishes after you forget to wash them for a couple of weeks."

"You're imaging things, Alex," Noel said, quickly pushing Alex off her. "Why don't you grab your schoolbooks and finish your schoolwork?"

"Can you help me? I don't understand everything that the teacher taught today."

"Sure, Alex. Go get your things, and I'll give you a hand."

"Yeah! I'll be right back!" Alex said, running into the next room.

Noel got up and sighed as she plopped down on the couch. Seeing that Alex was still gone, she quickly pulled out one of the little vials from her pocket she'd received from Dan earlier today. She couldn't help but dwell upon the words spoken during their meeting.

I did what I had to do. This is the only way for me to win the qualifier. I have to be number one, no matter what.

Yet, despite her best attempts to rationalize it, she couldn't relieve herself of the horrible sensation in her gut. The more she focused on it, the more she thought of Dex and the terrible way she had treated him. She knew that all he wanted to do was help her, and she realized it would be easier if she just returned to him for assistance. Despite what she had said earlier, deep down, she knew she would require some help to get mightier. However, stronger than her guilt was another emotion that had an ironclad grip upon her head and heart. It was this tenacious, emotional barrier that made her current state of suffering seem more desirable than admitting to Dex that she was wrong.

I don't need Dex; I don't need anyone. I always found a way to pull through without help, and now is no different with or without these weights. So why do I have a bad feeling about this?

She let loose a massive sigh and glanced at the ceiling for a moment as if waiting for some reply before returning her focus on the Gorilla Goo. She clenched the bottle tightly before pocketing it with an angry gleam in her eyes.

I can't change things now, and I doubt Dex would want to see me again. But I'm used to losing people in my life, like that good-for-nothing mother of mine. The only one I can count on is myself. Regardless, I'll still find a way to win, no matter what.

...

"Welcome, everyone, to the women's boxing semifinals!" Jesse B screamed into his microphone. "Tonight, we have two of the mightiest boxers that Battletown has to offer. Knockout Noel will face off against none other than the pride of Bagor Gym and my twin sister, Everlasting Edna! Both fighters are extremely formidable, but only one will have the opportunity to progress! Who will win and make it to the final round?! My brilocks are on Edna, but we'll find out together tonight here in the Battletown stadium!"

Edna rolled her caramel eyes at the introduction. She had a modest build with coffee-colored skin. Her head was completely shaved except for her eyebrows, which had a tiny portion removed from the left. She wore a gray-and-light-blue sports bra with matching athletic shorts.

Edna glanced curiously at Noel, who returned Edna's gaze with a glare. Noel tapped her foot, arms crossed. She wanted to hurry up and get this over with. Gorilla Goo only lasted a little while after consumption, and even though she had taken it shortly before entering the ring, she wanted to end this quickly before the effects started to wane.

After the bell rang, Noel dashed towards Edna, who stood still, resembling a hunter lying in wait for her prey to get close. Noel swung at Edna, but her opponent merely sidestepped. Noel turned and fired a jab-jab-cross combo, only for Edna to turn side to side to avoid the blows. Frustrated, Noel launched a series of rapid punches. With a focused look on her clear face, Edna effortlessly evaded every attack. Noel threw a left hook, which hit the air as Edna ducked and launched a barrage of quick uppercuts into Noel's stomach. It was like she was playing a symphony. The song of leather on flesh in a beautiful rhythm resembled the dance of machine gunfire. It must have been played in the major scale of B for "breathtaking" because Noel was having a hard time breathing.

Gasping, Noel swung at Edna, forcing her to jump back and immediately go on the defensive. Noel had barely thrown up her guard before Edna hurled punches right at her. She would throw a jab-cross before side-stepping closer and launching a series of uppercuts. If Noel tried to attack while Edna was close, she would either jump back and counter with a series of jab crosses or sidestep and throw punches at her blind spot.

Perspiration dripped down Noel's forehead as she struggled to keep up. Her heart ached; it felt like it was going to pop out of her chest. On the other hand, Edna looked utterly unfazed, as if she had just finished some leisurely activity.

"It looks like Noel has fallen prey to Edna's specialty: endurance trapping," Jesse B interjected. "Years of running laps while playing portable strategy board games, like 'FourThought' and 'Mind's I' have heightened her stamina and cognitive perception beyond most her age, if not all of Battletown. While she is no powerhouse like her opponent, her endgame has no parallel. I'm telling you, folks, a thousand years will pass before Edna needs to take a break. How does Noel plan to defeat a foe whose stamina is on a completely different level? Tonight, folks, we will discover what happens when the unstoppable force meets the immovable object!"

Noel gritted her teeth. Her breathing was heavy, and her arms and legs ached. She could feel the effects of the Gorilla Goo beginning to wear off. In a desperate attempt, she began wildly throwing punches at Edna, but Edna kept turning sideways to avoid the brunt of the blows.

How am I supposed to beat this chick? I'm already starting to ache, but she looks like she could go another ten rounds without breaking a sweat. I have to turn things around.

She racked her brain for an idea when a thought popped into her head. If she couldn't match Edna's stamina, then she would change the game. Noel ceased recklessly throwing punches and took a defensive stance. Edna's eyes widened in surprise as her opponent stood a foot away, still as a statue with arms raised.

"Would you look at that, folks!" Jesse B screamed in the microphone. "Noel has stopped playing offense and has switched to a defensive stance. Even Knockout Noel's nightmarish physical prowess could not prevail against Everlasting Edna's endurance-eliminating tactics, a true testament to my sister's hard work, which I, as her brother, strongly encouraged. However, Edna's fighting style is mostly defensive. Will Noel be able to defeat Edna in her own domain? I hope not because I have brilocks down on my sister winning, but we'll find out here tonight in the Battletown stadium."

Noel shot an irritated look at Jesse B, who shuddered slightly while attempting to hide behind his microphone.

That guy is annoying. Can he just shut up for a few moments?

Noel glanced at Edna's eyes, which softened in understanding. Edna nodded in agreement, and Noel nodded back before both returned to their defensive stances. For a few moments, they stood there staring each other down. The crowd grew silent in anticipation, but after a few moments, the action had died down to see who would blink the most. The crowd quickly began yelling at the two girls to start fighting with strong language that only grew in intensity.

Edna sighed before charging straight toward Noel. As she approached, Edna launched a left jab, only for Noel to block and counteract with her own left jab before Edna could react. It hit Edna on the nose, with the bald boxer losing her balance and falling to the ground. Noel was on top of her in moments, throwing punches left and right. She was quickly pulled off by Ajax, who looked more than a little unhappy about having to do so. After pushing Noel away, he went to check on Edna. She appeared dazed, with a crooked nose and several bruises on her face. Other than that, she appeared to be okay.

Edna coughed as she slowly sat up. With a dazed expression, she swayed slightly. Her eyes kept opening and closing. Finally, with a loud thud, Edna plopped straight down on her back with her eyes closed.

"Knockout!" Jesse B screamed as the crowd roared in excitement. "Knockout Noel has succeeded once again. She has proved that despite all odds, the unstoppable force will always prevail in the end! Now Knockout Noel moves on to the final round of the national qualifier. Will she win and qualify for the national female boxing championship, or will the unstoppable force known as Knockout Noel finally run out of steam? We'll find out the answer next time here in the Battletown stadium!"

Noel rolled her eyes as she walked out of the ring and into the locker room. After quickly shower and changing clothes, she picked up her earnings and left the stadium. Noel roamed the dark streets feeling a strange sensation, or lack of one. Typically, after a victory, she felt ecstatic, like she was the queen of the entire world. Pride would roar like a mighty dragon within her heart and warm her very being. Her body would hunger for the thickest cut of prime ribs, and her palate would salivate at the thought of tearing that juicy meat to shreds with all thirty-eight of her ivory daggers.

Yet, as she strolled slowly down the path she always took back home, she only felt cold, lethargic, and empty.

This doesn't make sense. I won, but ... it doesn't feel like a win, Noel thought as she looked towards the sky only to see dark clouds veiling the twinkle of the sparkling stars.

It was the loud ringing from her phone that snapped her attention back to the present. She looked at the caller ID with narrowed eyes before answering the phone gruffly. "Yeah."

"Wonderful job in the stadium tonight," a rich voice said over the phone. "Your performance was excellent. I look forward to the finals."

"Can it, Dan!" Noel snapped. "What do you want?!"

"I came to tell you that I require your assistance. Meet me at midnight tonight at Battletown High School."

"What? No! I have things to do. Bother someone else!"

"Unfortunately, the contract you agreed to states that you are to appear and assist with matters when called, with little to no wiggle room for negotiation in exchange for your precious supply of Gorilla Goo. If you fail to meet the expectations clearly established in our contract, then I'll be forced to enact the penalties for breaching the contract, including, but not limited to, cutting off your supply of Gorilla Goo. Then you will find yourself in quite the pickle against your upcoming opponent, who I hear will trump all of your past opponents. Have I clearly established your situation?"

"Yes," Noel muttered.

"And you will appear at the high school tonight during the darkest hour?"

"Yeah," Noel agreed reluctantly.

"Excellent. I'll see you then. Be sure to bring your A-game."

Noel hung up the phone and sighed. She pocketed the plastic device and stared glumly at the rocky road before her. Black clouds concealed the stars causing the path to grow darker. She took a slow, unsteady step forward with a very un-Noel-like expression: uncertainty. After shaking her head, her expression hardened, and she quickened her pace. As she journeyed home, she couldn't help but wonder about this deal she had made.

I have to make sacrifices to get what I want, right? It's okay as long as I achieve my goal. Right?

Chapter 23

Dan's Dirty Work

Noel glowered as she leaned against the giant metal cage that encased Battletown High. While waiting for Dan, she dwelled unhappily on what had just transpired before leaving her house and heading toward the school.

...

Noel had put Alex to bed earlier that evening. After throwing on her maroon hoodie, she left through the creaky, unhinged front door but heard the pitter-patter of small footsteps behind her. Noel turned to find Alex with eyes full of concern.

"Noel," Alex had asked, "why are you leaving the house now? It's late."

"I just have something to do really quick. Go back to bed."

"No!" Alex yelled. "I don't want to be here alone! You promised that you would always be here at night!"

"I'll be right back, Alex. I just have to take care of something at Battletown High."

"Sissy, you hate going to school! Why would you go there when it's dark?"

"I ... have a ... job that needs to be done."

"But you've been leaving the house more than usual lately, and that strange smell on you has only gotten stronger!"

"I don't know what you're talking about! I just have to go do something, and I'll be right back, okay!" Noel yelled, pointing towards her bedroom. "Now get back to bed, Alex! Now!"
A stream of angry tears burst from Alex's eyes as she stormed back to her room. Her sobbing pierced through the thin walls and rang loudly in the nighttime air even after Noel was far down the dirt road.

...

"Noel, I'm glad to see you joining us this evening," Dan said while strolling around the corner. He had his usual pack of six beefy henchmen, all dressed in white trench coats but lacking their usual glow, following closely behind. She only recognized Sanchez, who eyed her intently while fiddling with his finely waxed mustache.
"I trust that you are having a pleasant night," Dan said politely with an air of congeniality. "The school grounds are so much more enjoyable, covered in a succulent layer of darkness."
"I'm not here to talk and hang out with you, Dan!" Noel growled. "What do you want?"
"That's a pity." Dan sighed before pointing towards a decrepit building across from the school.
"That there is the old Douglas building. It was used to manufacture boxing gloves until Bobs put him out of business. Nowadays, the rabble of the streets meets there for various shady activities."
"Pot calling the kettle black much."
"Don't compare me to them!" Dan snapped. "I'm leagues above them."
"Sure," Noel said, rolling her eyes. "So, what do you want me to do?"
"Follow me. Everything else will be obvious once we get there." Dan and Noel approached the Douglass building, with Dan's bodyguards staying behind. Sanchez, in particular, gave Noel a look of warning as he firmly gripped his rifle in a ready stance.

After walking several drux down the darkened roads, they approached the sinister-looking alleyway beside the Douglas building. Sanchez and the other five White Caps were still nowhere to be seen. Noticing that Dan was without his meddlesome bodyguards, Noel wondered if she should take advantage of this moment to jump him, but sensing her thoughts, Dan turned his head and said, "I wouldn't try it. Just because my men aren't close doesn't mean they can't protect me." Noel growled but allowed Dan to lead the way as they walked through the alleyway beside the Douglass building.

The alleyway was grimy, smelled like rotten food, and was even the color of moldy fungus. The stench became even more revolting as they reached the back of the Douglass building. Noel clenched her nose as her eyes began watering. There was a giant dumpster with several cardboard boxes and tents with many newspapers scattered along the ground. Several children were hanging around, talking cheerfully with each other, until they saw Dan and Noel approach.

The only non-child present was a high schooler with dark brown hair who looked vaguely familiar. He wore a gray hoodie, matching jeans, and tennis shoes. Covering his medium afro was a gray cap turned sideways. Maybe she had seen him in class or lunch or something. She didn't commit much of what she saw at school to memory. The high-school guy immediately walked towards Dan and Noel, and all of the children's expressions turned fearful.

"Dan," the guy muttered with a low voice, "what are you doing here?"

"Just here on business, Doug. I have a proposition for you," Dan said casually with a swagger in his step as he got face-to-face with Doug. Doug was a bit taller with a jiggling jelly belly, but there wasn't a trace of fear within Dan's emerald eyes.

"Yeah? What're you here to offer?"

Dan reached into his inner shirt pocket and pulled out a

cigarette. After reaching into his pants pocket and pulling out a lighter, he lit his cigarette before placing it between his lips. "Submit to me. You see, I'm no fan of the methods you use when running your operation back here. I personally find it distasteful to use children for pandering and petty thievery because they could be used far more effectively. However, I recognize that you, Doug, have special skills in regard to communicating and coordinating joint projects with your team. That makes you invaluable. Follow me, and I will take you places you have never reached."

"I think not, Dan. I rather like the life that I've created here. I may not have the brains to create the things you do, but these children know who is in charge here. And it will never be you."

"That's a shame." Dan sighed. "I thought you could be reasoned with, but it looks like we'll have to do this the hard way." Dan looked at Noel, who until now had been trying to figure out why she even had to come back here, as it slowly began to sink in.

"Seriously?" Noel asked in annoyance.

"Seriously," Dan said, motioning her forward. With a sigh, Noel advanced until she was right in front of Doug.

"Noel," Doug said with a facial expression strongly resembling stone, "I see that you've become Dan's stooge."

Without hesitating, Noel threw a punch straight into Doug's face. He yelped in pain as he stumbled backward.

"I'm nobody's stooge!" Noel said fiercely.

"Only because you're about to die!" Doug yelled before charging Noel with a nasty punch. Noel swerved out of reach before landing a devastating jab-jab-cross combo on Doug. He hit the ground hard with a groan. He winced as he held the tender part of his face.

"Not bad, Noel," Doug muttered in begrudging admiration while reaching behind him, "but I'm not Ms. Jilper. I don't have to take your crat!" He grasped at the newspapers on the ground and threw them towards Noel. As they fluttered through the air, Doug grabbed a metal pipe and got back on his feet. Doug swung the pipe wildly at Noel. Noel kept backing up to stay out of reach, but she soon found herself cornered in the alleyway with the dumpster behind her.

"I've got you now!" Doug roared as he slowly advanced, pointing the pipe enclosed tightly within his clenched, pale fingers directly at Noel. He raised the pipe overhead and rapidly swung at Noel in a sledgehammer-like motion. Noel swerved from side to side, barely avoiding the pipe, but she couldn't keep this up forever. "Just get hit already!" Doug bellowed as he brought the pipe down. Noel ducked as the pipe clanged harshly against the dumpster.

"Aaarrggghh!" Doug yelled. His hands shook violently as the metal pipe fell to the ground.

"I gotcha now, punk!" Noel screamed as she quickly got within striking range. She fired several intense punches that sank into Doug's face and stomach. Doug grunted as he fell flat on his back, strongly resembling a recently felled tree.

"Don't think that I'll let you off that easy!" Noel yelled as she straddled Doug and continued to pummel his face in. After a few moments, Noel got off of Doug. His face was now severely bruised, and blood drizzled down from several places.

"Ugh," Doug muttered while coughing up blood. He grimaced at Noel. "You got me good. Too bad you're Dan's pawn."

Noel rammed her foot into Doug's stomach. He gasped sharply and clutched his stomach. Noel flipped him over. She tightly gripped his hair and lifted his head off the ground.

"I told you," Noel screamed while repeatedly slamming his face into the ground, "I'm no one's pawn!"

After Noel ceased planting Doug's face in the ground, his mouth began spewing more blood and a few broken teeth. He glared at Noel out of the corner of his eye. "You say that, yet you haven't realized why Dan had you attack me of all people.

This was a part of his plan."

"What are you talking about?" Noel asked as she flipped him over and put her foot on Doug's neck.

"I ... Isn't ... it ... obvious?" Doug said between gasps for air. "He wants ... control of ... the street gangs. By... eliminating the other ... gang leaders. Then ... he'll become ... the new ... underground boss of ... Battletown."

"Now, now," Dan said calmly while pulling a handheld device from his coat pocket. "Let's not get carried away." Dan aimed the device at Doug and clicked the button. Noel quickly leaped off Doug as a wire from this device popped out instantly and stuck to his body. Doug's body convulsed as several bolts of electricity coursed through every fiber of his being. There was a small smile on Dan's face as he turned to Noel. "Excellent job. You performed superbly."

"Whatever," Noel said in a brusque manner. "Is what he said true?"

"Are you really planning on believing the words of someone who takes advantage of children seriously? Clearly, he was only trying to confuse you. As I told you before, I'm a businessman specializing in delivering solutions for all of life's problems but solving them requires certain ... resources. And aggressive expansion is the only appropriate response for combating the ever-increasing flow of problems within the community."

"Other people's problems are not my problem. If you want to try dealing with everyone else's problems, then be my guest, but keep me out of-"

Noel stopped abruptly as she was approached by the group of children in the alleyway.

"Wow! So you're Knockout Noel!"

"Oh my Weatherman! I follow your fights at the stadium. I'm such a huge fan!"

"Me too! Tell me, what is your secret for getting so strong!"

"Me? Well..." Noel said, scratching the back of her head, trying to think of a good response. She usually would disregard any-one who tried to talk to her, but these kids strongly reminded her of Alex.

"It's simple," Dan said, jumping into the conservation. "The secret to Noel's strength is a special concoction of mine called Jaguar Juice. With just a tiny sip, you'll gain the strength of ten ferocious fighters."

"Really?!" the kids said wide-eyed in admiration.

"What?! No! I ..." Noel started to say before being interrupted by Dan.

"Yes, and I can also provide you with the same juice so that you can become as strong as Knockout Noel. You just have to join team Dan, and I will grant you the juice."

"Wait..." Noel said before being drowned out by the children.

"Yes! We want to be as strong as Knockout Noel!" they said unanimously with great enthusiasm.

"Excellent! Then leave this alleyway and make your way to my men wearing the white coats. They will tell you what you need to do next."

The children gleefully dashed out of the alleyway leaving only Dan and a trembling Noel.

"Why...?" Noel muttered.

"Why what?" Dan asked quizzically.

"Why," Noel asked in rage, "did you lie to those children?! I've never taken Jaguar Juice! All my strength is from me busting my butt every single day!"

"I hate to burst your bubble, Noel, but that Gorilla Goo you've become so fond of is actually a heavily diluted form of Jaguar Juice."

"What?! But you said that it would make me stronger," Noel yelled.

"All I did was tell you that you would no longer feel tired after you drank it. You chose to drink it afterward. You're the one responsible for being uneducated in the matter," Dan said, shrugging. "However, now you have the opportunity to be a role model for the youth here in Battletown, and with my assistance, you'll be able to have quite the ...outreach for the local youth."

"No, we're done, Dan. I'm not getting mixed up in any of this. I've made it this far on my strength alone, and I refuse to use Jaguar Juice to enhance my strength or brainwash children into taking it. Those are my lines, and I will not cross them for anything."

"Really?" Dan asked curiously. "Are you sure about that?"

"Yeah, I'm done with all of this, Dan."

"I see," Dan said calmly as Noel began to walk away, only for Dan to call out to her once more with a small smile. "Before you go, Noel, be sure to check your text messages one last time. You'll see something that may change your mind."

Noel whipped out her phone and began scrolling through her messages. At the top of the screen was a message from an unknown number. It had arrived less than a minute ago. Her jaw hit the ground as she began shaking uncontrollably after clicking it. It contained only a single picture, and Noel was horrified by what she saw.

Interlude 4- The Search for Answers

Shortly after Noel left the Mud Hut, the front door slowly creaked open as Alex peeked her head out. Before sneaking outside, she carefully scanned the dirt around the house and the other nearby shabby homes. The streetlights had stopped working long ago, with the city council prioritizing other projects over fixing the lighting. The world outside the Mud Hut was silent, and Alex couldn't detect another living being around the darkened area, not even around the WarWolves' shrine just a little down the road. Alex sighed in relief.

She had never been fond of the blinding shadows of night, and the day the streetlight bulbs died simultaneously had been one of the scariest days of her life and one she remembered with both fear and fondness. While she had sat trembling on the floor of the Mud Hut with tears gushing from her eyes, Noel plopped down beside her and enveloped them both with a warm blanket. With a hearty laugh, Noel handed her a can of bubbling crème soda before saying something that Alex never forgot.

"Darkness is a wuss! It may take someone's vision, but that's nothing compared to what I can do! Darkness should be afraid of me, and if it scares you, then I'll give it a reason to be afraid!"

The memory brought a smile to Alex's face, and she quickly shook her head before focusing on the dirt path that she and Noel took to school each morning.

She wore a white shirt with pink short sleeves and pink worn-through pants with several patches roughly sewn on. With a quick movement, she wiped the moist tears off her face using the sleeve of her shirt. As the tears were brushed off, the fear in her eyes disappeared and was replaced with a fierce expression. She reached into her pockets and pulled out a pink ribbon and pink bow choker.

That's it! I refuse to hide any longer! Sis is in some kind of trouble and needs my help! Alex thought as she donned the choker, tightened the ribbon around her waist, and tied it into a pretty bow. With an impressive burst of speed, she began running down the street.

I need to get to Battletown High fast! Sis has done so much for me. It's time I do something for her!

Unbeknownst to Alex, she was not alone. Hidden carefully in the thick cloak of darkness behind the house across the street were two sidvens dressed in white trench coats, each with a rifle strapped across their backs. Both were wearing a pair of funky-looking white goggles equipped with high-grade night vision.

"Looks like Knockout Noel's sister has left the house. This might be our best chance. Let's go!" Bryan said as he turned to face his colleague, only for Rorshe to give him a blank stare.

"Why?"

"Just come on, Rorshe!" Bryan said as he grabbed ahold of Rorshe's arm and pulled him forward. "Dan asked us to deliver him some insurance. Just shut up and follow my lead, okay?"

Rorshe scratched his head with an absent expression but followed obediently. "Okay."

...

Dex walked the streets of Battletown. His head was downcast, with both hands in his pants pockets. He sighed as his thoughts turned to Noel. He couldn't understand what was going on inside her mind.

How could she get involved with the White Caps?! Does she not realize how dangerous they are? Is she that desperate for strength that she would turn to them? I have to do something to help before she ends up too deeply involved with them.

Trying his best to push his heartache aside, Dex had gone out trying to gather information about this "Dan" that Noel had mentioned. However, he wasn't having much luck.

This Dan guy must be in charge of the White Caps, but everyone I've talked to doesn't seem to know anything about him. Either I'm wrong, or the guy has thoroughly covered his tracks, and I have a feeling that it isn't the former. So, what should I do next?

That was when he felt a familiar prick in his mind. Dex kept strolling as he tried to keep a blank face. His eyes darted around wildly. The spider-like itch now vividly crawling within his skin meant only one thing.

He was being watched, but he couldn't find the prying eyes anywhere. It had been a while since he had encountered a secret observer who could evade his perception, not since the Vorav Mountains.

This is troubling. It looks like I will have to kick things up a notch. Dex stopped and began leaning causally against a flickering streetlight. He closed his eyes and took deep breaths as he focused his mind solely on his hearing. Soon he began to make out sounds that he normally wouldn't have been able to hear. High-pitched whistles from the danger dog training facility, rumble bees buzzing in the acidic trees outside of town, and even the nightly chattering of every sidvan within Battletown. Dex winced at the vast audio sources entering his mind, but he focused on the general area around him.

In a nearby alleyway, hidden from his perception, were two sidven creeping within the tall shadows. He could tell they were wearing trench coats from the rustling of fabrics against the brick walls and concrete walkway. He could also hear a slight metallic clink whenever they shifted their positions, so they were clearly armed with dangerous weapons.

Most likely firearms. It must be the White Caps, but why are they watching me? Let's see if I can find out.

He focused his hearing on the exact spot where the two White Caps were hiding. Their heartbeats stayed a consistent, unchanged rhythm, so Dex knew they couldn't tell he was listening to them. He detected slight boredom from one and controlled anger from the other as they spoke to each other in low voices. Dex couldn't put his finger on it, but both White Caps sounded familiar.

"I'm so beat," White Cap #1 groaned. "Dan has really been putting us through the wringer lately. My voice is so sore from all the singing I've been doing around town."

"Hey, I'm just thankful to have work. There just aren't enough jobs these days," White Cap #2 responded gruffly. He had a side part pompadour and a chinstrap beard that rustled in the nighttime breeze.

"Come on, as long as you have a strong body, you could get almost any job you could ever want here."

"In the past, Jarek, back when you could literally beat all of your problems away with a pair of strong fists, but now life has become more complicated. It takes more than physical strength to hold a job these days. There are all of these 'rules' that you have to keep in mind besides the rule of strength. Break just one of them, and society decides to screw you over."

"Yeah, I heard what happened to you. It's terrible that some kids pulled a fast one on you. You lost your job, and it was a cushy one too."

"Yeah, I'm still angry about that, but I do feel a little better since one of the two kids has become Dan's pawn. She'll learn just how scary dealing with adults can be, and hopefully, the other one will get to learn the harshness of reality. Maybe if I'm lucky, I'll be able to play a part when that day comes."

"I'll keep my fingers crossed for you. Everyone deserves retribution when they've been wronged. What were their names again?"

"Knockout Noel was the first one, and the second one was … you know, I never heard the other one's name, but he is the geeky-looking kid with glasses that we're watching now. Dan said to keep a close on him and wait for a good opportunity. Dan is really keen on acquiring bargaining chips."

Oh no! Dex thought while he continued listening. *Noel is knee-deep in trouble with the White Caps. I need to come up with a plan so that I can …*

"Dex!" a voice yelled from behind him. Dex barely stifled his surprise as he turned to see Alex.

"Dex," she said loudly. She wore a brave face, but there was a slight tremble in her legs as she spoke. "Have you seen Noel tonight? She left the house late, and I…"

"Shh!" Dex said, putting his hand over her mouth. He closed his eyes and focused on the two White Caps, but upon Alex's arrival, they had ceased talking and resumed carefully observing Dex. He sighed before moving his hand away from Alex's lips.

"Alex, what are you doing out here? It's dangerous, especially at this time. Noel will be furious!" he whispered.

"Please don't tell her!" Alex whispered in a panic. "Ever since the War Wolves built that tiny shrine close to our house, Sis said I wasn't allowed to go outside late at night. Something about their animal costumes splattered in red paint makes her feel uneasy."

"Yeah ... they're a rough bunch. But enough about them; why are you here?"

"It's like I was telling you! Noel left the house really late tonight, and I was trying to find her. She said she was going to her school, but I couldn't find her when I went there. I don't know what she has been doing, but she has this really weird smell on her. I don't like it. She hasn't been doing some new type of training with you, has she?"

"No. Your sister has decided not to train with me anymore. She wanted to use a substance known as Gorilla Goo instead."

"That must be the weird smell that's been on her. So why are you out here so late at night anyway?" Alex said as a smug smile formed on her face. "You're not here to secretly watch my sister from afar, are you?"

"No!" Dex said, an intense blush covering his face. "I was trying to gather information about the people your sister has been hanging around lately. They're called the White Caps, and Noel seems to be in big trouble with them."

"What! Then what are we doing hiding back here? Let's go get them!" Alex exclaimed, grabbing ahold of Dex's arm and pulling him forward. With a cautious look, he glanced towards the alleyway with the two White Caps before pulling his arm from Alex's grasp.

"Alex," he said in a low voice as he ushered her away. "It's not safe for you to be here now. The White Caps have people watching me in the ally, to our side, with the largest shadows looming. You need to go back home and hide there until day-break."

"What?! No way!" Alex yelled as her eyes narrowed in the direction of the two White Caps. "They've been mean to my big sister! I'm going to make them pay!"

"Don't!" Dex yelled as he tried to grab Alex, but it was no use. With quick footwork, Alex dashed towards the darkest alleyway, much to Dex's horror as he chased after her. It was one of the rare moments that he wished that he could use his abilities outside of self-defense.

"Hey!" Alex yelled upon approaching the two White Caps. Both men jumped with startled expressions at the sight of a little girl screaming at them furiously as she sprinted toward them. Thankfully, their target, Glasses Boy, was chasing after the girl, so they readied their rifles. Now was their chance to complete their mission!

"Now that's enough, little girl!" White Cap #2 said with a clear, authoritative voice as he advanced beyond the shadows. Now glowing like pale phantoms from the afterlife, this White Cap stepped out of the alleyway. With a harsh gaze, he pointed toward Alex. "Now beat it! The only one I have an appointment with is Glasses Boy."

Dex knew that voice. It was Trash!

Why is he here? Are times so tough that he had nowhere else to turn other than the White Caps? Why, though? Surely there must be other options. Heck, going to live under Mother Nature's harsh hospitality would still be a far better option. At least then, we wouldn't have to deal with him now.

Dex turned his attention back to Alex, who was glaring down at the two White Caps with an unflinching expression not terribly different than her older sister.

"No! You've been mean to my sister, Noel, so I'm here to make you pay, you evil ghosts!" Alex said, pointing towards the two men.

"Oh, you're Noel's kid sister, huh? The gory apple doesn't fall far from the blood-stained tree," Jarek said as he stepped out of the dark alleyway. He was a dark-skinned sidvan wearing the standard, glowing White Cap trench coat with light blue dress shoes. Upon his short, shaggy hair with black curls was a glowing, white bowler hat with pink lace. On his back was an acoustic guitar. But Dex and Alex found themselves eyeing the menacing black rifle that he slowly aimed towards Alex. "We heard about you at our latest meeting, but your capture was another team's responsibility. It looks like you'll be coming with us, kid. Now surrender willingly before your life's song morendos."

"Never!" Alex exclaimed with a feral expression. A small cloud of dust billowed from the rocky road as she planted her left foot forward. Her knees bent like a beast, ready to pounce. She arched her back slightly, both arms outstretched with tense fingers. An uneasy feeling crept into both Trash and Jarek as they looked into the beast-like eyes of the girl before them.

With a loud bang, Trash pulled the trigger on his rifle, and a bullet shot out with incredible velocity toward Alex's right earlobe. Jarek shot a swift, disgruntled look at Trash, whose response was an indifferent shrug.

Trash was under Jarek's command and wasn't supposed to fire from his rifle unless given clear directives. However, Trash figured that the hierarchy amongst the White Cap's chain of command must have allowed for at least this degree of autonomy among the group. It was meant only as a warning shot to break the girl's spirit anyways, so what was the harm?

What happened next was beyond Trash's expectations.

With the agility of a wild monkey, Alex nimbly jumped out of the bullet's path.

"Alex, be careful!" Dex yelled, his body now a blur while the steaming bullets hurtled through harmlessly.

"No, Dex! These guys will pay!" Alex yelled with small but quick strides toward Jarek. As he turned his head back towards Alex, his eyes widened at the sight of the little girl just within arm's reach. He quickly tried redirecting his rifle at her, but she nimbly ducked between his legs. With deft fingers, she yanked the guitar off of Jarek's back. Shrieking a high-pitched war cry, she leaped up and brought down the guitar over Jarek's head as he hit the ground with a loud groan.

"You girls need to stop attacking my coworkers!" Trash yelled as he returned fire on Alex.

With a snarl, she held up the guitar. With a loud *bing*, Trash's bullets bounced off the musical instrument as Alex speedily approached.

She quickly leaped on the opposite wall, and before Trash could respond, Alex had launched herself off the wall and sent her foot flying into his face, which caused him to tumble into the wall with a loud thud. Without a moment's pause, Alex kicked Trash's rifle as it flew through the air and landed with a loud clang in the dumpster within the darkened alleyway.

With a groan, Jarek tried to redirect his rifle at Alex, but she hurled the guitar, which crashed painfully into his face.

"Hits me right to my very being," Jarek grunted before dropping his head against the jagged ground.

"You're asking for it now, little girl," Trash grunted as he got back on his feet. He raised a fist as he rushed towards Alex. He brought down his clenched, massive hand with great strength, but Alex was too quick. She ducked between his legs and kicked him in his groin. The man shrieked while displaying a lovely falsetto. He dropped his weapon while sinking to his knees.

"Ugh... you two are definitely sisters... blurf my cratty luck." He moaned while clutching at his aching crotch.

"That's only the beginning," Alex said, cracking her knuckles. Her cheeks were puffed, and she still came off as cute despite trying to act tough. "I'm going to make you pay for messing with my sister."

"Okay, time to go," Dex said, grabbing Alex by the hand and pulling her away. "These are grown men, and you are too young to get involved with them."

"Let me go!" Alex yelled, trying to break free from Dex's grip. "I can take them!"

"Yeah, no. We're leaving."

"No, you're not, Glasses Kid," Trash said while he and a badly bruised Jarek staggered to their feet. "I'm afraid that you both are coming with us."

"I'd like to see you make us, you big meanies!" Alex yelled.

Trash and Jarek locked eyes briefly before Jarek gave a quick nod. Both White Caps immediately pulled out the concealed black pistols hidden within their coats and aimed them at Alex and Dex. An uneasy feeling crept through Dex as the four guns faced them. Instinctively, he stepped in front of Alex.

"Gentlemen," Dex said slowly, "it's been a long night, so I'm just going to take my little friend here and leave."

"You can't escape us," Trash said with a sneer. "Save yourself the trouble and come quietly. These pistols were designed by Dan himself. The bullets fired from them will chase after anything with a beating heart. Don't make us put a few holes through you."

"I doubt that you could put a scratch on me even with your guns."

"Maybe, but if you dodge, then Noel's little sister will get hit instead. Is that what you want?"

"Don't listen to him, Dex! We can take them!" Alex said. "It's two against two."

"You may want to double-check the numbers," Jarek said with a smirk. He pointed behind Dex and Alex. They turned only to find a cluster of ten additional White Caps right behind them. In moments, both Dex and Noel were surrounded by fourteen guns, all pointed right at them.

"Sorry we're late," Bryan said nonchalantly as he aimed his rifle at Alex. Rorshe was standing behind him with one hand holding a sub-machine gun aimed at Alex while the other hand was firmly grasping onto a Happy Smackers double-stacker beef patty with cheese as he shoved it into his mouth. "Rorshe was hungry and insisted we make a quick stop to get dinner. While we were there, we regrouped with several of our coworkers, who had been sent by Dan to provide additional assistance with this task. Dan's foresight sure is remarkable. I'm glad he's in charge."

"Dex," Alex whimpered tearfully. All of her fury had evaporated like the morning dew in the sunlight. "I want Noel!"

"I know. You'll get to see Noel soon, but you need to be strong for a little bit longer," Dex said in a convincing voice while eyeing the White Caps nervously. He could easily escape if it were just him, but having Alex here complicated things. Seeing his limited options, he held up his hands in resignation.

"We'll come peacefully. Just don't hurt Alex."

"That can be arranged," Trash said with a wicked smile. "Just follow us, and remember, no funny business, or we will pop a cap in both of you. We'll drop you off at one of our warehouse bases per the boss's orders. We have plans for the both of you."

Chapter 24

Lost Fire

Noel was horrified by what she saw in the image. It was a photo of Alex and Dex tied and gagged in some dark room.

"What are you trying to pull?!" Noel yelled, storming towards Dan. He kept his calm demeanor as Noel grabbed the collar of his jacket and pulled him around until they were face to face.

"Just a little collateral, Noel. It's wise to collect a little ... insurance for every business transaction."

"You will release them!" Noel roared as she pulled Dan off the ground. "Do it now, or I will paint this alley in your blood!"

"No, you won't," Dan said without a trace of fear, "because if you do, my men will end them. So instead, you will put me down gently, and next time I give you a call, you will follow my every order down to every last detail. Once we both have what we want, I'll release those two back into your care, and we'll go our separate ways. Capisce?"

Noel gritted her teeth, but she did as he said. She lowered him back to the ground slowly. She continued to clench his collar tightly before reluctantly releasing him. Dan straightened his crumpled collar before returning his attention to Noel.

"Very good. Now, I must get going, but I will call you again soon with the details of your next job. Make sure you are ready," Dan said before walking away.

Noel stood in that alley, staring at the wall with clenched fists. If looks could kill, that wall would have died a painful death. Finally, after what seemed to be an eternity, she made herself turn around. The sound of her heavy steps echoed as she trudged out of the alleyway. The raging fires within her eyes dulled as she paused, her gaze lingering in the direction of her house. She found herself lost in thought for one of the few times in her life. She stood still and rigid for a few moments to process the intense emotions surging within her before deciding her next course of action.

I guess ... I'll head back to the Mud Hut. She thought, her hollow feet striking the rocky ground with slow, lifeless steps.

The way back seemed dimmer than she remembered. Sure, the path was dark on the way here, but before, there was always a light to return to.

Once she returned to the Mud Hut, she slowly walked up the steps and went inside. The cold silence embraced her as she collapsed on the couch. Her arms throbbed with pain, but she did her best to ignore it. The Gorilla Goo may have erased her fatigue, but it did nothing about the immense pain in her arms and legs. She glared intently at the ceiling while lying on her back, only for the grimy plaster to match her icy stare. Not that Noel was deterred for even an instant. Somebody or something was going to feel her pent-up wrath, and her ceiling had the unfortunate timing of crossing paths with an irate Knockout Noel.

"You got a problem with me?" Noel muttered in a dangerously low tone at the ceiling. "Keep shooting me dirty looks, and I will end you."

This did nothing to stop the ceiling's cold, condescending stare, and Noel was not going to put up with that. Not tonight.

"Stop looking at me like that!" Noel yelled as she grabbed an empty juice carton on the floor and hurled it at the ceiling. The carton harmlessly bounced off the unfazed ceiling as it stared at her with an unflinching and unsympathetic gaze.

"Get off my case!" Noel exclaimed as she quickly jumped to her feet. Without wasting a moment, she crouched down like a loaded springboard. Noel launched fist-first into the ceiling with an angry yell, and with a loud crash, her left hand broke through the wood and plaster. However, the tenacious ceiling stubbornly kept a firm grasp around Noel's left wrist and refused to let her return to the ground.

"Let go of me!" Noel yelled as she banged on the ceiling with her right hand. "Leave me alone! It's not my fault! I never meant for this to happen!" she screamed at the callous ceiling. Hot tears streaked down her cheeks.

"All I wanted was to get stronger!" Noel ranted between strikes. "So why did they take Alex?! She and Dex had nothing to do with any of this! I'm the one who made the deal, so I should be the one taking the heat, not them! But now, because of me, they're both trapped!"

The ceiling just glared coldly at Noel. There was not a shred of compassion in its gaze, only disgust and disappointment.

"Blurf you! I don't have to take this from you. You're no better than Mom," Noel screamed as she flipped her legs onto the ceiling. With mighty heaves, she began trying to free herself from the ceiling's firm grasp. After several moments of staining furiously and yelling profanities at the ceiling, Noel pulled herself free as she fell. Like a large bag of potatoes, she landed hard on the couch.

Noel gave the ceiling the stink eye and shot it a rude hand gesture, but it continued to glare at Noel with a quiet intensity. Noel leaped up from the couch with a loud grunt and trudged out the front door. The entire Mud Hut shook as she slammed the door behind her. Noel could no longer stand the ceiling or the sound of piercing silence.

She walked down the road farther than usual until she reached her destination, Stan's Soda Shack. It was a rustic little soda pub away from the busier parts of Battletown. Despite this, the sound of friendly chatter over brutal brawls reverberated through the smooth wooden walls. A low chime resonated from the ceiling every time a punch was thrown inside Stan's Shack, which smelled of sugar and blood. Legend had it that on the day of his retirement, the owner, Stan built the entire wooden building on a half-coherent bet. He had one week to make a functioning soda pub from the ground up. Then with a nonchalant expression, Stan completed the task in only three days.

Noel went inside and sat on a refurbished antique wooden stool. Crestfallen, she placed her arms upon the warm, polished counter to take the edge off her throbbing arms. Her wrist weights were in full view, but Noel couldn't care less if others noticed them. She had too much on her mind, but the pain wasn't why her face now resembled a storm cloud.

Noel reached into her pocket and tightly gripped the vial. It felt cold to the touch like a heart no longer beating. Not that she noticed. She only gazed blankly at the counter. A world once stained red with the blood of the weak was now nothing more than a lifeless gray hue.

How did I end up in this mess? I'm days away from the finals for the regional qualifier. I've trained for months for this match, but my blood isn't boiling at the thought of combat like it normally does. I knew I'd have to sacrifice things to get stronger, but why Alex? Why Dex? Why do I feel worse than before I started taking Gorilla Goo? These aren't the sacrifices that I meant to make, and what did I gain from it? This lousy vial that only grants a short burst of strength is what I got in exchange for my sister and Dex?!

"What was I thinking?" she muttered as she raised her arm. Things were about to get ugly if she didn't receive a cream soda soon. Downcast eyes full of anguish, she sat silent until a familiar face greeted her in the form of Stan.

Stan was in his early forties, with pale white skin and red hair. He wore a matching handlebar mustache that strongly resembled a fuzzy caterpillar and a green eye patch over his right eye. He was very well-built, and several awards were hanging on the walls from various fighting tournaments he had participated in back in his glory days. He was known as No Plan Stan, Stan the Man, and most noticeably, Stan the Unstoppable; however, since retiring, he was now known as Stan the Soda Man. Here at his place, anyone could come in from early morning to late at night to enjoy a nice cold soda. The business had been fair enough to keep him busy, but no matter how busy he became, he always had a knack for remembering the faces that walked inside his shack.

"Noel," Stan said with a friendly smile while standing behind the counter, "I haven't seen you in a while."

"I haven't had a reason to come in a while," Noel responded.

"I reckon so. I've been keeping up with you in the qualifier. Congratulations on making it to the finals. I've heard your upcoming opponent will be your toughest yet."

"Yeah," Noel said emotionlessly with a cold stare. Her eyes resembled a barren desert with a source of life in sight.

"But you've worked hard to make it this far. To think that in your first year of boxing, you've already made it to the finals of the national qualifier with nothing but hard work and sheer fighting prowess."

"Yeah."

"How is your little sister doing? It's been a while since I've seen her and her happy smile. Has she been practicing any wall-hopping techniques I taught her?"

"Just bring me the usual, Stan, and keep 'em coming," Noel moaned as she brought a hand to her forehead; the pain in her arm throbbed terribly.

"You sure?" Stan asked, both surprised and concerned. "Your match will be in just a couple of days."

"Just do it!" Noel growled, bringing her fist down on the counter with a loud thud.

Stan narrowed his eyes but silently turned to grab several bottles of cream soda. He placed them within Noel's reach. She grabbed the nearest bottle, and after twisting the cap off, she quickly downed the entire contents with several big gulps. After taking an enormous belch, she gulped down the remaining soda in front of her.

"More, Stan," Noel demanded impatiently after she finished the last drop of crème soda. She slammed the glass bottle as it shattered on the counter while Stan raised an eyebrow in disapproval.

"No," Stan said firmly as he slowly approached Noel. "You've had more than enough. You need to stay focused on your match and train. Once it's over, you can guzzle all the soda you want. I have this conversation with Mac-en-Clobber nearly every day, but I never would have thought that I'd have to have it with you. You always know what you want."

"What do you know, Stan?" Noel snapped. "You're just a has-been. You have no idea what's going on."

"So, we're having one of those kinds of days." Stan sighed, walked around the counter, and sat beside Noel. "What's going on, Noel? What's eating away at you?"

Noel remained silent; she had no intention of sharing her problems with anyone right now. Stan, realizing this after a few moments, broke the silence.

"About twenty years ago, I fought in the mixed martial arts tournament in Battletown. I had won the past two years and was the crowd favorite to win again. However, my wife went into labor on the night of the finals. I found myself trapped in a situation that I had never imagined. Either I could compete in the final round of the MMA tournament, or I could witness my child's birth."

"What did you decide to do?" Noel asked, leaning forward curiously.

"I went to be with my wife. I'd won many tournaments already, and I knew there would always be another one, but I wouldn't always have the chance to watch the birth of my first child. It was a beautiful memory I got to share with my wife, and if I could go back, I wouldn't hesitate to repeat it all over again."

"So you're saying I should give up the final round of the qualifier?" Noel growled.

"I'm saying that you need to determine what is the most important to you right now, because time is precious, and you don't get do-overs in life. So, choose to prioritize what's most important to you. Don't live a life that you'll regret later. If winning the tournament is the most important thing to you, then win it in a way you can be proud of, but is winning really the most important thing to you?"

Noel thought for a minute. Why did she want to win so badly? Why was it so important? The answer was clear.

I want to be number one, and I want to take care of Alex. That's why I want to win! That's why I must win! But if I win, I want it to be through the strength I've earned from the time I spent training in the gym and ... with Dexter.

Noel got up from the stool and turned to face Stan. "Please put this on my tab. I'll be back after I win the finals. Now I've got to get going. There is something that I need to take care of," she said with focused eyes as she headed toward the exit. Before stepping out, she faced Stan one last time. She reached into her pocket, grabbed a small bottle, and tossed it toward Stan. He caught it and, after glancing at the bottle of Gorilla

Goo, raised an eyebrow. "Stan, would you mind tossing that for me? I won't be needing it anymore."

Stan nodded as Noel walked out the door. He smiled as he dropped the bottle into the trash can.

"Good luck Noel. Now go get 'em."

Chapter 25

One Woman Rescue

After leaving Stan's Shack, Noel took to the dark streets, becoming one with the shadows as she made her way downtown. She passed several old buildings while scouting from the darkness with a deadly focus. After about a hin, she found what she was looking for; a single White Cap alone in a dark alley. Noel slowly crept towards him like a wolf, ready to pounce on its prey. The White Cap in question was leaning against the wall, trying to figure out how he would explain why he was out late again to his wife and much too distracted to notice Noel.

"Kelly is going to kill me. She already thinks I'm having an affair, and if this keeps up, she will make us resume marriage counseling. I hate counseling. Why should I have to pay some stranger to tell me how badly I'm screwing up in life? I know I'm not spending enough time with my kids, but that's not because I don't want to. If all of these bills would just magically disappear, then I'd spend every waking moment with my kids and wife. If only there were only a way to make that happen... Wah!" Bryan yelled as a shadowy figure quickly grabbed him by the throat and pulled him off his feet.

"Where are my sister and friend!" a voice yelled while the figure slammed him repeatedly against the wall.

"W-what?! I don't know what you're talking about! Who even are you?!"

The figure threw him to the ground. He landed hard on his back. He gasped hard as the air was knocked out of his lungs. The shadow figure, without hesitation, grabbed him by the collar and pulled him up till they were face to face.

"I'm Knockout Noel! Now, where are my sister and Dexter!" she yelled.

"K-knockout Noel!" Bryan's eyes widened in fear. "I can't tell you! Dan will kill me!"

"That's nothing compared to what I'll do to you if you don't tell me. Now spill. You don't want to keep Kelly waiting, do you?"

Bryan's eyes filled with tears. He trembled like a blender but sealed his lips firmly with no intention of talking.

"So you're going to be difficult," Noel said as she slammed him against the hard ground. Bryan groaned while Noel cracked her knuckles.

"That's fine. I was hoping to beat the knowledge out of you anyways."

The man closed his eyes as he braced himself. The pain he was about to feel was something that he would remember with perfect clarity for the remainder of his days.

...

Dexter was stuck, to put it mildly. They had tied his waist, arms, and legs to a chair that was bolted to the ground. Dex strained with all his might, but regardless of how much he struggled, he couldn't break out. After spending most of the night trying to free himself, his skin underneath the ropes had become raw. That pain paled in comparison to his concern for Alex's well-being. They had been separated shortly upon entering the warehouse, and he hadn't seen her since. To be honest, he hadn't seen much of anything since arriving. There were no lights inside or windows or openings throughout the warehouse except the doors.

I've got to break free and save Alex! I'm sure Noel is worried sick!

He had tucked away his pink wristbands in his pocket. If he could only get them on, he could easily break out of these ropes, but he had been unsuccessful at retrieving them so far. The White Caps had been smart enough to bind him and Alex immediately after capturing them.

"Darn it," he muttered. "These ropes are too tight to escape. But there has to be some way out of this chair."

After a moment of silence, an idea popped into his head. He rapidly moved his arms back and forth as much as his bindings would allow. Slowly the armrests became smoother while his aching, raw wrists began oozing a gentle crimson that slowly seeped into the ropes.

I wonder what will give first: my arms or this chair? Regardless, I must get out of here as quickly as possible before they ...

That was when a door opened slowly behind him with a loud creak.

"Well, well, if it isn't Noel's former sparring partner. I hope your stay with us has been comfortable."

"Not in the slightest. Who are you?" Dex asked.

The footsteps moved around him until their source stood in front of him.

"Just a businessman with a certain ... knack for working with people."

"Are you Dan?"

"My reputation precedes me, I guess," he said in mock surprise. "Yes, I am Dan, and you are Dexter. You work night shifts at the Jab-en-Grab close to the stadium. You live in a lovely house in the nicer part of Battletown. Your parents are hardly ever home because when they're not working, they're either busy with other projects or partying it up in some foreign country, and every night you go to bed, you have to have your teddy bear, appropriately named 'Huggles,' close by; otherwise, the inevitable truth of just how lonely you are will follow you even in your dreams."

"Whaaa! How do you even know all of that about me?" Dex asked, wide-eyed, his jaw gaping. His mind was reeling, trying to figure out how Dan knew so much about him. Some of those were things that Dex had never told another soul, either living or dead.

Dan gave a small, all-knowing smile before continuing. "I make it my business to know these kinds of things, Dexter. To be a successful businessman, the ultimate power comes through knowledge. With the right information in your hands, the whole world is literally within your grasp. Which is why you are here." Dan leaned in until he was face to face with Dexter.

"Your little friend Noel is having a difficult time grasping my vision for this town. I'm afraid that she may be too narrow-minded to understand the complexities of my plan to create a better life for Battletown and its future generations. I'm sure she will come to terms with my vision with time, but until then, she'll need a little persuasion."

"She'll never join you! She is too strong to be defeated by you!"

"In a fair fight, she could easily beat me and all my men. It could also be said that she could never defeat you in a fair fight, however ..." The air cracked as Dan struck Dex like a serpent attacking its helpless prey. Dex gasped at the sudden strike, his cheek smarting.

"Without light, you can't see me, and if you are unable to perceive my attacks, then you can't use your pesky Podge abilities to dodge. With your abilities neutralized, I've created a situation where even I could defeat you without breaking a sweat. With you and Noel's darling little sister trapped here,

I've created a situation where not even Knockout Noel can find victory!"

"Why are you telling me this?" Dex asked as he narrowed his eyes. "You don't seem like the kind of person to show his hand."

Dan gave a low, menacing chuckle as he grabbed Dex's shoulder's.

"You're teaching Noel about Podge, a type of martial arts that is as obscure as it is deadly. You represent another source of power that gives strength to the mighty, and it is my personal mission to humble the strong by showing them that even the weak can topple the mighty through hard work and cunning," Dan said with a sinister sneer. His grip tightened as a low buzzing filled the air around them.

"Aaargh!" Dex screamed as two strong currents flowed violently into his body. After a few moments, Dan released his hold, and Dex's head plopped forward with a twitch as Dan continued speaking.

"I've defeated many martial arts masters and skilled warriors from many countries through careful strategies, perfect timing, a pinch of theatrics, and unwavering dedication. Yet, you are the first Podge instructor to come to my town, Dex, or should I say Master Dexter Winji?" Dan said as he grabbed Dex's chin and forced his face up until they were gazing into each other's eyes.

Dex's dazed eyes widened. "Where did you learn that?"

Dan just shrugged.

"My information network is unparalleled, Master Winji. I know plenty of other secrets too, but none of that is relevant right now. What I want you to ponder long and hard about is your future."

"What are you talking about, Dan?" Dex asked with a guarded expression.

"Why you, of course!" Dan said while pointing his finger at

Dex. "Think for a moment what it would feel like to live in a Battletown, where the townsfolk have learned to put down their barbaric ways permanently and conduct themselves in a more civilized manner. Wouldn't you prefer waking up to the scent of peace and tranquility instead of violence and bloodshed every morning? Isn't that part of the reason you are reluctant to leave your house every day?"

"You, too, seem reluctant to leave your abysmal abode of darkness, Dan, but not because of fear," Dex said while focusing on the dark figure before him. "I see a vicious venom brewing within your shadow-infested soul. You lie in wait like a coiled serpent ready to strike at a moment's notice and spread your venom to all you encounter. Your 'vision' goes way beyond the boundaries of Battletown. I feel an ambition in your heart that is both great and sinister. Many have suffered because of you; many more will follow if you have your way. Your false peace will do more harm than all the bloody conflicts here combined."

Dex winced as he felt the clean, well-maintained nails hidden underneath Dan's gloves dig into his skin as a menacing buzzing filled the air around him. However, his resolve remained steadfast as he continued to address his captor.

"Tell me, Dan, what are your intentions with Noel?"

Much to Dex's surprise, he heard Dan take a deep breath as he felt Dan's grip loosen.

"Noel has become a valuable asset to my cause, and I have no intention of releasing her. She is a vital pawn that I will fully utilize until it's time to sacrifice her for something far grander."

A look of horror filled Dex's face; he opened his mouth to speak, but Dan put a finger to his lips before he could utter a word.

"Unless... you and I make a little arrangement. If you pass on your knowledge to my associates and me, I promise to release my hold on Noel. Not to mention I'll free both you and Noel's little sister from your ... current holdings. Refuse, and I'll have Noel serve as a living tribute to the White Caps while you and her little sister remain my prisoners for the rest of your days."

"I won't let you harm either of them!"

Dan just sighed before circling around Dex and placing a hand on his shoulder. Dex stiffened as Dan leaned forward and began speaking in a low, almost mesmerizing tone right in Dex's ear.

"Take a moment to think rationally about this, Dexter. You've seen how brutal and uncivilized things are here in Battletown. I believe you've even complained about the savageness of the sidvens who reside here. You, Master Dexter Winji, have a chance to create social reform here within Battletown. You can be part of something bigger than yourself that will forever change things here. Your training could be the catalyst that sparks a new way of life where people don't rely on the strength of their fists to survive but through perfect harmony with one another. Doesn't that sound nicer than our current reality?"

"No!" Dex yelled while shrugging off Dan's hand. "You won't deceive me that easily, Dan! This world is far from perfect, but the world you envisioned is far more unbearable. I'll never help you!"

"Then you forfeit Noel and Alex's lives."

Dex shot Dan a furious glare as he shook violently, trying to break free to no avail. Dan just shook his head while clicking his tongue.

"It's impossible to break out. I had you securely fastened so that even you can't escape. This time, you'll be unavailable to assist Noel unless you ..."

Suddenly a loud crash resonated throughout the warehouse. The door behind Dex opened suddenly, letting in just enough light for him to see Dan's shocked expression as a White Cap, whom Dex identified as Trash from the sound of his voice, came to his side and whispered something in his ear. Dex couldn't make out any of it except the last sentence.

"She's here."

...

Noel kicked the warehouse door down, and it skidded across the floor with a loud screech. Immediately a group of six armed White Caps greeted her, all with machine guns aimed directly at Noel. They opened fire, but Noel dashed to the side and vanished into the dark room behind a large stack of wooden crates. After a few moments of firing off rounds at where Noel had been standing, five of the goons ceased firing.

"Where did she go!" a White Cap yelled while firing his weapon wildly around the room. Like every standard underling, he wore a pair of black goggles designed by Dan, which enabled perception within even the darkest area. It was vital, especially in places with limited lighting, but he could not detect Noel even with these goggles. It was as if she had become one with the shadows.

The underling grunted in annoyance as he began firing aimlessly, figuring it was his best bet to put down the invader. Only the sound of the voice beside him caused him to cease fire.

"Knock it off, Ozzi!" Rick yelled with an irate expression. "This room is filled with valuable merchandise. Dan will be furious if you destroy any of it! Not to mention that all of your excessive gunfire will attract unnecessary attention, and the last thing we need is law enforcement showing up!"

"But we have to catch Noel! If we fail, then our lives will be on the line!"

"No, duh, Captain Obvious! Just don't destroy the cargo in the room! Use your head and think clearly, just like Dan always tells us. Why did this have to happen now, while Sanchez is away on clean-up?!" Rick exclaimed as he quickly pulled out the two pistols concealed within his trench coat. He and Ozzi, without a moment of hesitation, stood back-to-back while cir-cling the room.

"How about we turn on the glowing feature for our coats?" Ozzi asked with a proud look, clearly very happy with himself for coming up with another 'brilliant' idea. "Maybe she'll become frightened by our ghost-like appearances?"

"No, you twit!" Rick yelled harshly. "This chick is nothing like the superstitious saps here; the ghost shtick won't work on her. Our best bet is to keep our glow off, so that she can't see us. But we'll be able to see her with our goggles, so we must be vigilant. Besides, there are six of us with guns and only one of her with only her bare hands."

"Are you sure about that?" Ozzi said as his twitching eyes glanced around the room and his index fingers lightly pressed against the trigger.

"Did you see her packing any heat?!"

"No ... I mean, where are the other four guys that were in here with us?"

"What do you mean, they're right here..." Rick said as he turned his head, but even while wearing his night-vision goggles to see through the veil of darkness, he couldn't detect the other White Caps that had been with him, which meant only one thing.

"Noel got 'em! Quick, dumbblat, get over here! It's up to you and me! Once we find Noel, we'll take her!"

There was no reply from Ozzi. The only response he received was a silence so loud he could hear the sound of his rapidly-beating heart. A bead of sweat went down Rick's face as the back that had been pressed against his suddenly disappeared.

He started pounding on his chest in an attempt to quiet his heart, only for the sound to grow louder. Rick was glad that the room was dark because his legs were shaking so badly that it was taking everything just to remain standing. A low creaking reverberated on the other side of the room, and Rick unhesitatingly fired at the sound. After the dust settled, he made his way towards the spot only to discover the shattered remains of one of Dan's crates with the battered body of Ozzi lying motionless.

"Oh no!" Rick gasped, putting a hand over his mouth. He quickly backed up to create distance from himself, only to bump into another person. He froze in fear. His arms and legs became rigid as wooden boards. His heart pumped rapidly as his body entered fight or flight, but at the same time he realized that either was pointless. His fate was sealed, and there was absolutely nothing that he could do to stop it. But knowing that didn't cease the terror that hammered through his hyperactive heart.

"Oh blurf," he squeaked as he fell prey to a pair of angry fists.

...

"Oh. Well, well, it seems like things have become a little more complicated than I had initially anticipated," Dan said with a frown. "Nevertheless, I still do have a plan prepared for this scenario. You know what to do, correct?"

"Yes, sir!" Trash responded enthusiastically while slamming a fist into his open palm. "I can't thank you enough for this opportunity! I've been craving some payback for a while now!"

"Then I expect pleasing results, Mr. Trash," Dan said with a sinister chuckle. "Now get the weapon ready. Noel is making her way steadily throughout the warehouse. I think it's time that we greet our guest."

"Yes, sir!" Trash responded before turning his attention back to Dexter while flashing a wicked smile.

"H-hey, what's going on?" Dex asked nervously as Trash quickly approached him. The newly joined White Cap opened his coat and removed an item from his inner coat pocket.

Dex tried to identify the object, but the darkroom hindered his vision. Regardless, he strained his vision to its limits to make out the object, and when he finally did, he gasped.

"Hey, you're not serious! No! Get that thing away from me! Nooooo!"

...

Noel continued dashing through the warehouse. Her feet made no sound as they hurried across the concrete flooring, almost as if she were gliding on the shadows within the warehouse. Every White Cap she encountered was left bruised and bloody on the flooring. She would have rolled her eyes in disdain if she weren't in the middle of a one-girl rescue.

As if this new-age nonsense is going to beat me; who in their right mind thinks that guns can beat the power of my fists?

She continued quickly moving from part to part until she heard a familiar voice behind a closed door.

"Noel... Noel..."

"Alex! Alex, I'm here!" Noel yelled before ramming into the door. It groaned loudly as it swung open and banged against the wall to reveal a bright, white light bathing the room. Many large wooden crates were stacked upon each other and formed a towering maze. Her footsteps clanged loudly against the square, metallic panels that made up the flooring as she dashed inside and searched wildly for Alex. Her nose wrinkled at the scent of gunpowder and Gorilla Goo seeping from the crates. For the first time, she found a smell she detested more than Cal's pungent aroma, but she kept sprinting down the warped, seemingly endless pathways with crazed intensity. Noel grunted in annoyance; every twist and turn seemed to bring her back to where she started. Normally she would have just punched a path to Alex through the crates, but she couldn't risk igniting the gunpowder inside them.

"Alex, where are you?!!!" she roared at the top of her lungs. After a moment, her sister's nearby low moan responded faintly, and Noel immediately ran towards it.

After a few more twists and turns, Noel found Alex. Her head was drooped down with both eyes closed. She was strapped against a wooden chair that was painted garnet. Noel's tense expression softened but carried an intense combination of anger, fear, and relief as she dashed over to her restrained sister. With nimble fingers, she tore away at the thick ropes binding Alex and noticed her sister trembling.

"Noel..." Alex whispered as her eyes slowly opened. Tears welled while her expression contorted in fear.

"Hey, it's alright," Noel said gently, cupping Alex's face. "I'm here now."

"Noel... this is a trap," Alex murmured as the room's door closed with a loud crash and locked with an audible click that echoed throughout the room. A clap resounded twice, and shadows instantly consumed the room. Noel turned around and protectively stood in front of Alex while a certain voice that Noel was quickly beginning to hate spoke in perfect sync with the slithering shadows.

"Well, well, looks like a certain someone decided to drop by without advanced notice. Those are terribly bad manners, you know."

"Can it, Dan! You kidnapped my sister and my cake dropper! That's far worse than anything I've done!" she yelled while wildly looking around the room. Dan was nowhere to be seen, but his voice resonated from within the area.

"Don't confuse prudent business practices with petty vendettas, Noel," Dan said with condescension camouflaged by a pleasant tone, almost like he was talking to a child. "I have no desire to harm either of those two, but I'm afraid your unwillingness to cooperate in my master vision has forced me to make some rather ... distasteful choices, but in the world of business, you have to make sacrifices to be successful. So, submit to me, Noel, and I'll allow those two to walk away freely, but if you keep refusing, both will have to spend a little more time with me."

"Never, Dan," Noel growled as she crossed her arms. With an angry, resolute glare, she faced the direction of Dan's voice. "The only reason I turned to you was to get stronger. I have no intention of involving the children here in Battletown in your Jaguar Juice schemes. They are kids who will grow up and become mighty warriors one day, and I will not let you harm any of them!"

"So be it," Dan said with a sigh before hardening his tone. "I knew that spirit of yours would need some breaking. It's time to temper you into a perfectly trained steed. Go get her."

A double clap resounded again as bright light swallowed the shadows and bathed the room with its warm rays. Dan was nowhere to be seen, but standing before Noel was a massive male figure with his back toward her. His face turned to glance at her, and as she looked at it closely, it looked kind of familiar, but she couldn't place it at first. After a moment, she remembered where she had seen this guy before.

"You're that Trash guy from the hospital."

"Yeah, and thanks to your little stunt, both Smash and I lost our jobs, and with my reputation ruined, I couldn't find work anywhere. Dan found me after that and offered me a job, which I readily took. I admit the work is dirty and unsightly, and the shifts are irregular, but the pros definitely outweigh the cons. One of which is the chance to mop the floor with the same girl who took everything away from me."

"Keep dreaming, pal," Noel said, striking a ready pose. "I could beat you in my sleep. What makes you think that you even stand a chance?"

"Because of three things," Trash said while sticking out an arm with three fingers extended. "One, you stopped taking your Gorilla Goo, so your arms are tired. Two, you've been training non-stop every day, so your muscles are severely damaged, and three..." he said while turning around to face Noel, "is because of our secret weapon."

Chapter 26

Trash's Revenge

Noel's jaw went slack as her eyes became wider than her arms were aching. Right in front of Trash, hanging helplessly, was Dex strapped into a baby carrier. After silently trying to comprehend the situation, Noel broke the silence with a snicker, which soon morphed into a burst of hearty laughter.

"You look so stupid right now, Dex! Ha ha ha!" She laughed with delight while pointing at him. "You look like some grown man baby. Ha! Is your baby daddy afraid that you'll run away or something?! Ha ha ha ha!"

Alex gave Noel and Dex a bizarre look before joining in with a giddy giggle at the sight of her sister's "friend" in a baby carrier.

Dex was red-faced as he turned his head away. Noel was the last person he wanted to see this. He would have covered his face with his arms, but both of his arms and legs were strapped against Trash's matching appendages. He felt almost like some human marionette, or maybe it would be more accurate to say that it was like he was receiving a weird, never-ending hug from a violent, macho man. Regardless, Noel stifled her laughter and resumed her prior seriousness.

"You really think that keeping that cake dropper in your baby entrapment device is going to defeat me? I could still beat you without breaking a sweat."

"Then come at me," Trash challenged while beckoning her with his hands.

Noel charged Trash, throwing a vicious jab-jab-cross combo. She aimed for his face but felt her fists slightly lowering as she fired each punch.

Blaf! The weights! She cursed silently as all of her punches became chest level. To make matters worse, Trash's body became a blur every time a punch got close, and he evaded all of them.

"Surprised? We found out about your friend's special ability. Now his power is all mine, and I will use it to crush you once and for all!"

"Really? Do you plan on just walking out in broad daylight with an adolescent boy strapped to your body? Have fun fighting the police, child protective services, and most of modern-day society, you creep."

"But that's the thing, though. Who gave those entities that power? The power they have only exists because it was given to them by a higher power. But now, with this boy strapped to my chest, I have even greater power, and I look forward to admonishing every group of power that opposes us."

"Um..." Dex said meekly, clearly still very embarrassed by the whole situation. "This situation is really awkward for me. Can I please go back to being tied up in the chair? I'd prefer that over this."

"Shut up!" Trash yelled at him. "Now, you're an extension of my body, and you'll do what I say!"

"Hey, don't yell at him!" Noel roared, taking another swipe at Trash, only for Trash to dodge.

"Yeah, stop being mean to Dex!" Alex yelled, struggling to break free from her bindings. "Only Noel can be mean to him!"

"How about nobody be mean to me?" Dex asked hopefully.

"Nope," Noel and Alex said in unison.

"Drat," Dex said while looking downcast.

"Sucks for you, Glasses Boy," Trash said with a small smile as he dodged another punch while throwing one of his own. Noel barely blocked it, but the impact sent her a couple of drux back. Noel attempted to bring her arms back into her fighting stance but winced. Her left forearm began shaking wildly, and she quickly grabbed it with her right hand to stifle the tremors. Taking advantage of Noel's momentary pause, Trash rushed forward and began throwing wild punches. Noel grunted but blocked with both shaking arms, forcing them to stand firm against every blow. It felt like she was trying to withstand multiple attacks from a bat. The screams of agony from her arms only grew in volume with every passing punch. This tiresome dance lasted until Trash launched a punch that slipped between Noel's guard arms and exploded in her face. She groaned as she hit the ground hard, and her eyes began rolling around in her head. Both Alex and Dex were shocked to see Noel collapse on the floor.

"Looks like it's time to finish this," Trash said as he stepped toward Noel's barely conscious body and picked her up by the neck. Noel gurgled and struggled as Trash raised his other arm, now in the form of a clenched fist.

"No!" Both Alex and Dex yelled as Trash began striking Noel repeatedly.

"You'll be their punching bag for life, boy. You should be thankful that I'm beating her into submission."

"No! STOP!" Dex roared as he struggled with all of his might against Trash. "Stop hurting my friend!"

"Wha! Stop trying to resist me!" Trash yelled as his body began making crazy movements as if he were trying to perform some sort of robotic dance move, dropping Noel in the process. "You can't overpower me!" Trash bellowed as he forced his body to make choppy steps back towards Noel. He crouched down and began throwing punches, but with beads of sweat dripping down his forehead and pained groans, Dex redirected every punch. Whenever Trash would attack, every punch would swerve above or around Noel. Frustrated, Trash tried firing a double punch but grunted in pain as Dex redirected it back into Trash's face. He staggered, breathing with blurry vision as he felt the blood and swelling around his eyes. He growled angrily as he put his hand around Dex's neck and squeezed tightly.

"You think that you can defeat me, you little blip?! I just beat your little girlfriend unconscious, and if you don't stop, I'll do it to that little kid, too, before wringing your neck!"

"Noel ..." Dex gasped as the violent fingers crushed the air out of his body, "is still stronger than you."

"We'll see if you still think that after I splatter her sister," Trash said as he slowly approached Alex. Seeing the menacing man getting closer, Alex tried wildly to escape from her chair but was powerless against the bindings.

"I hope you enjoy the afterlife, kid," Trash said as he raised a fist.

"Nouuurghh!" Dex yelled before gurgling as Trash's free hand constricted his throat.

"Be sure to tell everyone at the Den's gate that more are on the way."

Alex closed her eyes as she braced herself for the blow. She knew that it was going to hurt, and that scared her. But what scared her more was that she would be leaving Noel. Hopefully, wherever the place was that sidvens went to when they were splattered all over the ground, Noel would be able to find her. Alex had always been kind of interested in knowing more about the world that came after death, but since Noel was against them going to places that taught about the afterlife, Alex never got to learn more about the place that everyone went to once life delivered the final knockout. Noel only used one name to refer to it.

It looks like I'm finally going to go to the Den of the Eternally Defeated. Noel, please come find me there.

Alex heard a loud crack as a body hit the floor.

Wow, it didn't hurt. My classmates always made it sound scary. Well, I guess I better make a campsite and kill something I can eat. Sara said there should be a giant meat locker filled with what could be preserved from everyone who entered. There might be some rats festering inside that I can devour too. You can't live forever if you don't eat and kill.

Alex slowly opened her eyes, which further widened in surprise that she was still trapped in her chair in Dan's warehouse. Trash was prone on the ground, still as a statue, with Noel standing above him, fist raised. Her face was severely bruised and bloody. Dex's arms and legs wiggled vigorously underneath Trash, desperately trying to convey that he couldn't breathe. Noel bent over, grabbed ahold of the slumbering foe, and, with a mighty heave, flipped him over like a giant pancake. Dex took a massive breath but gave a double thumbs-up signifying that he was okay. After a moment, she firmly squeezed his shoulder before stepping over him and staggering towards Alex. With a swift motion, she tore the ropes off of Alex before leaning in and whispering faintly in her ear, "Alex... you're safe now."

Tears filled Alex's eyes as she tightly embraced Noel's neck. Hot tears streamed down Alex's face and fell upon Noel, drenching her clothes. Noel returned the embrace, sighing joyfully as the room slowly became darker. After everything, this was the happiest she had felt in a very long time. This moment to embrace her little sister meant more to her than any number of championship belts.

Chapter 27

Dan's Fury

A loud double clap reverberated throughout the warehouse. The warmth of Alex's tight hug faded from Noel's arms as the lights quickly darkened.

"Well, well, you certainly do live up to your name, Noel. If anything, I must give you credit for your unwavering tenacity and your ability to find victory even in the direst of circumstances." Dan's voice echoed across the room. Noel tried to pinpoint his location but to no avail. It was like his voice was coming from all sides. Then, without any warning, she felt an ominous presence beside Alex, like a serpent ready to strike, as a familiar, menacing buzz filled the air.

"Get down, Alex!" Noel yelled as she turned to shield her, but not before she felt a cold, metallic grip around her arms.

"Aaarrgh!" Noel screamed as a devasting current of electricity traveled through her arm.

"Noel!" Alex screamed as she dashed towards her sister. Without looking away, Dan reached into his coat pocket and pulled out a revolver. He aimed it at Alex. With an angry glare, Noel swung her free arm toward Dan.

"So predictable," Dan said as he released his grip and leaped back before causally circling around Noel. "You are simply too stubborn to admit defeat. I admit you've made it a lot farther than I anticipated, but your tenacious streak ends here, Noel. Submit to me, and my plans, or you three won't be seeing the light of day again."

Noel's breathing was ragged as she staggered with every step. She swayed slightly as she forced herself to remain upright. Her right arm trembled while her left arm spasmed uncontrollably. A strange ringing filled her ears as bright, white spots filled her vision, yet the raging fire in her eyes refused to diminish.

"I'll never submit to you, Dan. Now, how do you want your beating: well done or medium rare?"

"Yeah! Let's get him, sis!" Alex yelled as she charged forward, only for Noel to shoot her an alarmed look.

"Stop, Alex! Stay back from ...!" was all Noel could say before a loud bang went off.

"Noel... I don't feel so good," Alex said, hitting the ground.

"Alex!!!" Noel screamed as she ran over to Alex's twitching body. She knelt and put a hand on Alex's chest. Her whole body felt stiff, but Noel gave a sigh of relief after feeling a steady heartbeat.

"Relax, Noel," Dan said coolly as he put his revolver back inside his coat pocket. "That was just a tranquilizer. She'll be up and running again soon. I would never end a child's life prematurely."

Noel warmly caressed Alex's face before standing and turning away from her sister. All heartfelt emotion present prior now was replaced with a fury that burned brighter than the stars in the nighttime sky as her eyes became a burning crimson. She raised her right arm as she took a fighting stance.

"You hurt my sister! I'm going to blurf you up, Dan!" she yelled as she stood still as a lion ready to pounce. There was nothing but silence surrounding Noel, but she refused to take a single step. Her fingers clenched tightly as every joint popped. The intense anger radiating within her innermost being boiled rapidly, but Noel took a few deep breaths instead of allowing herself to be swallowed by her fury. The animosity didn't disappear but coursed throughout her mind as she closed her eyes. The darkened room became defined within her mind's eye as her inner rage burned fervently.

With a barely audible whoosh, Dan appeared beside her in a manner not terribly different from a slithering snake. She threw a shaky right cross, but he halted it by grabbing hold of her wrist.

"Impressive, but not good enough," Dan said as he sent another surge of electricity into Noel. She tried muffling her scream by gritting her teeth but couldn't prevent a pained groan from leaving her lips. "You will not beat me in your current state, Noel. You've attained injuries from both me and my associates in addition to the fatigue from excessive training. Even with your abilities and prowess, you're fighting a battle with unreasonable stipulations. Just give up already before you wind up stone cold, but I know you well enough that you won't be deterred so easily. You require a complete beating at your finest to learn, so I'll humor you, Noel."

Dan released his hold and stood above Noel as she fell to her knees, both arms now convulsing wildly.

"Go ahead and swallow a bottle of Gorilla Goo. That'll rejuvenate you long enough to fight me at full strength. You should have one bottle left."

"I don't need that rank gunk to beat you!" Noel yelled as she slowly got back on her feet.

"Please, don't humor yourself," Dan said with a sigh as he put his hand on Noel's shoulder. She yelped as another wave of paralyzing electricity ravaged her muscles. She hit the ground hard with a low groan. "The strongest fighters in the world wouldn't be able to walk properly under the conditions that you find yourself in. Not even someone with the mark of dominion could turn things around here; now drink the Gorilla Goo and take your best shot at me."

"Even if I wanted to ... I can't. I gave my last bottle to Stan," Noel muttered against the cold flooring. She trembled as she tried to get up but couldn't get her muscles to move. It was taking everything just to remain conscious.

There was a long, eerie pause before Dan responded.

"What did you just say?"

"I gave my last bottle to ... Stan from the Soda Shack. Stan the Unstoppable himself got rid of that bottle of Gorilla Goo ... for me. I will never use that crat ... again," Noel said between pained gasps.

The low buzz surrounding Dan suddenly increased in volume as he approached her with slow, heavy steps.

"How dare you give my precious Gorilla Goo to that worthless coward!" Dan yelled as he reached for Noel's face. "I'll end you!"

"No, you won't!" Dex yelled as he jumped between Noel and Dan. He struck a fighting stance as he faced Dan, now wearing his pink wristbands. He turned briefly to glance at Noel's strained expression. "I'll take care of things here, Noel. You and Alex just rest up for a moment. This won't take long."

"O...okay," Noel whispered before her eyes slammed shut. Her breathing became slow as she succumbed to her exhaustion, but not before muttering, "Don't lose. That honor of beating you belongs to me."

Dex gave a small smile before directing a furrowed expression at Dan.

"If you want to harm Noel, then you'll have to deal with me first."

"Step aside, Master Winji. I already figured out the trick behind your abilities. Your powers are useless here in the dark while mine are at their peak. While cloaked in a protective layer of shadows, I can't be detected until it's too late. Spare yourself the unnecessary pain and step out of my way. One of the few things I hate more than those who utter that wretched soda keep's name are those who stand in the way of my goals."

Like a mountain, Dex refused to budge as he narrowed his eyes at Dan. "Not happening."

"So be it." Dan's body began to blend with the malicious darkness in the room. "You'll be the next one to fall."

With an intense velocity, Dan's hand reached for Dex's right leg, but Dex shot up out of Dan's serpent-like strike.

"How did ...?" was all Dan could say before Dex's left leg dropkicked his chest. He grunted as he stumbled back a few drux, but before he could react, Dex stood before him and launched a barrage of punches into his face.

"Get off me!" Dan roared as he tried to take a few swipes at Dex, but Dex easily evaded every attack and kept hammering Dan without pause.

"How are you doing that?!" Dan yelled as he leaped back. Blood dripped down his badly bruised face. "There isn't light in this room! You shouldn't be able to detect me or dodge my attacks!"

"You think I'm going to answer that!" Dex yelled as he closed the distance and continued to swing at Dan mercilessly. Dan threw up his arms in a desperate attempt to block, but he was still getting pushed back by Dex's merciless onslaught. "You and your men have caused so much harm to the people of this town! It ends tonight, Dan!"

"So now everything is my fault, Master Winji?! Dan yelled as he crashed against the metallic wall. Slowly, he slid down, his face in a grimace. With a loud crack, Dex slammed an open palm on the wall next to Dan's head as he prepared his other fist to strike Dan's battered face.

"Let me remind you that this town was barbaric before I formed the White Caps, and only through the interventions of me and my associates have things improved here in Battletown.

Violent gangs have been put down, those who take advantage of children have been removed from the streets, and strength has been given to the weak."

Dex hesitated for a moment with an unsure expression before hardening his resolve and launching a punch toward Dan.

"Can't you see a world where the White Caps govern with peaceful resolution is just within our fingertips? Where the weak don't have to hide in fear from the strong, and the sickly don't have to worry about everything they hold dear being ripped away from them by someone with more physical might? I'm making the world a better place, so why are you stopping me? Why are you defending the savage way of life here that you are so often critical of?"

Dex paused his fist a fingertip's length from Dan's forehead. He stared intently at Dan for a moment before responding.

"Battletown is a brutal place," Dex said with a narrowed expression. "It's full of sidven who are barbaric with terrible hygiene. They make poor dietary choices and always try to solve all of their problems with their hardened fists. What you're saying sounds nice, and several of your points are valid. However, there's a flaw with your vision."

"And what's that?"

"The way to help the weak isn't by destroying those stronger or using chemicals to boost the weak. The weak must learn to become strong so that they aren't destroyed by other sidvens or by life. You don't truly wish to help the weak; you just want to create a world where the White Caps, no, where you rule over those too weak to fight back."

"Spoken like a true, naïve simpleton unaware of the hardships of reality. No one achieves their goals without making major concessions, something that your friend Noel has come to learn. But her drive pales in comparison to mine. I will create my perfect world, Master Winji, no matter who stands in my way!" Dan yelled as he slowly reached for the watch on his right hand. With a click, he pushed a button, as the room began moving.

With a loud mechanical roar followed by several clangs, the floor shifted under their feet. But the madness didn't stop there, as the walls and ceiling started rotating with Noel, Alex, Dex, Dan, Trash, and everything else in the room tossed around like rag dolls. Dan gave a small chuckle as he quickly launched himself off the moving wall and flew through the exit during the brief moment it was in the center of the flooring.

"I underestimated you this time!" Dan yelled before disappearing into the shadowy chasm of the warehouse. "That's a mistake I won't make again!"

"You sneaky crook!" Dex yelled while somersaulting in the air. His anger dissipated as he saw both Noel and Alex flapping helplessly around the ever-changing room. Noel was thrown against the wall while Alex was thrown inside a large crate with a loud crack.

"Noel, Alex!" Dex yelled as he whirled around the room, dodging several falling crates. He righted himself using his arms to somersault back to his feet. With quick, fluid steps, he sprinted across the dynamic flooring towards Noel, who was descending like a falling star. With a light thud, the unconscious brawler landed in his arms.

He quickly hoisted Noel over his shoulder. Noel's body bobbed up and down as Dex held her with one arm as he dashed across the room towards the crate Alex was trapped in. With a loud crash, Dex's fist launched into the crate, as the top half shattered. Lying on a pile of firearms was Alex, with a surprised expression.

"D-Dex?"

"Alex, grab my hand!" Dex yelled as he stretched out his arm. With a strained gesture, Alex reached for Dex's hand and clasped on tightly. Dex grunted as he pulled Alex out of the remains of the crate and into his free arm before hoisting her on his other shoulder.

"Hang on, you two! I'll get us out of here!"

The room's exit kept changing constantly. It went from the floor to the left wall, then the back wall and the ceiling, before returning to its original place on the front wall. Dex was paying close attention as he chased after it. The room's entrance stayed beyond arm's reach as it moved at an alarming rate, and if he weren't carrying both Noel and Alex, he could have easily leaped through it.

Maybe I can throw them through from a distance and then bridge the gap ... No. I have no idea how the rest of this building's structure has been altered during the room's mobility or if the building's layout is continually changing as well. Splitting up is the last thing that we need right now.

"Hey, Dex," Alex said as she tapped his shoulder. "How are you able to see right now? I can't see a thing."

"Because I'm wearing my strength bands. They've enhanced my senses so that I can see, even in the dark. How is Noel?"

"She's asleep right now," She said with a slight quiver in her voice. She trembled slightly while tightly holding onto Dex.

"Are you okay?" Dex asked softly.

"Y-yeah," she replied with a sniffle before shaking her head. "I still feel yucky from that Dan guy's gun, but I'll be okay. I have to be ... for Sis right now."

"I'm glad you're feeling better, Alex. You've been very brave tonight. Noel would be proud," Dex said with a smile as they zoomed across a wall.

"Thanks!" Alex said with a gleeful smile that morphed into a devilish grin. "By the way, I see that you rescued my sister before me. Care to tell me why?"

"Um..." Dex stammered, now thankful that the room's darkness hid his flustered face. Unfortunately, Alex's strong imagination allowed her to picture the look on his face as she giggled with delight.

Dex cleared his throat before continuing. "Anyway, we need to focus on getting out of here right now. The room's movement comes off as sporadic initially, but I think I see a pattern. The walls are rotating clockwise horizontally for 180-degrees, followed by a 180-degree vertical rotation and then a 90-degree horizontal rotation. The room then rotates vertically another 90-degrees with one more 90-degree horizontal rotation, with the room's front entrance returning to the front wall at a 90-degree counterclockwise angle. If I time it just right, then we'll be able to exit the same way that we came in."

Alex said nothing as she scratched her head with a perplexed expression. She could feel steam escape her ears as her brain tried to make sense of what Dex had just said. Before she could respond, she felt a presence brush up against her legs.

"You're not leaving without me, Glasses Boy!" Trash roared as he whirled by Dex and grabbed ahold of the boy's waist. Dex's balance teetered briefly as he gasped in surprise before continuing to sprint across the madness of the shifting room. It took all of his concentration to maintain his form while carrying both Noel and Alex against the moving surfaces in the room. If he became distracted again, he might lose his balance and hurt Noel and Alex.

Realizing this, Trash tightened his grip on Dex before growling, "I'm only in this mess because of you and Noel, and I refuse to be left to rot in this room! Either you take me with you, or we all get pounded into paste together!"

"No! Get lost! Dex, let go of me!" Alex yelled while trying to pry Dex's arm from her waist.

"Are you crazy?! No!" Dex yelled back as he tightened his hold on her, and she continued to struggle.

"Trust me, Dex! Please!" Alex pleaded as she turned towards him. A familiar fire burned brightly in her eyes that he would have seen even without his strength bands. His grip slowly loosened despite the screaming protests within his mind. He never would have guessed that his faith in those fiery eyes was stronger than his own rationale.

I must be out of my mind. Noel, have mercy on my soul. He released his hold on her and said, "Fine."

Instantly, Alex grabbed onto his extended arm and performed a handstand.

"Um... Alex, whatever you're doing, make it quick," Dex said as his arm began to tremble. "It's taking everything I have not to drop you two."

"Just a bit longer," Alex said as she swung her legs back and forth.

"Try anything, and I'll bring you all down with me!" Trash yelled as his fingernails began cutting into Dex's skin, causing Dex to wince.

With a mighty war cry, Alex launched both feet backwards and right into the back of Trash's head. He groaned lightly, his eyes rolling as he let go of Dex, only to tumble to the ground and be carried away by the shifting flooring.

"See! What did I tell you!" Alex boasted as she took a seat on Dex's shoulder.

"Not bad, Alex! But can you handle this!" Dex roared as he sped up in the direction of the front wall. Alex squealed in delight as the three zoomed through the room's exit as it moved back to its original position. Dex gave a sigh of relief at the sight of a normal, darkened hallway; they'd be out of this warehouse in no time. That just left one more concern for Dex.

"Hey, Alex," Dex said with a low voice.

"Yeah, Dex?"

"Can we keep the last several minutes a secret from Noel?" Dex said as he felt a light sweat on his forehead. "I really don't want her to be mad at me."

Alex flashed him a rosy smile as she leaned forward with her fingers intertwined behind her back. They swiftly approached the light flooding through the broken front door.

"Pinky promise," she said with a mischievous smile before adding with a giggle, "I'll especially keep it a secret how you saved Noel first before rescuing me."

A blush appeared on Dex's face. "I'd appreciate that, Alex."

Chapter 28

The Finals

When Noel awoke, she was greeted by the noontime sun. She was lying in her bed with her pillow wet with saliva and her hair a mess.

"Whaa..." Noel said with a giant yawn while stretching her arms. They ached terribly and just raising them hurt. It felt like they had been stung by a swarm of rumble bees, yet a vast sense of relief washed over her seeing the wrist and ankle weights no longer attached to her.

"Are you awake?" Dex asked, walking into the room as Noel looked up, surprised to see him.

"Cake dropper, what are you doing here?"

"Sorry for encroaching, but after you passed out, I carried you back to your place. I was afraid that Dan might send more men after you, so I stuck around to keep you and Alex safe until you received the rest that you needed."

"You ... really did all of that ... for me? Why, Dexter?"

Dex smiled. His beautiful blue eyes seemed to sparkle behind his glasses. "Because I'm your friend, and no matter what you say or do, I will help you out."

Noel was speechless for a moment. The remark had surprised her because she knew that most people, her own mother in particular, were quick to bail if things got tough. A strange feeling welled up inside Noel. It felt like her heart was being pummeled by a different kind of warmth.

"Thanks, Dexter. You've had my back this whole time, and without your help, both Alex and I would be in some serious blip."

"Don't mention it," Dex said casually, trying to downplay his beaming smile that stretched from ear to ear.

"Hey, I know I ditched you for Gorilla Goo before, but would you help coach me again? I want you to train me in Podge so that I can reach that new level."

"Hmm, I don't know," Dex said, stroking his chin in mock deep thought. "If you'd prefer the easy way, then I don't know that this is the right choice for you. Podge is about choosing self-control over quick and easy fixes, remember?"

"Please." Noel grasped his free hand. "I was wrong to give up on you and your teachings. It was the biggest mistake of my life. One that I won't repeat, so please. I promise that I'll listen to you."

Dexter's expression broke, morphing into a giant smile.

"Of course, I'll train you again. I'll be here to help you."

"Great! So what insane training workout are we going to do first?" Noel said excitedly as she tried to sit up, only to groan as a fresh wave of pain coursed throughout her body. Apparently, more than just her arms were aching.

"First," Dex said, shoving her onto her back, "You will be staying in bed and resting until your muscles have completely healed. You've done nothing but drive them to near exhaustion since you began taking that Gorilla Goo. Once you've healed in about three days, then we can begin training."

"Three days?! You have to be kidding me. That's the day of the finals for the qualifiers. I can't wait that long!" Noel complained.

"Didn't you say that you would listen to me?" Dex asked sternly.

Noel was about to open her mouth but chose to say nothing as she slumped back on her bed with a slight pout. "Fine." She crossed her arms unhappily.

"Noel," Dex said calmly. "You've already done more than enough training to win the finals. The only thing you need to do now is rest. Give your body a chance to recover, and if you do, I promise you will start that battle with enough power to rival ten Knockout Noels."

Noel looked at him, surprised. "Really?"

"You better believe it. Now rest, and if you need anything, then just let me know. I'll be bringing you lunch in a little bit."

"Thanks. You can just get me the plate of ribs that I left in the fridge."

"No, I'm making you a hearty lunch of white fish to provide your body with an excellent source of protein."

"Wow, thank you..."

"As well as a big salad filled with vitamins and minerals."

"...Thanks."

"Now go back to bed, and I'll be back later," Dex said, walking out of the room as Noel groaned but obediently pulled the covers back over herself. As Dex walked through the main room, Alex was waiting for him with a smile.

"You do a great job of handling Sis. I'm impressed. No one has ever been able to tell her what to do before. You really are the perfect boyfriend for her."

"No!" Dex said, red-faced and waving his arms wildly. "We're just an athlete and coach. Nothing but pure professionalism between the two of us."

"Riiiight," Alex said with a sly smile and an all-knowing wink before heading to the shared bedroom. "I'm still rooting for you two. Noel could use a good friend like you."

Dex stood there for a moment, face burning like a campfire doused in gasoline. He quickly moved into the kitchen and began working on lunch. He didn't have time to dwell on fantasies, but that didn't stop him from humming a happy tune while prepping the food.

Noel gave an unhappy sigh as she pulled the blankets over her head with shaking fingers. She grunted as she rolled over on her side. She closed her eyes and tried to fall asleep, but an uneasy feeling welled up inside her. She tossed and turned in pain, but the feeling inside her chest refused to lessen.

She opened her eyes and gazed at the darkened blanket that lingered over her face. Her desire to hop out of bed and continue training was strong, but Dex's words rang loudly within her active mind.

Give your body a chance to recover, and if you do, I promise you will start that battle with enough power to rival ten Knockout Noels.

Noel's tense muscles loosened as her breathing began to slow. She could feel herself drifting off to sleep, but an air of uncertainty lingered within her mind.

Will this really work? Noel thought before closing her eyes.

...

The night before the finals of the qualifiers, a shriveled figure lay restless. Inside her drafty, small, and terribly messy one-room apartment, her bed creaked as she rolled side to side in bed while tightly grasping her shoulders. She sat up suddenly, her bloodshot eyes twitching wildly while her fingers fidgeted with the sheets before moving to her arms. She looked around the room with choppy turns, unable to focus on anything for too long.

"Need more juice. Need more juice," she repeated like a broken record while her fingernails began digging into her skin, and a thin trickle of blood oozed out.

Her supply of Jaguar Juice had run out, and now she was suffering through the terrible cravings of withdrawal. As the crimson flow thickened, her ringtone suddenly went off. Not ever bothering to check the ID, she picked up the phone and answered. "I need more juice."

"I bet you do, my thirsty friend," Dan replied, "and I have something prepared for you. It's waiting outside your door, Meg."

Meg quickly turned towards the door before pausing.

"Wait. I'm prepared to give you double your normal amount with a greatly increased concentration. There is just one thing that I need you to do for me."

"What?"

"I heard that you won your match against Terrifying Tina during the semifinals. Poor girl, I hear she may never walk again after you crushed more than just her spirit," Dan said with an air of insincerity.

"And?" Meg asked callously.

"You will be fighting in the finals against Knockout Noel for the national qualifier. I need you to brutally destroy Noel during the finals. Make it so that she can never box again, just like Tina."

"Is that all?" Meg said with a vicious smile. "Then consider it done. I beat that chump easy enough last time, and I'll crush her again, no problem."

"Then happy hunting."

As soon as Dan ended the call, Meg rushed to her door and opened it, and sure enough, a cardboard box was waiting for her right outside. She grabbed it and brought it inside before quickly closing the door. After ripping the box open, Meg grabbed one of the neatly packed bottles and downed the red-and-green juice inside. She could feel a familiar source of strength running through her. It was like a surge of burning electricity was coursing throughout her body. Her muscles twitched wildly while growing larger by the second as her once shrunken body returned to its Jaguar Juice-fueled glory.

"Yeeeeessss!" she roared while beating her chest. "Knockout Noel, I'm about to end your whole career!"

...

"Ladies and Gentlemen!" Jesse B screamed into the microphone. "The night that you have been waiting for is finally here! Tonight is the finals of the female boxing national qualifiers. Tonight, the two fiercest female boxers on the roster will fight for the chance to compete in the national qualifiers and collect the 4000 brilocks prize money! With a lot on the line, neither girl can afford to pull any of their punches, not that you have to be concerned about that. Both girls are known for their ferocious tenacity and merciless slaughter of their opponents. Many bodies have been bloodied and beaten beyond recognition for your viewing pleasure. So enough with the pleasantries, and let's get the night started! In the blue, soon-to-be-purple corner, radiating an intense aura, is the rage-filled rookie Knockout Noel! And, towering over the red corner, the beast who devours all of her opponents, Monstrous Meg! Now, both girls meet in the middle of the ring, and once the bell rings, the blood bath will start!"

Noel and Meg eyed each other as they both sauntered toward the ring's center. As they stopped in the middle, neither's gaze looked away from the other. They stood like unshakable towers with strength rivaled only by the other. The tension in the arena was thicker than a foggy nighttime sky as both Noel's and Meg's gloved fists crashed into each with a deafening crack. Both girls grunted lowly while their respective gloves tried to push the other's back and refused to budge an inch.

The entire audience cheered wildly from the sheer intensity of these two powerhouses colliding. A certain feeling filled the hearts of everyone in the stands as they roared loudly. This match was going to redefine the word "brutal," and the audience couldn't be more excited.

"Enjoy the cheers, Noel," Meg growled while leaning down until she and Noel were face to face. She was wearing a black-and-brown sports bra with matching athletic shorts that reeked of sweat, dried blood, and something else that she couldn't place but was by far the most repulsive scent she had ever smelt, next to Cal. Spittle flew on Noel's face from Meg's hot breath while Meg continued her taunting. "Because this is the last time that you'll be hearing them. Tonight, I'm going to end your boxing career."

"You wish, Meg," Noel said with a strained expression, her fist shaking while stuck in a deadlock against Meg. "Tonight, I'm going to beat the blurfing blip out of you."

"Ha!" Meg scoffed with a smug smile. "I'd like to see you try."

After another intense stare-down, Noel growled in frustration as her fist was pushed back slightly by Meg's huge, black glove.

Meg smirked as she turned to stroll back to the red corner with slow, heavy steps. Noel gave a frustrated grunt as she glanced at the slight tremors coming from her left glove.

It looks like Meg has an edge here tonight. This might get rough. Noel thought darkly. She turned her head while returning to the blue corner, her eyes narrowed, and her mouth upturned in a huge frown.

"Hey, Noel!" Dex yelled from outside her corner. Serving as her wingman, he spoke with a loud, clear voice. "Don't get rattled over Meg. You can take her; just keep your eyes open!"

Noel met his gaze before nodding her head in understanding. She emptied her mind as she focused her sight on her over-seven-drux foe in the opposing corner.

Alex cheered loudly for her big sister from the stands. Typically, she would be forbidden from breaking her bedtime to attend one of Noel's boxing matches, but to make up for all of her absences; Noel allowed her to watch this ONE match live. Not that Alex intended to let this be the only boxing match that she ever watched live. She would just have to break out her secret weapon again: her diamond eyes attack!

Meg was crashing her black-gloved knuckles together while continuing to glare at Noel menacingly. Noel returned the glare with a matching intensity as her relaxed arms shifted into a fighting stance.

She won't be as lucky now. This time she won't be walking away.

The bell-ringing resonated throughout the arena as both Noel and Meg charged at each other with fists raised.

Noel's blood boiled; she felt like a restrained beast finally freed from its cage. She had spent the last three days resting and forcing herself not to train. There had been plenty of times that she had nearly gone outside to beat the old, abandoned building across the street just out of sheer boredom. She even would have been up for practicing those Podge breathing techniques, but Dex's face, along with his words, would always appear in her mind. He promised that if she had rested for the three days, she would be more than ten times as strong, and now, as she bolted towards her towering foe, a new strength coursed throughout her. Now it was her turn to leave Meg bruised and bloody.

Meg launched a punch, which Noel dodged, and then, giving a mighty roar, Noel threw a punch that crashed right into Meg's jaw. Meg swayed back as she bellowed in pain. Besides giving her heightened physical prowess, the Jaguar Juice also increased both her durability and pain tolerance to the degree where nothing short of guns and large knives could hurt her. She stood there stupefied as she felt a sensation that she hadn't felt in a long time. As something that definitely wasn't a trickle of sweat went down her jaw, she wiped it off with her glove. Her eyes narrowed, and her nostrils flared as she stared at the blood on her glove. Meg's murder-filled gaze immediately shifted toward Noel.

"How dare you hurt me, you dirty blit!" Meg roared before dashing towards Noel. She began wildly swinging her sledgehammer-like fists at her foe. Noel, without flinching, blocked Meg's first blow, evaded the second, and blocked another punch right before counterattacking with a vicious left hook.

Meg gasped as Noel drove her glove even deeper into Meg's jaw. With a loathsome look, Meg snarled as she hurled a left jab at Noel's face. A loud smack reverberated. Meg growled, her left glove now halted by Noel's intercepting right one. Meg tried pushing the glove back, but it refused to budge.

Unflinchingly, Noel's left fist flew toward Meg's face.

Instinctively, Meg threw up her arms to guard her face, only for Noel's punch to swerve underneath her guard. With fast feet, Noel closed in on her adversary, crouched down, and began rapidly uppercutting Meg's gut. Before Meg could respond any further, a swift punch from Noel shattered her guard and smashed right into her face.

Meg groaned as she went flying through the air and crashed into one of the ring's corners. Noel's body moved with ease as a new source of strength flowed through her as she slowly approached Meg, intent on finishing her off. Seeing Noel close the gap, Meg grabbed onto the ropes and tried to stand, but her shaking legs buckled quickly and hit the ground as if they had chosen to abandon her.

"What's wrong Meg?" Noel said with a smug expression. "Isn't this where you're supposed to finish me? Or maybe you're nothing but talk."

"No... I... will... not... lose," Meg muttered as she rapidly brought down her arms, and her gloves flew off and shot towards Noel. Noel brought her arms up to block the first projectile with quick reflexes but gasped in pain as the second glove crashed into her gut. Noel paused for a moment, giving

Meg just enough time to reach into her cleavage, and pulled out a large vial filled with a red-and-green liquid. She smashed the top of the vial against the ring's corner and poured the contents down her throat.

"You're dead!" Meg exclaimed as her eyes became blood-shot. Her left pupil glowed a green hue, and her right pupil turned crimson as her body grew. Her arms expanded until they became as thick as tree trunks, and her now-ten-drux figure bathed the entire ring in her shadow.

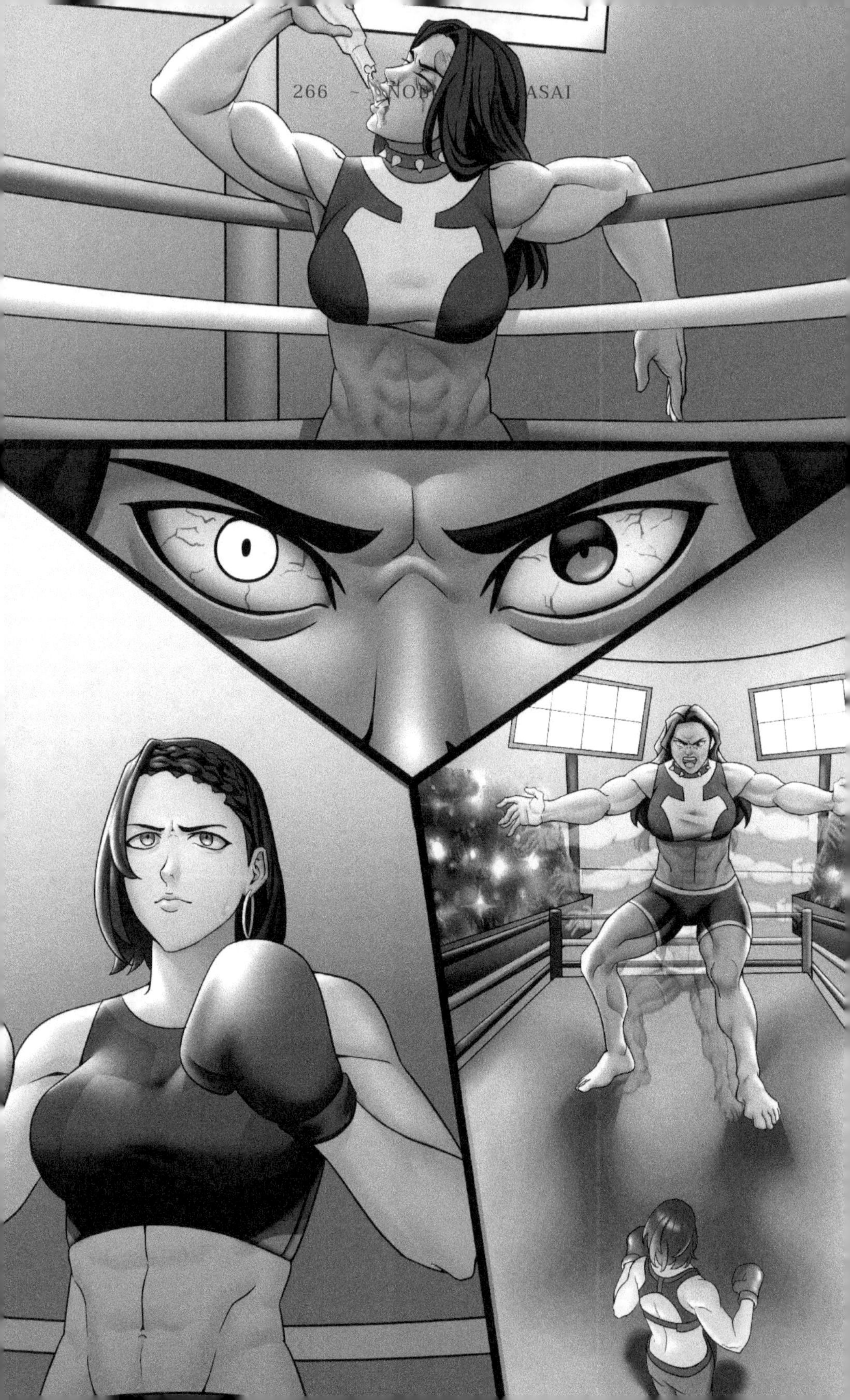

Chapter 29

Facing a Real Monster

"Holy blurf!" Jesse B screamed into his microphone. "Monstrous Meg has downed an entire bottle of what appears to be Jaguar Juice! A major violation, which will result in an immediate disqualification from the referee."

With a loud whistle, Ajax came between Noel and Meg.

"Monstrous Meg is disqualified for illegal substance use!" Ajax yelled, making an X with his arms as he quickly stepped between the two girls. "Knockout Noel is the winner!"

"Shut up!" Meg said as she swung a meaty fist at Ajax, but the battle-hardened ref effortlessly knocked it away with his forearm.

"That's quite enough, missy! No one breaks regulations in my stadium. Now stop!" Ajax said firmly with a calm expression. His right fist turned blood-red as he struck an intense fighting pose. With knees slightly bent and his right arm pulled back like a coiled spring, he narrowed his attentive eyes upon the monstrous girl staring down at him.

With a roar, she swung her other fist, but not before Ajax launched his crimson knuckles into her abdomen.

"Ajax attack!"

Meg gasped in pain before violently coughing up blood. With every breath, blood oozed from the red fist print on her stomach. The skin wasn't broken, but somehow her plasma was leaking out. Despite this, Meg continued to stand tall with a look of murder in her eyes that only intensified.

Ajax's technique is incredible. I'm glad I didn't get hit by that, Noel thought with both awe and fear.

"Dealing with teenage girls is such a pain," Ajax muttered with a sigh before hardening his expression. "Meg, you cannot defeat me. Leave this ring willingly now and never return, or I will drag you out by force. What will it be?"

Meg sneered, grabbed Ajax, and effortlessly lifted him over her head. He tried to break free, but even this old veteran was struggling against the chemical-induced might of Meg's unbelievable grip.

Blat! What the blurf is in Jaguar Juice? It's like I'm up against someone several weight classes above me, Ajax thought as he futilely attempted to grasp onto her arm with his right hand, but not before Meg threw him up in the air. As he came crashing down, Meg grabbed him by the ankles and swung him around like a violent cyclone.

"Get lost, Ajax! This match isn't over until I've beaten Noel into a red puddle!" Monstrous Meg bellowed before hurling the referee above the stands, where he landed painfully in the announcer's booth with a loud crash.

"Holy crat"! Jesse B screamed into the microphone he now held with a fearful look in his eyes. His announcing table shattered before him, with Ajax's now unconscious body lying motionless on the table's remnants. Jesse sighed in relief when he detected a light snore from Ajax before returning his focus to the fight.

"Monstrous Meg has literally yeeted the referee out of the ring! Thankfully Ajax is alive with nothing more than some nasty cuts and bruises: however, it looks like the rules have been thrown out of this match! Folks, I do not know how this match will play out, but I can tell you this! This fight is about to be more brutal than you could have ever imagined! Don't turn your eyes away, viewers, because this fight will be talked about for generations to come! Now let's see what happens in round two of Knockout Noel vs. Monstrous Meg!"

Noel kept a firm fighting stance but had a slightly wary look in her eyes as she focused on the behemoth in front of her. With the sound of a falling tree, Meg sent a fist crashing into the ground right where Noel had been standing. Thankfully, Noel had jumped out of the way, but the impact caused the ring to tremble, with Noel losing her balance and falling on her side.

Noel quickly rolled over and jumped back to her feet. While Meg pulled her massive hand from the ring's flooring, Noel dashed towards her colossal adversary. With a loud grunt, Noel leaped up and launched a mighty left jab into Meg's jaw. A loud smack echoed throughout the entire arena with no interference from the speechless audience. Noel's eyes widened, her mouth gaping in disbelief.

Noel's punch, strong enough to defeat Mac-en-Clobber, Dangerous Dana, Right-Hook Rheyna, Everlasting Edna, and many of the other folks within Battletown, now harmlessly nudged Meg's rock-like cheek. Her foe's face contorted into a wicked smile as she slowly rose until her towering figure covered Noel in shadow. Her dilated pupils focused on Noel from up above with a hunger-like intensity.

"Come at me, you blit! Even you don't stand a chance now!" Meg bellowed at the top of her lungs, both arms raised. With bent knees, Meg's arms rained down upon Noel in a flurry of punches that fell like meteors, creating massive craters within the ring.

Fiery determination filled Noel's eyes as she leaped back to avoid a thunderous blow. Without a moment's rest, Noel continued to evade the airborne strikes with deft footwork. After a few moments of bouncing around the battered ring while staying on her toes, she found herself breaking more than a moderate sweat.

This blit is bringing the heat tonight! Not only is she bigger and stronger, but her skin is harder than any rock I've ever felt. My punch didn't even faze her. I need to land a good hit on her again somehow, but she's not leaving an easy opening. I can't reach her ugly face, and I can't reach her gut while her punches are raining down. I'll just have to make my own opening, Noel thought as she ran around Meg's punches until she reached Meg's right leg. Without a moment's hesitation, Noel threw a left jab into Meg's knee, only for it to connect harmlessly. Growling in frustration, Noel circled around Meg's leg while continuing to mercilessly attack the hairy, throbbing extremity.

A booming laugh escaped from Meg's moist lips at Noel's growing frustration. Noel ignored the obnoxious noise while continuing to punch Meg's knee, a mistake she would regret, as Meg's hand swiftly grabbed ahold of her left arm and abruptly pulled her off the ground until she found herself eye-level with Meg.

Her beastly foe flashed a cruel smile while shaking Noel in the air like a rag doll. Noel's eyes rolled around wildly, and her left arm felt like it was going to come out of its socket as her body was violently whipped around. Once the motion ceased, it took Noel a moment for her vision to focus. The first sight she beheld was a close-up of Meg's hideous face as she dangled a drux away.

"Well, Noel, this looks like the end for you," Meg said sinisterly, her hot breath still reeking of Jaguar Juice. "Any last words you'd like to say before I break you?"

Without missing a beat, Noel launched a right cross into Meg's left eye. Monstrous Meg bellowed in pain as she instantly dropped Noel and blindly stomped around the arena with a hand over her left eye. Noel landed on her butt with a groan, but not before being spotted by Meg's seething vision. With her left eye now puffy, she shrieked like an injured animal before turning towards Noel.

Without hesitating, Meg tried kicking Noel off the stage, but Noel managed to avoid the brunt of it by quickly rolling out of the way. This was not enough, as the force of the bottom of Meg's foot lightly rubbing against her sent Noel sprawling into the red corner. Noel grunted upon impact, and after opening her eyes, she saw that the ring was attached to the ceiling, with two Monstrous Megs now at the blue corner. Noel slapped her face a couple of times to find that the ring was back on the ground, with only one Meg pulling the blue corner out of the ring. She broke all three of the wires threaded through the blue corner with a loud snap as Noel stared with an incredulous expression.

Oh, blurf! Just how much strength does that crat give you?!

Meg slowly approached Noel while gripping the blue corner like it was a bat. Noel jumped to her feet and took a step back as she continued to eye Meg warily. She didn't like that Meg now had a blunt weapon; if she wasn't careful, she would be pounded flatter than a plasma patty. Noticing that she was standing near Meg's gloves, she swiftly dashed toward them and kicked them, sending them flying in the direction of Meg's face. Meg batted both gloves back towards Noel with powerful swings, who dodged both by quickly crouching down. After jumping back up, Noel zoomed towards Meg but swerved out of the way as Meg tried to smash Noel with a shattering swing. Noel was forced to keep backing up until she felt one of the white corners behind her as Meg kept swinging wildly at her. Noel's nostrils flared as she gave Meg a frustrated scowl.

"What, can't beat me in hand-to-hand?" Noel taunted.

"I'm not going to beat you. I'm going to demolish you!" Meg yelled, swinging the blue corner down on Noel. Noel rolled out of the way, avoiding the blow by a hair's width, as the white corner shattered to pieces after taking Meg's blow head-on. Noel jumped back on her feet and began running around Meg, trying to attack her blind spot. As she got close, Noel dashed towards Meg and launched an attack. Meg, expecting this, quickly swung the blue corner around and nailed Noel in the stomach. The crowd oohed as a loud snap crackled from Noel's abdomen. She gasped for air as the blow sent her flying out of the ring only to land on the painful concrete flooring outside of it.

"Noel, are you alright?!" Dex asked as he hurried over to where she had landed.

"I'll manage." She muttered while sitting up with a light groan as she clutched her side.

"Let me take a look," Dex said as he put his hand on her side and began applying light pressure. Noel bit her tongue, trying to keep in a yelp of pain as Dex started feeling around the hurt area.

"You have a broken rib with some nasty bruises, but other than that, you're fine."

"That's a relief," Noel said as she began to get up with a wince. Seeing her struggle, Dex offered her his hand, and after hesitating for a minute, Noel grabbed ahold as Dex pulled her back on her feet.

"Thanks," Noel said before heading back toward the ring.

"Wait a minute!" Dex said, grabbing her hand. "You can't fight in this state! We need to get you home so that you can rest!" he insisted passionately, but Noel just shook her head.

"Even if I wanted to, Meg isn't going to let me leave unless it's in a body bag. She's been very clear about that. Besides, even if she did, that wouldn't change things. I've worked too hard to get here to throw everything away for a broken rib. It doesn't matter how much I'm hurting or how hopeless things look. I always face my problems until they disappear. I've got a reputation to uphold and a kid sister to look after."

"But..."

"Hey, who do you think I am?" Noel said as she gazed into Dex's eyes with a serious expression. "I'm Knockout Noel, and I always find a way to win. Do you doubt me?"

"I just don't want you pushing yourself when you're hurt," Dex said with a worried expression.

"You can play nurse when I'm done here. Just give me a few minutes," Noel said with a reassuring smile before shuffling back into the ring. Meg stood in the center, still holding the blue corner in her big, meaty hands.

"So you came back willingly. I thought you would have wet your pants and fled out of terror. At least it saves me the trouble of having to chase you down," Meg said with a smug, menacing grin on her face.

"Then you don't know me very well. When we are done here, your body will be unconscious and bloody on the ring floor."

"Ha!" Meg snorted. "You're the one who is going to get beat. You'll be nothing more than a red puddle after I'm done with you. It's fitting, though."

"What do you mean?"

"Your very first match was against me. It was humiliating, losing to someone who had never set foot in the ring before. Now the last fight of your life is against me, and it will be your worst day ever."

"Wait, are you Miny ...?"

"Enough talking!" Meg exclaimed, swinging the blue corner wildly at Noel. With a loud groan, Noel ducked below the blue corner as it swung overhand. The ground trembled every time Meg brought it in her attempts to crush Noel, but Noel nimbly kept jumping back while staying safely out of reach. While grasping her side, she forced herself to breathe deeply through gritted teeth. Her body was aching, but she buried that pain deep within her iron resolve.

I'm winning here tonight, Noel thought as she charged toward Meg. The towering beast brought the blue corner down like a giant sledgehammer with a ground-shattering crash that broke the ring in half. The crowd stared in awe, not at the fractured ring but at Noel. As the blue corner came down, she leaped onto the badly abused corner and quickly dashed up the stick while still clutching at her side. Before Meg could react, Noel had driven her fist right into Meg's nose. Meg roared in rage, dropping the blue corner and stomping wildly before swatting Noel away with her bare hands. Noel hit the ground hard and struggled to get on her hands and knees as Meg picked up the blue corner and ambled towards her.

With a grunt, Meg swung the corner downwards. Noel rolled over, barely avoiding it as it hit the ground with a loud crash. The ring rippled intensely with the aftershock, sending Noel sprawling across the ring. She landed painfully on her back, gasping for air with a pained expression. Her left arm was against her aching chest as she tried to sit up, only for a giant foot to knock her back down.

"I've had enough of you, Noel!" Meg yelled while her foot repeatedly came crashing down upon her.

With arms up, Noel guarded against the ruthless assault. The pain in her left arm increased with every stomp blocked, but Noel fought through it.

"Is ... that ... all ... you've got ... blit?" Noel jeered between the merciless shower of Meg's punches.

"Try blocking this, blit!" Meg yelled as she threw the corner to the ground and bent her knees after firmly planting both feet on the ground next to Noel. With a beastly roar, she leaped an impressive height of ten drux before hurtling downwards towards Noel.

"Blurf," Noel muttered as both of Meg's feet came crashing into Noel's guard. An audible crack came from the collision.

"Noel!!!" Alex and Dex screamed in unison. They stared wide-eyed with horrified expressions at Noel's still body. Meg stood triumphantly with one foot on Noel's chest and both arms raised.

"I've done it!" she roared victoriously to the silent crowd. The only reaction the audience gave was crossed arms and disapproving looks.

"Hey, what's the deal?! I won! I've finally won, so applaud me already!" Meg yelled at the massive crowd while every sid-van gave her a thumbs-down and booed her.

"Shut up!" Meg yelled in a baffled tone while pointing to the audience. "I beat Noel, so why are you booing me? Noel batters her opponents all the time to the crowd's roaring approval, so why are you turning against me?! Maybe I need to teach you all a lesson too ..."

Before Meg could continue her rant, she sensed a pair of hands grasping her shoes. She glanced down and saw Noel with a dazed expression as her fingers stubbornly held onto Meg's foot.

"Haven't you had enough yet, Noel?" Meg sneered while applying pressure on Noel's chest with her foot. Noel groaned, but her eyes focused with unyielding tenacity as she tightened her grip on Meg's foot. With a sudden, deft motion, Noel twisted Meg's ankle. The behemoth yelped as she lost her balance and fell off Noel with a loud thud. The crowd cheered loudly, only to boo as Meg got back on her feet, demonstrating a slight limp while picking up the fallen corner, and slowly made her way back to Noel. A crimson river trickled down Meg's nose as she glared at Noel with bloodshot eyes.

"I'm going to kill you," Meg growled.

"Go ahead and try," Noel said with a pained smile. "If your legs can take it. I'm surprised you can still stand after that loud snap they made after you jumped on me. I bet they're soft enough to break now."

"Die!" Meg yelled as she raised the blue corner overhead once more, only to be drowned out by the crowd's booing.

"Hey! Leave Noel alone, you dirty blit!"

"Noel was winning until you cheated, you Jag drinker!"

"Stop using a weapon, you giant cheater!"

"Of course, she is using a weapon! The freak would lose without it!"

The crowd began hurling even nastier insults down at Meg as she looked around at the angry mob with a pure loathing burning deep within her eyes. The breaking point came with a loud clang when an aluminum soda can was hurled by someone in the stands; it harmlessly bounced off Meg's head. It was just the forebearer because soon after, Meg found herself being pelted by soda cans, handfuls of popcorn, and several pieces of greasy, boneless chicken wings. Meg's pupils dilated with an almost audible click. She gave a fearsome look resembling a deranged monstrosity as she hurled the blue corner straight into the stands.

Screams broke out as some of the audience tried to flee from berserk Monstrous Meg, who, with a low growl, ripped out the red corner. She leaped out of the ring and walked towards those trapped underneath the blue corner. Several of the nearby spectators stood with arms crossed opposing Meg, while other viewers worked diligently to pull those who had been hit to safety.

Meg glared at the remaining crowd with intense anger as she pointed the corner at them. "This arena will be painted in your blood!" she yelled at the audience, but those who opposed her didn't falter. They stood like statues with a deep resolution within their eyes because within the heart of every true inhabitant of Battletown lay one basic principle: You never flee from evil. You face it head-on. So, as Meg approached with the ring's corner raised, there was no trace of fear within their eyes because they would do all in their power to protect their fellow townsfolk from the evil abomination before them.

"Stop!" A shrill voice rang out from within the ring. Everyone, including Meg, turned their heads in surprise only to see a small girl yelling at the top of her lungs while in a strange fighting stance.

"Leave those people alone, you big meanie!" Alex yelled while standing in front of her fallen sister. "You hurt Noel, and now you're hurting other people. You need to stop, or else!"

"Or what, little girl?!" Meg growled with a fit of anger burning in those bloodshot eyes as she turned and walked back into the ring and towards Alex. She had seen this child somewhere before, but she couldn't put her finger on it. All Meg knew was that this little girl was about to pay the price for opposing her.

Now fearful for Alex's life, the crowd tried to silence Alex and get Meg's attention.

"Shut up, kid!"

"Stop that monster, or she'll hurt that kid!"

"Everyone attack her at once!"

The crowd charged towards Meg, but she sent them flying into the stands with a single swing of the red corner. When Meg was within striking range of Alex, she paused while recognition filled her eyes.

"I've seen you before. You're Noel's kid sister. You saw what I've done to Noel, and you think you can tell me what to do, little girl?!" Meg growled as she slammed the corner down. With a loud crash, it hit the ground right next to Alex before the behemoth picked up the corner and continued to slam it into the ground.

Alex's legs shook slightly and felt as sturdy as a pair filled with cotton stuffing. Tears drizzled out of her eyes as she felt her mouth trying to twitch into a frown. *No, now I need to be strong for Sis,* she thought as she forced her fear into the deepest part of her being.

Slowly, she stepped away from Noel with Meg's gaze closely following the little girl's movements.

At least now, Monstrous Meg's attention won't be on Noel or anyone else here, Alex thought. Her body stiffened as Meg quickly closed the distance with a few thunderous steps until Alex found herself covered in Meg's shadow and unable to see anything other than the towering behemoth's murderous eyes.

So, after gathering every ounce of her resolve, she clenched her fists tightly and belted at the top of her voice with her most menacing Noel-like glare, "I will end you!"

Animosity reappeared in Meg's eyes as she raised the red corner overhead and took aim at the little girl in front of her. "Then you can die too!"

She brought down the white corner upon the little girl with all of her strength as the ground became splattered with her blood.

Chapter 30

True Strength

Or, that's what should have happened. Monstrous Meg was red-faced, putting all of her strength into bringing the red corner down, but no matter how much she exerted, the pole refused to budge.

"Hey!" a familiar voice said behind Meg. "**No one** threatens my sister!" Noel yelled while holding down the opposite end of the corner with both hands. Sweat poured down her red face as her shaking arms strained to keep the ring post from spattering Alex. The pain in her ribs was pure agony. It felt like they were going to shatter, but she ignored it.

"Your fight is with me! I will end you!" Noel roared as her eyes shimmered a bright crimson. Her left bangs flapped wildly with her now-visible birthmark burning with an intense red heat. Those in the crowd gasped, many holding up clenched fists before cheering louder for Noel.

Another loud snap reverberated throughout the stadium as Noel drove her foot into the back of Meg's knee. Monstrous Meg screamed in agony as her leg buckled, and she fell to the ground with a loud thud as Noel yanked away the corner.

"Alex! Are you alright?!" Noel yelled as she dropped the corner and dashed towards Alex. Her little sister shook her head that she was fine. Noel quickly hugged her before picking her up and lifting her overhead with her right arm.

"Dex, catch!" Noel yelled as she hurled Alex towards the startled boy standing outside the ring.

"Noel, are you crazy!" Dex yelled as he jumped up and caught the giddy ten-year-old. Upon impact, he grunted as the hurtling girl pushed him back. He felt the air whishing around both him and Alex before their painful landing in the bleachers.

"Whoa! That was fun! Can we do that again?" Alex said with a giggle as she hopped off of Dex.

"Hard pass," Dex groaned as he slowly got back on his feet. "Your sister throws way too hard, and your head felt like a rock when it slammed against my sternum. How about running a race or going a few rounds in food fighters?"

"We should do all three at the same time!"

"You really are Noel's sister," Dex said with a smile before changing to a serious expression as he returned his focus to Noel. Alex followed his gaze and adopted a worried expression. She grabbed Dex's shirt and gazed into his eyes as he turned to face her.

"Do you think Noel is going to be okay?" she asked with a slight tremor in her voice.

Dex's expression didn't change as he picked up Alex and put her on his shoulders. "If anyone could find a way to win in these odds, then it would definitely be Noel. When she sets her mind on something, nothing can stop her."

With Alex out of harm's way, Noel turned to face Meg, who was back on her feet. With muffled groans, the massive girl limped with heavy steps that caused what remained of the ring to shake. Meg held tightly onto the corner, which she now held as a crutch, while hobbling towards Noel with her free arm over her chest. Her face paled slightly as blood continued to seep out of her abdomen, but she showed no signs of quitting anytime soon.

Noel wasn't faring much better. She clutched at her throbbing side, and every step, both hers and Meg's, set off a new wave of excruciating pain. Plus, her aching body was adorned with bloody bruises. Noel clicked her tongue; she didn't like her odds here. Even with a leg kicked out, it would take more than a few punches to bring down Meg, especially while Jaguar Juice was flowing through her.

I'm not going to last much longer. I've got to bring this blit down, and fast, Noel thought as she glanced at her trembling arms before returning her glance at Meg as an unpleasant emotion came over her.

I don't know how I'm going to pull this off.

This thought swirled around in her head until the voice of a familiar face caused it to dissipate.

"Noel!" Dex yelled with both hands cupping his mouth. Noel abruptly turned her head and met the gaze of his blue eyes as he continued speaking from the bleachers.

"Close your eyes and describe her!"

"Are you crazy, Dex?! Now is not the time for that!" Noel yelled back.

"Trust me! Just close your eyes and breathe deeply!"

Noel's body went rigid while glaring at Dex from the corner of her eye. After beginning to say something, she cut herself off and went silent for a moment before taking a deep breath and responding.

"Okay ... I'll give it another try," Noel said as she turned to face Meg, but instead of putting up her guard, she dropped her arms to her side.

"What are you doing, Noel?!" Meg bellowed while Noel calmly closed her eyes and began taking a few deep breaths. "Praying won't save you from me! Now come at me so we can finish this, blit!"

Noel heard none of Meg's remarks as the world around her dimmed into one of darkness. She became like a single pebble thrown into a pond as the sounds of everything around her blurred into a distant murmur. In this space, she and only she existed.

How do I even do this? I can't afford to mess around, so I'm going to have to make this work, Noel thought as she put her right hand over her heart while continuing to breathe deeply.

I can feel my heart beating. I can feel bad pain in my left arm and ribs. I have several bleeding cuts, and I'm covered in sweat. I can feel ... a tiny portion of the area around me, about a drux. It's not much, but I can sense things that I don't normally see.

She grimaced slightly while the sensations she was experiencing began to flicker, and the invisible boundary lines of this place began constricting her. Noel felt an incredible mental strain but stubbornly refused to yield.

This is hard. It's tight, like an exercise band that's squeezing against me while I'm pushing it away. I'm doing good so far, but I have to go farther. Let's try this! Noel thought while dropping her shoulders and unclenching her fists. She turned her opened palms outwards, and with all of her mental might, she pushed against the boundary lines surrounding her. Slowly, bit by bit, she stretched out the surface area of what she could sense. More and more of the remnants of the ring fell within what she could sense, but just as this boundary line reached Meg, it suddenly recoiled. Noel tried desperately to force it back out, but now the space refused to expand.

Noel gave a frustrated sigh but opened her eyes. While it had been for only a fraction of a zin, in that one brief moment, she'd felt a burning abnormality coming from Meg's abdomen where Ajax had punched her prior.

So, with gritted teeth, Noel dashed towards Monstrous Meg.

Seeing Noel approach, Meg began standing solely on her good leg as she quickly raised the corner once more overhead.

She's going to try smashing me by bringing the corner down again. All I have to do is dodge and attack once I get close, Noel thought before her eyes widened in surprise. Instead of a downward strike, Meg feinted and swung the corner in a downward spiral.

With a pained gasp, Noel quickly arched her waist backwards. Her knees bent at acute angles while barely evading the corner as it flew over her. The wind displacement from the corner caused Noel's hair to flap wildly out of her contorted face. She yelped; the pain in her side was nearly unbearable at this point.

"I won't lose to you, Meg!" Noel yelled as she crouched down and launched herself right at Monstrous Meg. With a ferocious expression, she threw a punch with an animal-like intensity aimed at her opponent's mid-region.

Meg screamed in agony as Noel's attack connected. She vomited a puddle of blood as Noel's fist sank into Meg's abdomen, exactly where Ajax had attacked her earlier.

"You dirty... blit," Meg gasped as she swung at Noel, but Noel dodged by dropping down. Before Meg could throw any more punches, Noel leaped up and drove a second fist into Meg's gut. Another burst of crimson liquid with streaks of green ejected from Meg's mouth. The scent of iron filled the stadium. Fresh blood was a scent that Noel personally enjoyed, especially from a platter of ribs done medium rare, but not here. This blood smelled nasty. It was almost as if Meg had been drinking every household chemical that she could find lying around.

So, this is what Jaguar Juice smells like when mixed with blood. Disgusting! Noel thought as Meg's shaking hands suddenly dropped the ring post with a loud thud. Without missing a beat, an irate Meg launched an uppercut at Noel. She tried to bring up her arms to block but was a smidge too slow. Noel gasped, and pain shot throughout her body as the impact hit her jaw. But the force was far less lethal than her previous attacks, which could only mean one thing.

The Jaguar Juice is wearing off, and since she just threw up everything she drank during our match, she must be running out of steam. Now is my chance!

Noel quickly wiped the blood and saliva off of her mouth with her forearm before readying her fists.

Meg gave a pained roar but began throwing a barrage of wild punches. Like a cornered beast, she knew that she couldn't let Noel get any closer.

Noel stood silently and threw up her arms to guard against the onslaught. Every blow caused Noel to wince, but the pain from every punch was lessening. Noticing that even the speed of Monstrous Meg's punches was declining, Noel began to press forward.

Meg, desperately trying to keep Noel at a safe distance, licked her bloody lips for the trace amount of Jaguar Juice residing on them. A sliver of the vile gunk mixed with her bile entered her mouth as she quickly swallowed. She roared as she felt a fraction of strength return to her as she threw another mighty fist at Noel. Upon impact, both girls screamed.

Meg's blow connected with Noel's jaw and sent her flying, but not before she kicked out Meg's other leg with a loud crack.

Meg screamed as she fell hard and flat on her stomach. With a grunt, she slowly pushed herself up to glare at the battered Noel, who was glaring right back at her from the other side of the remnants of the ring.

Slowly, Noel rose from the broken ring flooring. Now with the addition of a bloody bruise on her left jaw, she trudged towards Meg until she stood above her.

With a whoosh, Noel's left jab flew toward Meg's right temple. Meg growled with a feral expression as her mouth opened.

Revealing a set of sharp teeth, Meg's head lurched forward, and she sank her teeth into Noel's glove.

"Ow!" Noel howled. There was a loud crack as her free hand crashed into Meg's right temple. The monstrous girl's jaw loosened significantly as Noel yanked her gloved hand free of Meg's mouth. A huge chunk of her left boxing glove was missing, with a trickle of blood seeping out of the gaping hole. None of that mattered to Noel as she delivered a harsh kick to Meg's side. Monstrous Meg groaned as she tried sitting up, but she could only manage a half sit-up before falling flat on her back with a thud.

Noel jumped on top of Meg and, with heavy steps, ambled until she was right in front of Meg's head. Her face was contorted in pain, but Noel paid it no heed as she began pelting her face with a barrage of furious blows. Meg's grunts of pain soon morphed into a dull moan as she became a lump of flush composed mainly of bruises and bloody scrapes.

After delivering a sound beating, Noel slowly got off of Meg. She threw off her gloves before briskly walking up to the red corner. With a pained grunt, she picked it up and walked around Meg until she was standing right above her head. Noel raised the ring's corner with a giant heave until it dangled vertically over Meg's face.

"Good Grisipi!" Jesse B, who had chosen to stay at the stadium, screamed into his microphone. "Knockout Noel is hanging one of the corners over Monstrous Meg's face in what appears to be an attempt to smash her face in. Normally this kind of act is far from what's allowed, but the rules state that those who act with the intent of murder forfeit all protection from the Decree of Brutality, and after witnessing Monstrous Meg's rampage tonight, there can be no mistaking her murderous intent. So what will become of Monstrous Meg with the corner now in the hands of Knockout Noel, the female powerhouse known for merciless rage and unbridled fury? Remaining viewers, quiet your breathing as we watch the thrilling finale of Knockout Noel vs Monstrous Meg!"

With a focused look, Noel held the pole over Meg's face as she slowly raised it higher.

"Finish her! Finish her!" the crowd chanted louder and louder throughout the stadium. Noel glanced at Dex and Alex from outside the ring. Both had clear looks of concern on their faces, especially Dex.

"Noel..." Meg said faintly before turning her head and vomiting up one more puddle of blood.

Slowly her body began to shrink. The massive muscles shriveled up as she began twitching wildly. Her sunken skin turned a deathly pale as she now resembled more of an exhibit piece for some preserved, barely four-drux mummy display than the ferocious, monster-like boxer that Noel had just faced.

"You really are Miny Megan," Noel muttered as realization dawned upon her face. The corner fell from her grasp, her arms falling to her sides. "What the blurf has Jaguar Juice done to you, Megan?"

Noel looked into her swollen, bloodshot eyes. There was no remorse but something else deep within. Noel couldn't put it in words, but she sensed a kind of emptiness and void of purpose, like salt that didn't taste salty.

"Just do it already. Finish me off. There isn't ... a point being around anymore. I always lose when it matters, just like when we first fought."

Noel's eyes narrowed as she picked up the fallen corner and held it above Miny Megan. With a grunt, she drove the pole down with a loud crash. Everyone in the stadium gasped. Noel had driven the pole straight through the ground ... right beside Monstrous Meg's head.

"Threaten my sister again, and you'll live to regret it," Noel warned before turning away and standing in the middle of what was left of the ring. She raised her left fist with a solemn expression, and the remaining crowd broke into thunderous applause. Her eyes turned back to their usual brown, the crimson shimmer of her birthmark fading to a light brown.

As she turned to leave the ring, she crossed paths with Ajax, who had just come to from his injuries, as he went to check on Megan. He nodded with a small smile as he slugged her shoulder.

"Good job, kid," he said in passing. Noel returned a smile.

"I do not believe it, folks!" Jesse B yelled. "Against all odds, Knockout Noel has defeated an opponent fueled by Jaguar Juice and has won the female boxer's regional qualifier. Not only is the 4000Ƀ brilocks prize money hers, but she will now be competing in the national female boxing championship. Folks, I'm not one for making predictions, but I foresee our dear Noel facing Invincible Inaya for the national title. Truly another moment that will make history, and I hope to witness all of it with you!"

Invincible Inaya. I'm coming for you. Noel thought as she made her way to Alex. Seeing Noel's badly bruised body, Alex's eyes watered up.

"Noel," she said with a sniffle, "are you ...?"

Before she could finish, Noel enveloped her in a giant hug.

"Yeah," Noel said warmly with a giant grin on her face, "but next time, leave the fighting to me. You're too young to bloody your knuckles."

"Hey!" Alex said with a slight pout. "I'm tough now. My skin barely gets scraped anymore."

"I never said your blood." Noel snickered while she playfully ruffled her hair before whispering in her ear. "I'm proud of you for standing up to Meg, but don't do anything that dangerous again. You had me worried to death."

"I can't promise that," Alex said while sticking out her tongue. "I am your sister, after all."

"Then maybe I need to remind you that I am still your big sister!" Noel mock threatened.

"Maybe if you can catch me!" Alex said while quickly running away.

"I'll give you a head start, so go ahead and wait for me by the exit. There is one thing I have to do here first."

"Ok." Alex said before dashing out of the stadium's exit as Noel made her way to Dex, who had a perplexed expression.

"You didn't kill her."

"Nope," Noel said nonchalantly.

"Why? I thought you didn't believe in mercy."

"I don't. But I also don't think I need to destroy everyone weaker than me. Isn't that the new level of strength that you have been trying to help reach?" Noel said with a small smile that Dex returned with a nod. Noel's face then turned serious as she put her hand on Dex's shoulder.

"Dex, I'm sorry that I bailed on you before. I was wrong to choose Dan's help over yours. If I had kept taking that Gorilla Goo, then I would have become like Miny ... no, like Monstrous Meg," Noel said as her throat tightened. She squeezed Dex's shoulder more intensely. He winced as he tried to ignore the pain, and Noel continued, oblivious to Dex's discomfort. "I said I was willing to pay any price for strength, but that's a price even I wouldn't pay."

Noel paused for a moment. Now noticing Dex's growing discomfort, she let go of his shoulder. Dex gave a sigh of relief as he tenderly grasped his aching shoulder, only to stare wide-eyed as Noel extended an arm toward him.

"I will need a lot of training before nationals, so ... will you train me again? I need your help, and this time I'm in all the way."

A huge smile appeared on Dex's face as he accepted her hand.

"Of course!" he said without hesitation.

Epilogue- Could it be Tonight?

The stars shined brightly in the nighttime sky. Rays of multi-colored light illuminated the horizon during the sun's absence. This evening, Battletown was bathed in the fiery, red starlight. The townsfolk's eyes diluted with a beast-like intensity. Their breathing became heavy as their animalistic impulses were unleashed in full force and filled every fiber of their beings. Snarls and maniacal laughter echoed throughout town as violent brawls filled the streets under the radiant crimson lights.

Far, far away from the violent atmosphere of Battletown, across many lakes, valleys, and seemingly-endless prairies, there was a shining city. Under the lustrous, white starlight, the stained-glass buildings sparkled with a brilliant gleam. Without a single speck of dust anywhere on the crystal roads, this town, known as Torshleki, was the very definition of pristine.

The entire town shimmered like precious gems in a treasure chest, but one building's beauty stood out by far. Standing a staggering 120 drux tall was a splendid structure that could only be referred to as divine. The walls were covered with reflective glass that spread the sky's beautiful light throughout Torshleki. The roofs consisted of alluring crystals lovingly carved from the rarest minerals. Known as the Constantine Cathernacle, this building was the grandest chapagogue in the entire world, where many who believed in the God known as the Weatherman came to worship regularly.

Highest upon the Cathernacle was an angelic suite that was off-limits to the general public. Several snow-white drapes covered the walls of the room. In fact, only a rare few were permitted to step inside briefly, but only one person was permitted to reside indefinitely.

The flooring was a perfectly unblemished white carpet divided with white tiles. Resting on the tiles was a beautiful alabaster kitchen counter with several working white appliances along with a decorative figure of the "Weatherman," standing upon a mountain while holding out his majestic weather staff. Upon the carpet stood a marble dining table with four matching chairs. In the farthest corner was a lovely bed lined with warm, silken blankets upon an antique wooden bed frame painted ivory.

"The stars sure are lovely tonight. I wonder how they look from the other side?" a voice belonging to a petite young lady said from the suite's outdoor balcony. Her long, wavy, beautiful brunette hair, which reached all the way to her lower back, swished in the gentle evening breeze. Her slim, enchanting face was perfectly chiseled with high cheekbones and a narrow nose, almost as if she had been hand-crafted by the divine creator himself.

She held onto the masterfully crafted and smoothed crystal railings as she looked out into the vast sky with a wistful expression. She had a breathtaking view of the entire city, but it wasn't the splendor of the city's nighttime grandeur that gave her such an expression of longing.

"I wonder if tonight will be the night?" she thought as she heard a light fluttering in the distance. A small smile broke out on her face as a snow-white dove flew straight toward her. The beautiful young lady held out her arm as the creature gracefully landed upon it. The bird met her gaze with intelligent eyes as the young lady greeted her with a charming smile.

"It's good to see you again, Berneigh. What have you got for me?" she asked as she removed from the bird's left leg a folded piece of parchment.

"I'm so thankful Pastor Markus tied the message to your leg this time. The housekeeper in charge of cleaning this room scolded me after she had to clean up the spot where you regurgitated your last message."

Berneigh cawed quietly as she turned her head in embarrassment. The young lady chuckled as she stroked Berneigh's feathers.

"Don't worry about it; you're not in trouble. Honestly, I thought it added a nice splotch of color to this white blot of a room."

With graceful fingers, the young lady quickly unfolded the parchment. With a strong, melodious voice, she read the message written within.

Dear Inaya,

After a thorough investigation, we have determined the location of the sidvan you have inquired about. He is currently located in Battletown. His address and contact information are listed below. If you require anything, please message me. I'm pleased to assist in any way possible, and I look forward to your continued cooperation with the Counsel of Chapagogues. May the Almighty Weatherman continue to use you to shine his light down upon us.

With warm regards,

Pastor Markus Rinestone

An excited gleam appeared in Inaya's eyes as she quickly tucked the message in her shorts pocket. Her smile was ravishing as she took several steps back before crouching down.

"So Battletown is where that scaredy cat is hiding. I have to give him props; it's the very last place that I'd expect to find him. He really is determined to conceal his presence from me. He must still be rattled over what happened last time. But, no matter," she exclaimed while breaking into a full-blown sprint. With every step, she grew bulkier. Her slim figure changed as her muscles enlarged and rippled. Her physique was on par with a world champion weightlifter, but her feet had the grace of a ballerina as she dashed towards the rail with many light steps. With an impressive aerial flip, she leaped over the rail and dived downwards with flawless form.

"I'll find him, no matter where he hides."

Those down below heard giddy laughter coming from the sky, but when they looked up, they saw nothing but a few silver feathers fluttering playfully in the night air as the wind quickly changed direction.

Glossary

- **Blaf**- A profane term meant to curse an undesirable person, place, event, or situation.
- **Blit**- A profane term meant to describe someone the user hates with a burning passion.
- **Blurf**- A profane term meant to strongly curse an undesirable person, place, event, or situation.
- **Brilocks**- The currency of Battletown/ all of Zoofria. They consist of smooth rocks infused with blood. They are created using a secret technique that only a few know.
- **Degree of Brutality**- Degree of Brutality- An official order created by the founding Fathers of Battletown over 3000 years ago to end thoughtless death/murder. It states that the right to rule/subjugate others belongs to those who prevail in a conflict. Those in power subjugate others to their will; however, murder is strictly prohibited. Those guilty of murder are marked for death. Those marked by the Degree of Brutality can be killed consequence-free.
- **Drux**- A unit of measurement equal to 15.6 inches.
- **Hino**- A unit of time equal to 1 hour. Also equivalent to 100 yosmins. 32 Hinos are equivalent to an entire day.
- **Kadrux**- A unit of measurement equivalent to 5,000 drux. Also equivalent to 78,000 inches.
- **Luxcium**- The world that this story takes place in. It's inhabited by a wide variety of people scattered across multiple geographical terrains, both seen and unseen.

- **Plasma Patty**- A traditional Battletown flat, breaded food made from red flour. Due to its simplicity to make, it was often eaten in the past whenever food was scarce.
- **Sidvan/Sidven**- The most common race of people residing in Luxcium. Many of the sidven of Battletown are particularly strong and resilient due to a powerful bloodline passed down from their forefathers.
- **Raios**- The nation south of Zoofria, abundant with water and vegetation. The two nations are not on the best terms due to religious/cultural differences, past conflicts, and poor diplomatic relations.
- **Weatherman**- A deity believed to control/regulate the weather. He is most commonly worshiped in Raios.
- **Yosmin**- A unit of time equivalent to 100 zins.
- **Zin**- A unit of time equivalent to 1 second.
- **ZHSAA**- AKA the Zoofria High School Athletics Association, is responsible for organizing and overseeing all high school-aged sporting activities with Zoofrai.
- **Zoofria**- the nation that Battletown resides in.

Nobutaro Masai is the author of Knockout Noel. He lives in Pensacola, Florida with his dog Indy and two cats, Tanjiro and Nezuko. He enjoys playing video games, spending time with friends, and of course writing stories.